# A BEAUTIFUL FEROCITY

## CULLEN'S CELTIC CABARET - BOOK 2

## JEAN GRAINGER

My idea is this, that when you only love a little you're naturally not jealous – or are only jealous also a little, so that it doesn't matter. But when you love in a deeper and intenser way, then you're in the very same proportion jealous; your jealousy has intensity and, no doubt, ferocity.

**Henry James**

# THE STORY SO FAR....

In 1917, two Irish boys flee their old lives to join the British army. One, Peter Cullen, comes from the slums of Dublin; the other, the Honourable Nicholas Vivian Shaw, is a scion of the Anglo-Irish aristocracy. Despite the class divide, the two boys forge an unbreakable friendship in the flames of the Great War and discover a mutual love of singing and performing. With three other talented soldiers, the acrobat Enzo Riccio, guitarist Ramon Wilson and Scottish comedian Two-Soups, they develop a variety show to entertain the troops. Later, they bring Cullen's Celtic Cabaret to London, where they team up with dodgy theatre owner Teddy Hargreaves. Meanwhile, their love lives are not going according to plan. Nick is passionate about his singing partner, Celine Ducat, but she acts like they're just good friends. And Peter is having second thoughts about his engagement to the headstrong May Gallagher...especially now flamenco dancer Aida Gonzalez has joined the show. Not that he's interested in Aida. Nor she in him.

NOW READ ON...

# CHAPTER 1

ETER

Peter Cullen sat in the breakfast room of Mrs Juddy's boarding house near the British Museum, studying the theatre reviews in the morning papers.

'An-oth-er tri-umph for Cullen's Celtic Cabaret...' he spelled out slowly, moving his finger from word to word. His literacy skills were improving, but he still found reading hard. When he was eight, he'd been so badly beaten by the Christian brother who was supposed to be teaching him that he'd refused ever to go back and had spent the rest of his childhood earning pennies by running errands for the Gaiety Theatre in Dublin and trying to protect his mother from his violent alcoholic father. Then he got the job in the brewery, so that meant all education was off the table. He had the rudiments of reading and could write enough to get by, but he wasn't fluent. He knew May wished he'd written longer letters during the war. Some were detailed enough, but the majority were just one-paragraph notes. Writing took him ages, and reading her lovely but long letters took forever.

The only thing that had kept him going through the years before he joined the British army at seventeen was his determination to get into acting. Theatre was Peter's drug, his life, and at one point, it looked like he had a promising career ahead of him as a Shakespearian actor on the Dublin stage. He was blessed with a photographic memory, so while learning scripts off by heart wasn't easy, he managed and could easily visualise the page before him in his mind's eye.

The Great War had put paid to that dream though, and now he ran a ragtag troupe called Cullen's Celtic Cabaret.

The morning's reviews, once Peter had deciphered them, were wonderful. Cullen's Celtic Cabaret was the mainstay of Teddy's show, and despite the initial run only being scheduled for six weeks, it was performing nightly to full houses and still going down a storm, so Teddy extended their contract.

The article in *The Times* praised Enzo's latest stage routine as part incredible acrobatics and part comedy with impeccable timing. It raved about Nick's warm Irish tenor that blended so seamlessly with Celine's sultry French alto, a surprising sound from a girl so young. Two-Soups, got a pat on the back for being clean, unlike so many other smutty comedy acts aimed at returning soldiers. And as for the flamenco duo Ramon and Aida...

Just as Peter was reading about them, the door opened and Aida herself entered. She was wearing her usual red day dress, which clung tightly to her taut, slender body. Peter got to his feet and pulled out a chair for her.

'Good morning, Aida. Look at this.' He handed her the Sunday newspaper and pointed out the part of the review that referred to her and Ramon.

She scanned it, saying nothing, and handed it back to him with an inquiring smile.

'Sorry, I know reading is harder than speaking.'

Though her English had vastly improved in the last few weeks since she'd arrived in London from Spain, she was still even slower to read it than Peter himself. 'Spellbinding, compelling, alluring, thrilling… That's what the writer is saying about you.' He smiled, and when she looked uncertain, added in French, '*Il a dit que tu étais magnifique, passionnée…*' He knew no Spanish, but both of them knew some French, and it was how they communicated when English wasn't enough.

'*Sí.*' She nodded calmly. '*Naturalmente.*' She knew that she and Ramon were an exceptional team.

He grinned. 'You're a cool customer, Aida, I'll say that much for you.'

She smiled and shrugged, then poured herself a cup of coffee from the pot on the table, sipping it with a shudder. She was disgusted by all the English wartime food, but especially the coffee.

Peter sat back down in the chair opposite her. 'Ramon says you call the coffee here "hot pond", which is funny. Maybe we should have you telling the jokes instead of Two-Soups.'

She gave him a hint of a smile. 'And the Scotsman will dance with Betty?' she asked.

He laughed, delighted she had understood him and amused by the thought of the huge, clumsy Two-Soups prancing around the boards with his large-boned, freckle-faced girlfriend Betty.

Nick the tall, stocky Irishman, came in then and helped himself to tea and one of the hard-boiled eggs Mrs Juddy had left in a bowl on the sideboard, peeling it and spreading it on the thick, white toast that Aida seemed to despise but that the rest of them really liked. 'How are the reviews this morning?'

'All good.' Peter passed the paper to him.

'Enzo overheard Teddy being d-d-delighted with himself about us,' remarked Nick as he scanned the review with satisfaction. 'He's taking all the c-c-credit, of course. He was telling someone that when he found us, we were useless, but he polished us up. Utter rubbish, b-b-but sure that's show business for you.'

'Peter make the show good, not this Teddy,' said Aida, and Nick smiled from her to Peter in surprise.

'G-g-good English, Aida. You're a fast learner.'

She shrugged, calmly accepting his praise.

Nick looked at Peter. 'He'd better p-p-pay us for last Monday, even if the theatre was d-d-dark,' he added.

'Don't worry, he will,' said Peter resolutely.

The Acadia had nearly caught on fire a week ago, thanks to the state of the electrics. A spark had set the ventriloquist's dummy on fire in the dressing room, and its owner had wept so many buckets over his scorched, disfigured puppet, you'd have thought it was his child who'd died. There had been an immediate angry gathering of performers, who threatened to walk out unless Teddy Hargreaves, who wouldn't spend Christmas if he could help it, got the wiring fixed. Everyone had paid for their own props, and they couldn't afford to replace them.

Hargreaves had made a big effort not to pay the extra night. He gathered the entire cast to address them, wearing his usual checked suit and smoking his enormous cigar, which was a fire hazard all by itself.

'Right, you lot. Myself and Charlie here are going to need twenty-four hours to fix these few tiny problems, so we'll be closed on Monday…'

'Charlie's not a proper electrician, is he?' shouted someone.

Teddy scowled ominously. 'Luckily I'm an electrician myself.'

It seemed highly unlikely, but no one argued with him. Rumour had it that some woman had once accused him of going AWOL from the army, of not being the war hero he claimed to be. Teddy found out who she was and made sure her landlord threw her out of the house, and she lost her job as a housekeeper at Claridge's. Everyone knew you didn't cross Teddy Hargreaves and get away with it. He did not like being publicly challenged, and it didn't end well for anyone who did it.

Having reduced them all to an annoyed silence, Teddy took a long puff on his cigar and blew it out, his head encircled in pungent smoke. 'So, as I was saying, seeing as you lot are going to have a cushy day on Monday, I'll be cutting your next week's take-home.'

The complaining and grumbling started right away, though under their breath for fear of the wrath of Teddy. Theatres were traditionally dark on Mondays, so they should be having that time off anyway, but with the huge numbers of returning soldiers passing through London, not to mention the patriotic British public, there was peak demand. And while that was the case, Teddy Hargreaves had been making hay and pocketing most of the proceeds.

Peter cast a warning glance at their troupe. They were only part of the show; there were other freelance performers too, and Peter was going to let them fend for themselves. *Say nothing*, he warned his own group with his eyes. *I'll deal with this, but this isn't the time or the place.*

After everyone had retreated, muttering, to their dressing rooms, he'd tracked Teddy down. Hargreaves was a bully, and Peter had learnt in the tenements of Dublin that the only way to deal with a bully was to fight back, harder and stronger. Teddy needed Cullen's Celtic Cabaret – they were the lynchpin of his show, and they both knew it – so Peter could afford to be tough. No soft soap, no fake friendliness. Peter had made his demands and told Teddy he knew he was too tight-fisted to have insurance, that he should be bloody grateful the performers had insisted on him closing for repairs and that it was a miracle the place hadn't gone up before now as there were so many dangerous oversights. He explained how every dressing room had naked bulbs, how the oil-painted sets were stored under the stage and how they'd go up like an inferno in seconds with one spark.

'It's negligent, Teddy, and you're risking lives.'

'Oh, you Paddy, comin' over here tellin' me about innocent lives, are ya? I've 'eard it all now.' He laughed, a bitter bark of a thing.

Peter was used to the way people spoke about his country. They didn't understand that eight hundred years of subjugation had driven Irishmen to rebel and fight back. As far as Teddy and many others were concerned, Paddies were murderous drunks and were not welcome.

It had been an ugly scene, but Peter was sick of Teddy's wheeling and dealing and lack of generosity. Peter knew he would never behave like that if he owned his own theatre. With his own troupe, he was open and honest. Teddy paid Peter a lump sum, and then Peter divided it out. Each of them got the same after he'd taken fifteen percent for management and another ten percent for expenses like travel, bed and board and repairs to costumes, and if the budget over-ran, he paid the difference out of his own pocket.

Teddy had gone mad, of course, but Peter had calmly explained to him that the management of the Palladium and the Adelphi both wanted their troupe too, so if Teddy was unhappy with them, then of course with the deepest regret, they would have to part ways. It wasn't actually true, but Teddy didn't know that, and he had backed down pretty quick.

'And he's g-g-going to stick to his word?' asked Nick.

'If he doesn't, I'll find us another slot somewhere else altogether.'

Nick nodded, satisfied, and Peter hoped his promise wouldn't be put to the test. It was a heavy burden for him, feeling responsible for them all having enough money to live.

Enzo was the next down to breakfast. He was a born-and-bred Londoner, despite being from an Italian circus family on his father's side, and his parents had a two-up, two-down terraced house off the Clerkenwell Road. But the tiny house was incredibly crowded, what with three of Enzo's six grown-up brothers still living at home, so Enzo and Ramon had recently moved into Mrs Juddy's with the rest of the troupe.

The acrobat threw himself into a chair, winking at Aida. The pair had got off to a very bad start, but something had happened between them to soften their relationship a little. Tossing his rich black curls, grown back since the army haircut, he made a big show of yawning as he accepted a toasted crumpet from Mrs Juddy, who had rushed in to serve the gorgeous, lithe, muscular Enzo with a starstruck smile while letting everyone else fend for themselves with the boiled eggs and slices of cold toast.

Two-Soups was next to appear, his red hair standing on end and flame red stubble on his chin. He too helped himself.

'How'd you get on last night, Enzo?' asked Nick.

'We're all waitin' to hear.' Peter grinned. Enzo's adventures with rich women was a running joke.

Enzo had been out late as usual. Yet another lady such-and-such –

Gamminston or something – had picked him up in some gin palace and offered to buy him dinner at the Savoy. Enzo had come to Peter for an advance of his wages – he wanted the free meal, but he'd nothing decent to wear. Peter had had a better idea. There was a woman who performed at the Acadia called Millie Leybourne, and she dressed as a bloke, top hat and tails. Peter had talked her into allowing him to borrow her black evening suit, white silk scarf and white tie off the rail in wardrobe, although she made him promise faithfully to bring it back in one piece. Millie had her eye on joining Cullen's Celtic Cabaret, and though Peter wasn't taking on new acts at the moment, if he was, it would be her. He delivered the suit to Enzo, making him swear not to let this Lady Gamminston rip it off his back.

'Ad a great time,' said Enzo, yawning even wider. 'Guess wot? I thought I'd seen it all, but this took the biscuit. Lady Gamminston and a bunch of her fellow hoity-toitys go round dressin' up and arranging themselves in the shape of famous paintings for people to come and look at. Not actin' or nothin', just standing there. Some posh bird called Lady Lavery is behind it apparently. Sounds daft to me, but what do I know?'

'And they don't move at all?' Peter was fascinated. Was that the sort of thing posh people really wanted to see? He was intrigued but a bit intimidated by aristocrats. They often had the strangest tastes, sometimes cultured, sometimes not.

'Nah, mate, sounds barkin', but there you 'ave it. She picked up the bill for the whole night, though, so she must be loaded. But like my mum would say, "She might have a title, but she ain't no lady."' A lascivious wink at his male friends made them laugh, though Aida rolled her eyes.

'Go on,' prompted Two-Soups, grinning.

'Well, she spent the whole night rubbing my leg wiv 'er foot under the table at the Savoy, and then we went on to a club in Soho, downstairs beneath a tea room. The place was a fug of smoke, and she said there was an opium den at the back, as if that was perfectly normal. But the dance floor was full of young people dancin' to a jazz band,

and all the men in the band were black as the ace of spades, and one woman as well.'

He had his audience now; everyone was listening to him. Even Mrs Juddy was enthralled at the descriptions of how the other half lived.

He went on. 'Well, this bird, right, she drunk a bucket of gin fizz and she snorted cocaine, would you believe. She said she bought it off a soldier who had been prescribed it for medical reasons. Then she suggested we go back to her place on Sloane Square. Can you imagine what my brothers would make of it if they saw me strollin' through the city, in me evenin' suit and white silk scarf, with a genuine lady toff on me arm at two in the mornin'?' Enzo's brothers all worked on a building site off Tottenham Court Road.

'I'd think they'd have plenty to say, none of it repeatable.' Peter grinned again, and Enzo laughed.

'Exactly right, mate. Then in this posh big dining room, she poured us more fizz, and then she got out this board she called a Ouija board. It's all the rage, she says. It had letters all around it, the whole alphabet, an' she put her glass on it and then made me put me finger on the rim and she did the same. And she asked, "Is anyone there?" And the glass went mad. It went whizzin' around spelling out "Wally", and she thought that was very funny because the idea is the glass is supposed to be a way of speakin' to the dead and the only Wally she knows is very much alive – her sister used to go out with him.'

'Wally?' asked Nick as he frowned and peeled another egg. 'Wally who?'

'No idea. Anyway, she said I must be pushin' the glass, it was goin' so fast, but I wasn't. I reckon it was her pushin' it. And anyway, we had to give up. It just kept spelling Wally, Wally, Wally, so we got bored of it and we retired for the evening.'

He grinned around at them, the inference clear. Peter caught Aida's eye again. She'd clearly understood enough of Enzo's story to not be impressed. She and Enzo might be friendlier now than they had been, but it still annoyed her when he talked about women like they were only there for his pleasure.

'Hey, Nick,' Enzo added, 'I've an idea. 'Ow's about tonight you come out wiv me and this lady? Bit of dancin', a few drinks? She wants to meet again, but I could do with a bodyguard. She's a bit too 'ot for me to 'andle, mate, if I'm honest, so I'd appreciate a pal by my side.'

To Peter's surprise, Nick agreed. 'Sure, sounds fun.' Then he remembered that Nick was from the aristocracy himself, so while Lady Gamminston seemed mysterious to working-class boys like Peter and Enzo, maybe Nick thought of women like her as completely normal.

'And I'll ask Celine if she wants to c-c-come,' Nick added, the tips of his ears flushing bright red.

'Ooh...any luck with the mademoiselle?' Enzo asked, with a cheeky wink towards the door. Celine hadn't appeared yet. She was always the last up, even later than Ramon, who slept like a log.

Nick blushed furiously at the question. 'G-g-goodness no. I wouldn't expect... I'm not her t-t-type.'

'Do not be silly man, Enzo,' said Aida, shooting a disapproving glance at the Londoner and bestowing a gentle smile on Nick, which made the poor fellow blush even more.

*Poor Nick*, thought Peter, sighing to himself. The lad had a terrible crush on Celine, ever since she'd sung a love duet with him on the stage of the Aigle d'Or during the war. Since then, she and Nick had got engaged...but only to convince Celine's father, Remy, that it was safe and respectable to let his daughter join a theatre troupe.

Nick was still hopeful of winning the girl's heart in real life when, as he confided in Peter, 'she grew old enough to be interested in men'. But Peter didn't share Nick's optimism and doubted that Celine was too young for love at eighteen. It was true that she had shown no obvious interest in the opposite sex so far, but something told Peter she was not the innocent little French girl his friend thought she was.

The door flew open again, and this time it was Betty. The Scottish girl was back in London and sleeping on a mattress in the girls' room when she wasn't sneaking upstairs to Two-Soups. The stairs always creaked under her plate-sized feet, but luckily Mrs Juddy slept like a log and was blissfully unaware of the Scottish late-night antics going on under her very proper roof.

'Hey, Peter,' said Two-Soups, 'can I go on before Nick and Celine tonight? It's Betty's last night, and we want to go somewhere nice for dinner and dancing.'

Aida caught Peter's eye, and he saw the amusement there. The elegant flamenco dancer clearly found the idea that the most ungainly people she'd ever seen in her life might want to go dancing endearingly funny. He thought it was lovely, though, and sometimes he wished he could have what Betty and Two-Soups had. They might be an odd-looking pair, but they were so connected and found each other adorable.

'Sure thing, Two-Soups,' he said kindly. 'Don't mention it to Teddy – just do it. He won't want to allow it, especially after I made him pay us for Monday, but since it's her last night...well, better ask for forgiveness than permission and all of that.'

'Thanks, Peter. Ye're a wee star, so y'are,' said Betty, clapping him on the back and sending his tea flying.

'We do our best.' Peter grinned, wiping tea off his side plate and the table with his napkin. Aida caught his eye once more, and he held her gaze for a fraction of a second. Her eyes were so dark, they could almost be described as black, and they flashed with passion and intensity. Whatever the opposite of easy-going was, that was her, but he found himself intrigued by her.

But only, he told himself sternly, because he wanted *everyone* in his troupe to be happy.

# CHAPTER 2

*ICK*

NICK HOPED he didn't look too desperate, hanging around in the breakfast room after everyone else had gone. Mrs Juddy had already given him three cups of tea and an enquiring eyebrow, and he was sure she knew he was waiting for Celine. It couldn't be helped. He was determined to ask the French girl about going out with Enzo and his friend tonight, and if he left it for too long, he wouldn't have the courage.

As it was, with every tick of Mrs Juddy's Royal Doulton china clock on the mantelpiece, his nerve was deserting him.

But then she appeared, wearing a simple dark-blue dress; it was his favourite colour on her, contrasting with her strawberry-blond hair.

'Ah, Celine. G-g-good morning,' he managed as she went to help herself to the remains of the buffet.

'Ça va, Nick?' She smiled as she took the seat opposite him, setting down a plate with two thick slices of cold white toast and some jam. She always ate a lot, but somehow she never put on weight. Her face was so thin and narrow, it made her amber eyes, flecked with gold, look huge. 'I mean, are you well?'

'*Oui, bien, merci.*' He loved speaking French to her, because somehow he could imagine himself as someone completely different from his awkward tongue-tied Irish self – a dashing, romantic continental, far too self-confident to stammer and blush. '*Enzo et son amie, une dame, vont danser ce soir après le spectacle, et il s'est demandé…*'

'English, please, as you promise me,' Celine said sweetly. 'You know, Nick, I must learn.'

He sighed and went back to English. 'Enzo and a lady friend of his are g-g-going d-d-dancing and d-d-dining t-t-tonight after the show, and he wondered if we'd like to j-j-join them?' He fought his way to the end of the sentence, swallowed and blushed; he dearly wished he could stop stammering like a lunatic every time he was nervous, which was always.

'*Oui, certainment.* I mean, yes, certainly. It sounds like some fun – let's do it.' She beamed at him, and he nearly died of joy and relief.

\* \* \*

HE WOULDN'T EVEN NEED to change when the curtain went down – he was already in his black tie and tails, which Enzo had told him he had to wear, because according to his la-di-dah date, they were 'going somewhere fabulous'. Enzo was going to borrow Millie Leybourne's suit again; he'd acquired a bottle of champagne last night that he'd gifted to her to say thanks.

Now there was just the show to get through…

Fifteen minutes before curtain, Enzo brought his new girlfriend into Celine's dressing room, where Nick and Celine were running through a new duet, 'Love Is Everywhere' by Matthew Ott, which was very popular.

Nick was in the middle of singing – 'When we're loving man and wife, dear, through life, dear, we will glide…' – when he found himself enveloped in a perfumed hug by a beautiful and familiar woman.

'Wally, darling.' Florence Postlethwaite's voice was slightly slurred.

14

*Bloody hell. So Enzo's date is Florence. Gamminston must be her newly married name.* Nick only knew her as one of the Postlethwaites. He and his brothers had played with Florence and her sisters as little children; they'd all been one big gang. And then his brother Wally had had a dalliance before the war with Florence's older sister Gertrude. And now, with a few drinks and who knew what else on board, Florence thought he was Wally. Nick had always known he looked like a version of his older brother; teachers at school were forever confusing them.

'N-n-n-n... I'm n-n-n-n...'

As he mumbled and stammered and couldn't get a word out, Florence turned to Celine with a loud, patronising laugh. 'So this is your latest girl, is it, Wally? Naughty boy. You know poor Maud Banting-White is pining away for you back in Ireland, ready to abandon old Blimpy to be your mistress.'

'She's n-n-n-n...'

Celine looked like she didn't know where to put herself, but Enzo, getting over his shock, came to Nick's aid. 'This is Celine. She ain't no chorus girl – she's a professional singer. And this chap ain't Wally, Florence – this is my old mate Nick.'

Enzo, like Peter and Celine, was in on Nick's secret; he knew his friend was actually the Honourable Nicholas Vivian Shaw of Brockleton in Cork, but he also knew that Nick had fallen out with his parents and never wanted to go home, and, along with Peter and Celine, he'd sworn to keep the Irishman's secret.

Lady Gamminston punched Enzo cheerfully in the arm. 'Don't be ridiculous. I've known the Shaws since I was a little girl. That's the Honourable Wally Shaw of Brockleton.'

'I'm not talking nonsense, Florence. That is the 'umble Nick Gerrity of Waterford's finest grocery store.' Enzo was unequivocal. 'Right, Nick and Celine, this is Florence. Florence, Nick and Celine. Now come on – you need to take your seat. We need to get on stage.' And he ushered her, protesting and confused, out of the dressing room.

'Everyone in costume please. Fifteen minutes to curtain.' Charlie the stage manager shouted up and down the corridors in his usual state of grumpy frustration.

Nick hurried back to his own dressing room to get into his make-up. He felt a bit shaken by his past life nearly catching up with him, so instead of going back to Celine, who was bound to want to talk about it, he went to stand in the wings and watch the acts that came on before him.

Millie – stage name Amelia – was on first; she was a great hit with the returning soldiers and the perfect act to warm up the audience. An androgynous-looking woman, she was very slight, with dark hair cut short and waxed down to resemble a cap, prominent cheekbones and dark-brown eyes. She sometimes dressed as a police constable, or as a dandy, and sung comic songs made famous by Vesta Tilley. She was a good singer, in her own laconic but effective way. Nick had vamped along with her on piano a few times, when Millie's rather sulky accompanist, Mary Joyce, couldn't make it.

Celine was very fond of Millie, and that was a good reason for Nick to like her as well, which he did, enormously. But it was more than that. He respected Millie's skill and found her far less terrifying than other women for some reason. It seemed the liking was mutual; he suspected Millie had been encouraging Celine to go on a date with him, and that that was why the French girl had agreed so easily to come this evening.

Out on stage, Millie had the crowd singing along to 'Jolly Good Luck to the Girl That Loves a Soldier', and then 'I've a Bit of a Blighty One', and by the time she came off, grinning at Nick as she passed him, the tone of the evening was set.

Next there was a chap, Alfred Cox, who looked a bit like Charlie Chaplin and did mime, but Nick suspected he'd get the chop soon. Silent comedy was hard, and besides, compared to Two-Soups he just wasn't funny. Alfred had been angling to become part of Cullen's Celtic Cabaret if and when they moved on from the Acadia, but Peter wasn't interested. Teddy's show was a mishmash of good and bad, but Peter wanted only the good.

Then there was a woman called Cecily Duffy; she had a Maltese terrier named Sparky who did clever tricks, like jumping through a flaming hoop. Sparky was a vicious little rat of a dog, and he was universally despised because of his love of snapping at ankles, but he would do anything for Cecily. She and Sparky were so devoted to each other that she kissed him on the mouth all the time, which turned everyone's stomach. Enzo joked that it was as well that the dog didn't seem to mind kissing her, because poor old Cecily was so ugly, even the tide wouldn't take her out.

The chorus girls came on next – Teddy had recently added them to the bill – high kickers in sparkling costumes that showed off their legs and gave the demobbed soldiers a thrill. It had caused a bit of a stir and some stuffy reviews, but Teddy loved a bit of controversy, said it brought the crowds, and to be fair to the brash Cockney, it did. One of them winked at Nick as they sashayed past him onto the stage, and another passed closer than was strictly necessary, but he was sure it was only because they knew they could make him blush and it amused them.

Then the girls ran off and the five-strong Chinese show went on, a funny thing based on *Ali Baba and the Forty Thieves*, with a contortionist who had everyone bewildered as to how he got his limbs into that shape. Enzo said they came from Limehouse in the East End, where all the Chinese lived.

Next came an American ex-GI turned magician. His real name was Gill Brown, but his stage name was Magus Magicus and he said he'd prefer to be called that. He was a Cherokee Indian and devilishly handsome, dark and brooding, never smiling, with jade-green eyes, pale skin and black hair. On stage he sported a black cloak lined with crimson silk, and he made audiences gasp in amazement at his illusions, particularly when he sawed one of the chorus girls in half. The girls loved it; they were always fighting among themselves to be his latest victim. But he was a surprisingly shy man. He showed no interest in their advances and never socialised with anyone.

Peter arrived in the wings beside Nick. 'Everything going all right?' He dropped his voice. 'Enzo tells me his girl Florence mistook you for someone called Wally. He's your brother, isn't he?'

'Yes. Wally went out with her sister G-G-Gertrude. Enzo did a good job of covering up for me, but I think I'd better give going out with him and Florence a miss. I hope Celine won't be too d-d-disappointed if I don't come.'

'I'm sure she won't even want to go without you,' said Peter kindly.

When Magus finished his magic show, by conjuring up a pair of live doves he had trained to fly backstage and into a cage, Peter walked out onto the stage, booming in his best Kitchener-style voice. 'Ladies and gentlemen, tonight Cullen's Celtic Cabaret needs *you*, the audience...'

Nick enjoyed Peter's introductions. His friend was a born showman; he knew how to get a crowd going and did it effortlessly using that deep, sonorous theatrical voice of his. Enzo often joked that Peter was the ringmaster and they were all his show ponies. Teddy knew it too, and he was always trying to mix up the show, with Peter's acts split up between the poorer performances and Peter introducing everything. But Peter had always refused. Cullen's Celtic Cabaret was a section that stood apart; it was the highlight of the show, and its manager, Peter Cullen, wasn't watering it down for anyone.

'And now' – Peter was finishing up – 'all the way from Scotland, the famous comedian, Baxter Campbell, known to all his friends as... Two-Soups!'

'A funny thing happened to me on the way to the theatre...' Two-Soups bounded past Nick onto the stage, and a moment later, Peter returned to Nick's side. Enzo came to join them in the wings, and the three friends, who had sworn undying loyalty to each other in the trenches what seemed like centuries ago, stood watching as the Scotsman had the audience wiping tears of mirth, telling joke after joke for fifteen non-stop minutes.

When he came off, leaving the audience begging for more, Enzo clapped him on the shoulder. ''Ave a nice night wiv Betty, mate, and don't do nothin' I wouldn't do, eh?' He made a slightly lewd gesture with his hips. Enzo was wearing a brand-new emerald-green satin costume that Peter had had made for him to replace the Edwardian bathing suit; the skintight leggings and vest clung to his body, leaving nothing to the imagination.

'Oh, Enzo, my auld flower, I'll be doin' worse than you, so I will, and that's really sayin' somethin'.' Two-Soups guffawed before running backstage to remove his greasepaint and get ready for the love of his life, who would be waiting at the stage door by now.

Enzo twisted to stare after the Scotsman as he went. An odd shadow passed over his face, and his whole body shivered. He turned to Peter.

Nick saw the unspoken conversation between them and wondered what was happening.

Enzo took a step towards the dressing rooms, but Peter grabbed him by the arm. 'No. I'll go. You go on stage,' he said firmly.

'But...'

'We're performers, Enzo. The show must go on.' Peter turned to Nick then. 'Can you do the intros?'

'Of course I will, but...what's the matter? Where are you going?'

'Nowhere, hopefully. See you later.' And Peter was gone, hurrying back to the dressing rooms, while Celine, who had just arrived, grabbed Nick's arm and pulled him with her out onto the stage, where the audience was getting restless.

Nick took a deep breath and sat down at the piano. He wasn't going to try introducing their act; he'd only stammer like a mad thing. Best to get straight to the music.

The audience quickly settled, and Celine was a huge success as always. There were a number of wounded and maimed soldiers in the audience tonight, sitting in their wheelchairs at the back, and as she had done when they sung in the base hospitals, she left the stage and went in among them and stroked their faces as she sang soft love songs. She never winced or looked squeamish, no matter how horrific the injury. She sat on their laps and kissed their cheeks and ran her hands flirtatiously through their hair, and they loved her.

It made Nick sad to see it, because that was the only bit of female attention those poor men were likely to ever get again, but at the same time, he was proud of her for meeting that need, the memory of a gentle kiss from a beautiful woman that they could take away with them and dream about.

Peter had been talking about getting playing cards made up with Celine's picture on them, and Aida's as well. Not mucky cards like the soldiers had passed around at the front, just ones of them posing in their costumes. Peter reckoned if he sold them at the door after the concerts, they would go like hot cakes and make a tidy little profit for the company. Maybe Enzo in his skintight green silk costume as well, for the ladies. Nick already knew Peter was a shrewd businessman, and he was beginning to think his friend would soon be running rings around Teddy Hargreaves.

Celine returned to the stage. Nick and she sang, 'Love Is Everywhere', and then his favourite duet, 'If You Were the Only Girl in the World', and after that Celine ran off, waving and kissing her hands to the applauding audience. Nick stood up to bow. Lady Florence Gamminston had got a seat in the front row, and she waved enthusiastically to him; he suspected she still thought he was Wally.

Ramon and Aida went on next and brought the house down as usual, and then Nick returned to the piano and sat down to play Enzo's introduction, building suspense with volume and lots of key changes.

After a few seconds, Enzo somersaulted onto the stage in his skintight green costume, and Nick couldn't help glancing towards Florence as the London boy spun and cavorted. The lady's eyes were popping, and Nick grinned to himself. If Lady Gamminston hadn't yet dipped her toe in that particular water, she certainly knew what she was getting now. He wished Celine would look at him that way, just the once, with her eyes out on stalks. But he was just a big clumsy lump of a man, so there was little chance of that.

He played a set of deep chords and then a run of nervous arpeggios, climbing the piano, building suspense. Over the weeks since they'd been there, the remarkable Betty had helped Enzo build an elaborate set of seesaws, high-wires, ropes and parallel bars, and for tonight Enzo had rehearsed a new sequence, in which the Londoner was going to shoot himself out of a cannon that Betty had constructed at his request.

It was a simple enough trick actually; Enzo had rehearsed it several times, and it always worked. There was a spring-loaded platform within the cannon that the acrobat could release when he was ready; this would cause the board to spring up and give him the velocity he needed to soar out of the cannon's mouth, do a couple of somersaults and then grab a rope and swing down.

The audience gasped and oohed and aahed as Ramon and Enzo pushed the cannon onto the stage, and then Enzo acted as if he was terrified to get into it. Nick played a dramatic scale. Peter was supposed to be here now, 'forcing' Enzo to climb into the cannon's mouth, but clearly their manager was still missing because Ramon stayed on stage to act Peter's part. He did a good job of it, looking dark and satanic and getting lots of boos. Enzo had the audience in stitches by trying to climb back out of the cannon, and Ramon made a comical show of shoving him back in.

When it came to firing him out of the cannon, Betty had supplied a big, long fuse, and again Ramon stepped into Peter's role, making a great show of lighting it. Some people in the audience clung to each other in fear, and Florence in the front row had her hands over her eyes, peeping through her fingers.

Nick played a 'drum roll' on the piano, sending a ripple of laughter through the audience that released the tension, and then came a huge cloud of smoke and a loud bang caused by Ramon secretly dropping a match into the metal bowl behind the cannon, which held a small amount of gunpowder. As soon as Enzo heard the bang, he activated the spring and there he went, catapulted out of the mouth of the cannon, flying through the air, turning twice, swinging from the rope, before landing perfectly, his arms outstretched to the audience.

It was such a great finale to the show that Nick rose to his feet, applauding furiously along with the rest of the enormous audience, who were whooping and stamping their feet while maintaining thunderous applause. Ramon and Celine and even Aida ran onto the stage to pat Enzo on the back and shake his hand, and there came the incorrigible Florence, scrambling over the footlights to congratulate him as well. Enzo ran to give her a hand up, and she gave him a big smacker of a kiss, which caused the audience to roar and shout even louder.

Peter was back from wherever he had run off to; Nick could see him peering in through the side curtains. Nick beckoned to his friend and manager to join the rest of them on stage, but for some reason, Peter seemed reluctant to come on and share the glory, so Nick ran over to get him.

'That cannon trick went down a storm. Come on, take a bow with the rest of us. Even that Florence has jumped in on the act...'

But then he saw Peter's face. His old friend was as white as a sheet, his jaw set in a grim line.

'Peter, what's happened? What's the matter?'

'Nick, just come with me. Get this over with and follow me, you and everyone, right now. Something awful has happened...'

# CHAPTER 3

ETER

BY THE TIME he'd reached the dressing rooms fifteen minutes earlier, after stopping to have a quick word with Ramon about playing his part in the cannon act, Two-Soups was gone; he must have changed like lightning, he was so keen to see Betty. Knowing everyone could keep the show going without him, Peter ran down the back stairs, out onto the street.

Instinct sent him out of the theatre and around Kensington Gore, and there he saw the gathered crowd, with women screaming and policemen trying to disperse the onlookers.

*Please let Enzo have been wrong for once*, begged Peter as he ran. *Please let it be some other poor soul...not Two-Soups – he is too full of life and fun*. But Peter knew all too well how life could be snuffed out in a second.

His lungs hurt as he doubled his speed. He knew what he was going to see. He'd known it was coming the moment he'd seen the shadow across Enzo's face and when Enzo visibly shivered.

Peter knew that look. Enzo didn't like to admit it openly, but he had an uncanny knack of knowing things; he had the sight, he knew when soldiers at the front were going to die, and that look had said that this was one of those times. And Peter should have acted faster; he should have let Enzo go after Two-Soups himself, or at least not wasted precious moments giving Nick, and then Ramon, directions of what to do without him, as if the show was the only important thing in life.

He reached the crowd of onlookers and pushed through them, dreading what he was about to find.

But there, to his relief, right at the front, towering over all the other heads, was that familiar mop of red curls. Two-Soups wasn't dead. Relief flooded Peter's veins, and he exhaled the breath he hadn't even realised he was holding. He was so glad to be wrong, to have got here in time to warn the big Scotsman to be careful, to change his plans for the evening, not go dancing, just go safely home to bed with his beloved Betty on his arm.

Someone had been hurt, though, that was obvious. A car was crashed into a lamppost ten feet away, and a cart was overturned in the middle of the road, with its produce – potatoes – strewn across the street. A man, presumably the owner of the cart, sat on a box, someone holding a cloth to a bleeding gash on his head. The car driver stood by the wreck of his car, being comforted by a well-dressed woman. Two medical orderlies lifted a stretcher into a FAS ambulance. The Quakers had set up the Friends' Ambulance Service at the start of the war; many of their members were conscientious objectors – conchies, as they were called – so it gave them a way to participate without harming anyone.

The long body on the stretcher was covered with a white sheet.

As Peter reached his side, Two-Soups made a sudden effort to get into the ambulance with the stretcher. A couple of policemen had to pull him back, and the medical orderlies closed the doors to the ambulance, then ran around and climbed into the front and drove off.

Peter's heart sank as he looked around; Betty was nowhere to be seen. 'Two-Soups?'

The Scotsman looked down at him. Huge fat tears ran down his long, sad face. 'The car. She was hit by the car. I tried to pull her out of the way, but it was too quick and now she's... Peter, she's...'

His knees were going, he was swaying, and Peter pulled him into his embrace and let his huge friend sob on his shoulder. *So that is what happened. The death that Enzo saw stalking Two-Soups came for Betty, not for him.*

'I want to be with her,' sobbed Two-Soups. 'I need to see her.'

A London bobby was trying to shepherd them out of the area along with everyone else. Peter caught the policeman's eye. 'Where are they taking her, officer?'

'Richmond Mortuary most likely,' the bobby replied. 'I'm sorry for your loss, sir.' He nodded at Two-Soups. 'But you need to move along.'

'I'm going there. I need to be with her.' Two-Soups wiped his eyes with his fists.

'No, give the ambulance time,' said Peter quickly. He meant give the mortuary time to make Betty's body look better, as he knew she must have been badly injured if she got hit by that car trying to avoid the cart, or whatever had happened. 'Come back to the theatre and rest for a moment, and I'll get Enzo and Nick. Ramon can take Celine and Aida back to Mrs Juddy's, but we'll go with you. You can't handle this alone.'

Two-Soups wasn't capable of arguing, so he allowed Peter to escort him back to the theatre. Peter settled him on the couch in his own dressing room and gave him a glass of whiskey, then headed for the stage, where the sound of the crowd shuffling out let him know the show had just finished.

The curtains were pulled, and Lady Gamminston poured everyone who had gathered on stage a glass of champagne.

Nick came running over to meet him. 'That cannon trick went down a storm. Come on, take a bow with the rest of us. Even that Florence has jumped in on the act...' But then he saw Peter's face, and said, 'Peter, what's happened? What's the matter?'

'It's Betty. She was hit by a car swerving to avoid a cart. She's dead.' He could barely get the words out.

Nick went white and put his arm around Peter's shoulders. 'Oh no. P-p-p-poor Betty and T-T-Two-Soups…'

Enzo looked over at them with a face of dread.

'We have to tell Enzo,' Peter said.

Nick beckoned to him, and the Londoner approached cautiously, as if not wanting to hear what was about to be said, with Florence doggedly at his heels. Peter nodded at Nick to explain because he was afraid he would break down in the telling, and soon the word went round the troupe. The jubilant atmosphere vanished, and everyone was in tears, even Florence, who had never met Betty.

Enzo looked as if he was about to be sick. 'I should have gone after him myself…'

'Don't be silly, Enzo darling,' soothed Florence. 'How could you possibly have known?'

Ramon, Celine and Aida agreed to go and tell Mrs Juddy, who would be so upset; she loved Betty. And Nick, Enzo and Peter returned to Two-Soups, who sat, defeated and heartbroken, in Peter's dressing room, the glass of whiskey clutched in his big hand untouched.

It wasn't until they were out on the street that Peter realised Lady Florence was still tagging along with them. He was inclined to tell her to get lost but then didn't have the heart to do it because Enzo still looked so haggard and guilty; maybe it would help him to have someone.

Peter felt even more guilty, for two reasons. One, because he'd put the show first instead of running after Two-Soups straight away and possibly avoiding this tragedy. And two, because his brain was *still* putting the show first, however much his heart was breaking for Betty.

How was he going to manage without Two-Soups? They needed comedy in the show, and it was hard to picture the Scotsman cracking jokes again any time soon. Peter supposed he could do more himself, imitating different politicians and generals, even the king – everyone enjoyed that. And he could ask Enzo to revert to his hilarious dancing with Ramon playing guitar, and then Aida could come on stage and try to teach him to do it properly; that would be funny enough to fulfil the comedy side of things. But what if Aida refused? She was so proud of the flamenco and hated Enzo making a joke of it, and Peter couldn't imagine ordering Aida to do anything she didn't want to do. How about Nick then? He'd shown he could write a comic song in the past; maybe he could come up with a few of those.

Peter thought he might invite that Millie Leybourne to join them. She had a very funny number where she was dressed in a top hat and tails on one side of her body and a long cream gown on the other; she played the man trying to seduce the woman, and it went down very well.

Teddy would be raging to lose Two-Soups, and he'd probably try and cut their money, but Teddy would just have to lump it. He'd be whining of course, but when did he ever do anything else? The sooner Peter could save up enough money and move on from Teddy, the better. Though where else was he going to play to two thousand people every night and twice on Sundays?

# CHAPTER 4

$\mathcal{N}$*ICK*

THEY WAITED in a room off the mortuary, Two-Soups sitting rigidly on his chair like a boy outside the headmaster's office, Peter pacing up and down. Enzo was slumped on a seat in the corner with his face in his hands, still shivering despite having changed out of his skimpy acrobat's costume into his ordinary clothes and coat. Florence had her arm around him, but Nick was uncomfortably aware that she kept looking across at him with a puzzled expression, clearly still trying to work out why Wally Shaw had turned up as a singer in a variety show and was calling himself Nick Gerrity. She'd not seen him since he was a boy, so he'd changed of course, but she wasn't stupid.

A creepy-looking man in a black suit, with a long face and a pointed beard that made him seem like the baddie in a children's story, opened the door. 'Is anyone here the next of kin of Miss Elizabeth McGroarty?'

Two-Soups stood up.

'You are her brother?' His nasal tone and piercing eyes gave his supercilious attitude a menacing air.

Two-Soups said hoarsely, 'Er...no, I'm Two...Baxter Campbell. I'm her fiancé. We're getting married... We were going to anyway...'

'So you are not her next of kin. Are her parents living?'

'Her father is, but he's old and lives outside Glasgow. Oh God, I'll have to tell him.' Two-Soups looked stricken at the prospect.

Peter stood then, taking charge. 'Baxter Campbell was Miss McGroarty's fiancé and therefore surely as good as her next of kin. He's the reason she was in London – they were planning their wedding. Mr McGroarty is in no position to travel, so it's best you deal with us and my friend.'

'And you are?' The creepy man arched a pointed eyebrow; everything about him was pointy.

'Peter Cullen. I'm Mr Campbell's manager.'

'Manager?' The man barely suppressed a sneer. 'What aspect of this gentleman, pray tell, do you manage?'

'We are actors and performers. Our show is on in the Acadia. My friend and colleague here has been bereaved by this terrible accident, so I think a little bit of compassion and flexibility wouldn't go astray now, would it?'

'You're Irish?' asked the mortician suddenly, disdain oozing from his tone.

'Yes, I am. Why d'you ask?' In his agitation, Peter had slipped back into his old Dublin accent, something Nick knew he'd purposely abandoned to avoid the anti-Irish sentiment that was rampant here in London.

'Murderous, ignorant race,' muttered the nasty little man. 'And the Scots aren't far behind you. The deceased will be released for burial once the coroner is satisfied no foul play took place. Leave details of where you can be contacted to be advised of same. Good day to you all.'

And then he was gone.

'Can't I see her? I want to see her...' Two-Soups looked at Peter, confused and distraught.

'I'm so sorry, Two-Soups.' Peter flushed with anger. 'It seems the authorities don't recognise you as Betty's next of kin. They don't seem to like the Scottish or the Irish here. I don't know how to deal with people like this...'

But Nick knew how to deal with them.

He jumped to his feet, crossed the room and rapped hard on the door the mortician had just slammed shut. When there was no answer, he knocked again, a firm, peremptory knock. 'Excuse me.' he called, reverting to the accent of his youth.

The door opened, and the man appeared again, ruffled and indignant to have been disturbed but also looking more cautious. 'And you are...?'

'Perhaps you should begin by telling me who *you* are, my good man,' said Nick haughtily.

'Mr Adrian Hedgely,' the man answered, looking belligerent but not as sure of himself.

'Well, Hedgely...' Nick deliberately dropped the 'Mr'. 'As Mr Cullen here has already informed you, Mr C-C-Campbell...'

*To hell with this stammer. Act the part.* He spoke in the clipped tones of his English public-school education, every inch the son of a baron. He didn't dare look at his friends but could imagine their reaction.

'Mr Campbell wishes to see his fiancé. Please facilitate that immediately.'

'It won't be possible,' Hedgely said, but he was on the back foot. He'd dismissed Nick's friends as Irish, Scottish, actors – not people he needed to treat with any respect – but he was clearly worried he was facing something different in Nick.

'Oh, I think you can make an exception in this instance. My uncle is Lord Alsward, he's the representative for Richmond Park, and I'm quite sure he would be grateful if you were to afford us your c-c-cooperation in this matter.'

An expression of scepticism crossed Hedgely's pointy face. Probably he'd remembered they were a troupe of actors and found it highly unlikely that Lord Alsward's nephew would be mixing with such riffraff.

'And Lady Alsward, she is well?' he asked smoothly.

Nick stepped back in horror, exaggerating his shock. 'Mr Hedgely, I would have thought you would be aware that Lady Alsward, my dear aunt Winnie, and her infant daughter, Isabella, were tragically k-k-killed in a boating accident in France in 1903. My uncle never remarried. The p-p-poor fellow lives alone with only the staff and his three-legged spaniel, Jeff, for c-c-company.'

Hedgely's demeanour changed utterly; he looked flustered and started grovelling. He clearly believed Nick now. 'Well, given the circumstances, I will, of course... If you wouldn't mind waiting for just a few more moments...' He obviously wasn't going anywhere without a name.

'You are addressing the Honourable Nicholas Vivian Shaw,' Nick replied, in a clipped, dismissive tone. There would be no convincing Florence he wasn't Wally after claiming Lord Alsward as his uncle, and frankly he'd rather be Nicholas Shaw to her than be mistaken for his philandering brother. 'And please don't keep us waiting for longer than necessary.'

'No, sir, of course, Your Lordship...' And the sinister little man, reduced to a shadow of his former self, backed out of the room.

Nick turned to find poor Two-Soups staring at him in bewilderment, while Peter, who already knew, winked at him gratefully. Enzo still had his head in his hands, but Florence was looking very smug, realising she'd been right all along. Well, nearly right. Not Wally, but his younger brother.

'You're a lord?' asked the Scotsman hoarsely.

'No, just an honourable. Long story. I'll t-t-tell you later.'

The door opened again, and Hedgely reappeared and invited Two-Soups to walk through. He beckoned Nick to come as well – presumably so the aristocrat could keep an eye on the Scotsman, who might be capable of anything. Nick indicated for Peter to come, and Hedgely scowled but didn't dare protest. The three of them followed him down a corridor with stone floors and walls painted a horrible green, and Nick wondered if this was the best they could do in a place that stored the dead.

Two-Soups, pale and walking slowly, was clearly determined to do this but frightened as well.

Hedgely took out a set of keys and unlocked a door.

Was it really necessary to lock the corpses away from the living, Nick wondered, as if they were something utterly untouchable?

They entered a small room with tiled floor and walls. A metal trolley was the only piece of furniture, and the place smelled of a chemical of some sort, something Nick didn't recognise. The body on the trolley was still covered with a white sheet, as it had been on the stretcher. Hedgely crept forwards – he seemed to make no sound as he walked – and folded the sheet down.

Betty lay there, her light-brown hair unwound and loose around her shoulders. Her face was unmarked, thankfully, but alabaster white, her once-red lips now blue.

Nick had seen so much sudden death, but the sight of Betty deeply moved him.

A young, vibrant woman, finally finding love, a dream life marked out for her and Two-Soups, who she always called 'my Baxter'. All over the country, young women were grieving for their boyfriends, husbands, brothers, fathers. But to see Two-Soups just looking at the girl he adored, tears flowing unchecked down his face, all that potential joy and love snuffed out before it even had a chance to flourish…

It was heartbreaking.

The Scotsman remained frozen to the spot, unable to move any further, unable to approach her.

Peter, always able to read the room, broke the tension by stepping forwards, bending down and kissing her forehead, then saying a quiet prayer over her body. 'Eternal rest grant unto Betty's soul, oh Lord, and may perpetual light shine on her forever, may she rest in peace.'

'Amen,' murmured Nick. He then stepped forwards and kissed her forehead as well. 'Goodbye, Betty. You were the only girl that didn't scare the living d-d-daylights out of me. We'll see you in heaven, and don't worry, we'll l-l-look after Two-Soups for you.'

It was very strange, but he could see now how beautiful she was, maybe not in the classical sense, but there was something about her face as she lay there, so serene and composed. Betty McGroarty had loved life, and that made everyone love her, and she was beautiful.

Two-Soups shook himself and stepped forwards. He just stood for a moment, gazing at her. Then he reached into his pocket and pulled out a simple gold wedding ring.

'I bought this weeks ago. I know you have your engagement ring on, but I saw this and I had the money 'cause we got paid. So I bought it, ready for our wedding.' He turned the sheet back further. Her dress was stained with blood, and her hands were lightly crossed on her breast.

Hedgely went to stop him – this wasn't allowed obviously – but Peter stepped between him and the body, giving a slight shake of his head. Hedgely looked like he was ready to call a policeman, but then Nick fixed him with a hard, cold stare and he wilted again.

Two-Soups pushed the gold band onto Betty's finger, with a little difficulty, over her engagement ring.

'With this ring, I thee wed,' he said quietly. He bent then and kissed her, not her forehead but her cold pale lips, and stroked her hair.

'*Mar sin leat*, my sweet lass. I'll never feel about anyone the way I do about you. *Caidil gu math mo ghràdh*.' They'd heard Two-Soups speak in Scots Gaelic with Betty before, so it was no surprise that he spoke it now. He turned then, looked at his two friends and gave them a stoic nod. He could leave her.

'Please have the undertaker send his bill to me, at this address.' Peter handed the mortician a card; he'd had business cards made up using Mrs Juddy's address.

Hedgely nodded and took the card, his brow furrowed. Clearly he had no idea what was going on here, but equally clearly, he knew it wasn't what it seemed.

* * *

ENZO STOOD up to meet them in the waiting room as they returned from the mortuary. 'I'm sorry. I'm so sorry. I wish I could have done somethin', he started saying to Two-Soups, but Peter stepped between him and the Scotsman.

'Enzo, there was nothing any of us could have done.'

Lady Florence advanced on Nick with a triumphant gleam in her eye. 'Nicholas! Of course you are, I see it now, but the last time I saw you, you were in short trousers.'

He drew her aside, away from Two-Soups, who had broken down again and was being comforted by Peter and Enzo. 'Florence, it's splendid to meet you, but d-d-do you mind not saying anything to anyone at home for now? I'm keeping a low p-p-profile at the moment, having a few adventures, that sort of thing, and if Mother found out I was gallivanting around t-t-town... I've sort of es-es-estranged myself from them, and I w-w-want to keep it that way.'

She clapped her hands lightly, delighted to be his confidante. 'I heard you joined up, and everyone assumed you were killed. Not a word shall pass my lips! But isn't your grandmother Floss still alive? She must be worried about you, Nicholas. You were always her favourite, as I recall.'

He felt immediately guilty; since coming to London, he'd been so busy and having such fun, he hadn't even given his grandmother his address. 'You're so right, but she knows I'm alive. She's the only one, though, and she's keeping my secret. Florence, I promise to write to her if you promise not to mention me to Mother or Father, or anyone who knows them.'

'Nicholas, my dear, mum's the word. Your secret is safe with me, and in return, be sure not to mention to Lord Gamminston that his wife is...friendly...with an acrobat, will you?' She smirked and put her finger to her lips.

'I certainly will not,' promised Nick sincerely, who had no intention of putting Enzo in harm's way. He knew the aristocracy could be very handy with their shotguns.

# CHAPTER 5

 ETER

COULD he have saved Betty if he'd acted faster? Could Enzo have saved her if he'd not followed Peter's orders and gone on stage?

Or was human destiny written in the stars?

Maybe there was nothing anyone could have done. Maybe if it hadn't been the car, something else would have happened later. The only thing Peter was sure of was that there was no point in anybody telling Two-Soups anything about Enzo having second sight. It would only make things worse.

Everyone was still up in Mrs Juddy's, despite it being the early hours of the morning when he opened the door with his key and he and Nick helped Two-Soups across the threshold. Enzo had gone home from the mortuary to see his family; he'd said he needed to be with his own folks tonight.

Mrs Juddy rushed out of the living room to greet them, throwing her arms around the bereaved man and wailing, 'Poor Betty. Poor Baxter.'

Peter could see Ramon in the parlour, walking towards them, looking more brooding than ever, coming to shake Two-Soups's hand. Celine and Aida were also on their feet, their faces soft with sympathy.

Behind them, sitting on the sofa, was a third young woman in a pink dress and coat, with an elaborate and expensive-looking hat on her lap and a small brown suitcase at her knee, looking suitably sad for the occasion but also self-assured and confident.

A range of emotions flooded through him.

That she should be here, now, in the same room as everyone, his old life walking out of the blue into the new... This was all wrong. She belonged in Dublin, not here in London. And yet, after everything that had happened today, it was so very, very good to see a familiar face from the old days, before the war, before everything. A young innocent girl, untouched by tragedy of any kind.

'May?' he managed to say. 'Is it really you?'

* * *

'MAY, please tell me you're jokin'.'

She winced slightly, and Peter was conscious he'd reverted to his Dublin accent for the second time that day, but there was nobody around at this hour of the night to hear him as they strolled up and down the street outside the lodging house half an hour later. Mrs Juddy had ushered everyone to bed, and gratefully they went. She gave Two-Soups two tablets that her husband had been prescribed for strong pain, and she whispered to Peter that they would knock him out for a few hours at least.

When they were alone, May had suggested a walk.

'No, I'm not. They said I couldn't come, and I said I was an adult and I'd make my own decisions, and so I just left.' She stuck her chin in the air, daring him to criticise.

'Without saying a word, May?' He went back to his new middle-class English accent. 'They'll be going out of their minds with worry.'

He couldn't believe she'd been so reckless, just turning up without even writing ahead.

'I wanted to see you,' she answered mulishly.

'But to sneak away like that...'

'I thought you'd be pleased,' her disappointment at his reaction clear. 'You wrote saying how much Two-Soups was looking forward to seeing Betty, and so I assumed it was a hint but that you didn't like to ask.'

'Oh, poor Two-Soups. He loved her so much...' He stopped dead, a wave of grief washing over him, putting his hand to his eyes.

When he dropped his hand again, she was there facing him, bathed in gold by the streetlight behind her. 'I'm sorry, Peter. I didn't mean to upset you by reminding you. It must be so sad for the poor man, losing his girl. I do hope you'd feel the same way if it happened to me.'

'Of course I would, May. How could you ask me that?' His mind was still on that poor lonely corpse in the horrible bleak morgue.

'You just don't seem very happy to see me.'

He forced himself to focus on her. 'I am happy to see you, of course I am...'

'To be totally honest with you, Peter, I'm not sure this trip was worth the bother.'

'Yes, well...' He fought back the temptation to agree with her. 'The truth is, I... Look, I'm so busy and now Betty... I won't have time to show you around or take you out to nice places or anything.'

For some reason this seemed to make her slightly less cross. 'You don't need to entertain me, silly, or take me out to fancy places. I want to help you, and I can. You know I can. I've always helped you before, haven't I?'

She wasn't wrong. If it hadn't been for May, he'd never have made it through the war, never had the idea about putting on a show in the Aigle d'Or, wouldn't be living his dream.

'You have, I know you have.' His heart softened as he looked at her anxious face. She really was very pretty.

'And I see what you're doing here, Peter. I've noticed that you've worked on changing your accent, you're dressed so smartly, and I suppose you mix with all sorts at the theatre – and I can help. I'm not gentry, but I'm solidly middle class, and it may not be the most romantic thing to say, but I can elevate you. I can show you how to be, and I can charm people. You know what they say, that behind every great man there's an even greater woman. I want to be that for you, Peter, and I love you. That's why I'm here. Is that so bad?'

His heart had melted entirely now. He put his arms around her and kissed her. The prospect of sharing the load of responsibility, having someone he could confide in, was appealing. 'Not bad at all,' he whispered.

She kissed him back enthusiastically, then stood smiling at him. 'So what about our plans for the future, Mr Cullen? When are you setting up your own theatre?'

He laughed and took her hand as they strolled back towards the lodging house. 'I wish I could do it tomorrow, May. I can't wait to get out of the Acadia. It's a deathtrap, and Teddy Hargreaves who owns it, he's an awful scrooge.'

'Tell me all about it.'

He told her everything in a way he couldn't with the performers. He had to present them, even Nick and Enzo, with a rosier picture than the truth to ensure they didn't worry and have that affect their performance.

'The electricity still sparks even though Teddy claims to have fixed it, and now there's a gas pipe leaking by the gentlemen's room, and he told the poor stage manager – Charlie's his name – to plug it with a rag instead of calling someone out from the gas company.'

It felt wonderful being able to unburden himself to someone who seemed so interested. 'That place needs so much maintenance, but he won't do it, won't employ proper tradesmen, just gets poor old Charlie to patch things up as best he can. And meanwhile he tries to pay everyone a pittance – I'm always having to fight with him over money – and makes us work seven days a week while he trousers the profit. The amount of money I could make from a theatre of my own, May – I wish I could work it out on paper, but you know me, I'm good at the day-to-day stuff, but a big, complicated budget...'

'Isn't it just as well you've got me, who's been working as a factory office manager for more than two years and knows everything there is to know about accounting for a business?'

She looked so sweet and pleased with herself that he had to kiss her again.

'First thing tomorrow, May, before anything else, you're going to telegram your parents and say you are fine and that you have a respectable lodging house to stay in and that I am taking good care of you.'

'I will, and I won't say you're in the same house – they'd have a conniption,' she teased, digging him in the ribs with her elbow. She had cheered up mightily now.

'And you understand that I'm going to be tearing around trying to keep the show going and looking after Two-Soups and sorting out the arrangements for poor Betty. And I've only just got Ramon and Aida back on track after their last fight – they are like a pair of snakes when they get going. God spare me from the Latin temperament.'

She looked pleased at this revelation about Aida. 'Yes, Spanish women fight with their men all the time, like that horrible Carmen woman in the opera. I don't blame the soldier for stabbing her. But I'm not like that at all. I'll help you with everything. Let me deal with the undertaker – I can make all of those arrangements. Will she be buried here or in Scotland, do you think?'

Peter could feel the weight lifting off his shoulders. Everyone always expected him to know what to do about everything, and it felt good to have someone offer to share the responsibility. Nick was his right-hand man, and he did discuss things with him, but he didn't like to burden him too much, or any of them. It was his job to smooth everything over. May was headstrong. She was more besotted with him than he was with her if he was honest, but she was pretty and fun and it was true – she could be a great help. And she was right about one thing: She knew much better than he did how to deal with people higher up the social ladder, people who were still something of a mystery to him, particularly the men. Maybe her showing up wasn't the worst.

39

When they got back to Mrs Juddy's, the whole house was quiet.

In the parlour, the sofa was made up to be slept on. Mrs Juddy's first suggestion had been for May to take poor Betty's place on the mattress in Celine and Aida's room, but it had seemed far too soon, and so they'd settled on the front room.

Peter had a sudden thought. He went over and ruffled the sheets and blankets, then came back to May, who looked at him with a small smile. He pointed upwards and gestured to her to be quiet, and she removed her shoes and tiptoed up the stairs behind him, not making every step creak like Betty used to do with her huge feet... *Poor Betty.*

The door to Two-Soups's room was closed, and the Scotsman was snoring very loudly behind it. *Well done, Mrs Juddy.*

Peter opened the door to his room. May gave him a look that asked a thousand questions.

He'd had such a long and terrible day that the thought of taking May to his bed, feeling her hands on his tired body, kissing her sweet skin, was too much for him to resist.

'Will you come in?' he asked so quietly, he almost mimed it.

She nodded.

\* \* \*

THE NEXT MORNING, their naked bodies a tangle of limbs and sheets, they were woken by a pounding on the front door below. Peter sat up blearily, taking his new pocket watch from the side table.

'What... It's not even seven...' Then he heard Mrs Juddy answer the door and a loud, angry voice he recognised bellowed something unintelligible. He jumped up, pulled on his trousers and stuffed his shirt hastily into his waistband. 'Stay here, whatever happens. Promise me?' He knew May was impulsive and likely to appear if she felt he was being threatened, but Teddy Hargreaves was on the rampage about something and he didn't want her exposed to a string of threats and swear words, not to mention the look from Mrs Juddy if she thought May was in his bed.

He slipped out of his room and spotted Nick in his pyjamas at the top of the stairs, his hair standing on end.

'Let me handle this. Stay where you are for now,' Peter said as he passed his friend, but he could hear Nick following him down.

'Really, Mr Hargreaves, I suggest you come back later when you're making more sense.' In the hallway, Mrs Juddy was trying to stand firm, but the heavy man pushed his way past her in a deranged state, his checked suit filthy and his face blackened with soot, blind drunk and stinking of whiskey. As soon as he saw Peter, he charged at him, fists flailing.

'You burnt my theatre, you thick Paddy. I knew I should never have let you inside the bloody door...' He swung a punch at Peter's nose but missed wildly.

Peter grabbed his arm and Nick grabbed the other, trying to contain him as Teddy thrashed and lurched around, cursing and trying to kick them, sending a side table with china ladies flying.

'Teddy, just calm down and tell us what happened.'

'The Acadia b-b-burnt down?'

'Oh my goodness, your theatre, Peter!' gasped Mrs Juddy, her hand to her mouth. You'd swear she herself owned it, she looked that upset. 'But surely you're insured, Mr Hargreaves?'

'How could I afford insurance? Every penny I made went to my performers.' Teddy wailed, tears of rage, frustration, self-pity and drink streaming from his eyes as he tried to elbow Peter in the face and head-butt Nick at the same time; he was far too drunk to manage either, though the fumes from the booze he'd been drinking were enough to fell an ox. 'And it's your bloody fault, you dangerous Paddies! Gunpowder in the theatre, tearing off last night, leaving the back door open and explosives lying around on stage. It's sabotage, so it is. I'm going to call the Old Bill on you lot, see if I don't!'

'Teddy!' Peter shouted back at him as he and Nick struggled to hold on to the big bruiser's arms. 'Calm down, man. I'm very sorry for your loss, but there was no sabotage, and I'm sure the gunpowder wasn't the problem. I pointed out to Charlie that the storage of all the old backdrops, with their oil paint, beneath the stage was a danger. All it would take was one spark from a footlight for the whole place to go up like a tinderbox, and he told me he passed it on to you and you told him to tell me to mind my own business –'

'I'm going to get the law on you, take you for every penny you have,' Teddy roared. 'There's not a judge in the country will take an Irishman's side when there's explosives involved!'

'You will do no such thing, Mr Hargreaves, and stop trying to blame others for your own failings,' said a cold, clear voice from the top of the stairs. 'Peter's already told me all about your theatre, with the electricity sparking and the gas leaking, and there's plenty of witnesses to the place being a deathtrap. And not having insurance was reckless and negligent on your part.'

May descended the stairs, fully dressed, her hair pinned, her face powdered. She held herself with such confidence, her chin in the air and her hand on the banister. 'You're very lucky nobody was killed, like the theatre in Exeter years ago, where the fire started backstage and 188 people died. So stop trying to threaten my fiancé for your own failings, Mr Hargreaves, and thank your lucky stars the Acadia burnt down when it was empty. Now stop acting like a savage, or I will ask Mrs Juddy to call a policeman. I'm quite sure they'd love to hear testimony from all your performers about the shortcuts and shoddy practices you employed in your theatre. I'll be surprised if you don't face a charge of criminal negligence.'

Something about May's stern tone made Teddy Hargreaves pull himself together. He stepped back from Peter and Nick and roughly straightened the lapels of his checked suit, and when he spoke to Peter again, it was more measured, though he was still flushed with alcohol and revenge.

'You might think you can get away with this, Cullen, but rest assured, you'll never play another theatre again, because no one will have you.' Teddy was gimlet-eyed and quietly menacing. 'I'll be telling every theatre owner in the country how you burnt down the Acadia with your gunpowder, and no one will let you in the door. Us theatre people stick together in this country, and we won't allow rings to be run around us by Paddies and other foreigner saboteurs pretending to be better than they ought to be. You're fooling nobody, Peter Cullen. You can change your accent to an English one and try to mimic your betters, but we can see through you. You're a pig-ignorant Paddy and a danger to the realm, and you always will be.'

The silence that followed Teddy's awful threat was pregnant with expectation. Celine and Aida were awake; they'd come up the hall from the back of the house with their dressing gowns on and were looking out from behind the stairs. And Ramon had arrived on the landing above in his pyjamas. Nick and May were also watching Peter. Everyone wanted to see how he would respond to Teddy's vicious attack.

Peter knew instinctively that he had to take leadership. He had no idea if Teddy had the power to get his troupe blacklisted from every theatre in the country, but he wasn't going to show any fear. Or even act like he was taking the man seriously at all.

'Righto, Teddy. If there's nothing else, we might all get back to bed.' He smiled brightly, and that infuriated the big man still further.

'You do not dismiss me, Cullen!' he shouted, waving his fists again, and this time it was Mrs Juddy who intervened.

'Get out of my house now, Mr Hargreaves, or as Miss Gallagher has suggested, I will call the police.' And when Teddy tried to protest, she started shooing him as if he were a stray cat who'd wandered in. 'Go on, get out, or I will call for help to the nearest bobby I see.'

Teddy Hargreaves was a backstreet bruiser who could handle himself well in a fight, but the combined authority of May Gallagher and Mrs Juddy, and Peter's open contempt, had cowed him, and he backed away down the steps of the lodging house, still muttering dire threats of revenge. But at least he was gone. ·

Peter turned to face them all then, Nick, Ramon, Celine and Aida. And May as well – she'd proved herself part of the team. 'Well, you all said you badly needed a break, so here you have it. Leave the rest to me. Our priority now is to look after Two-Soups when he wakes up and get poor Betty's remains released for burial, and we'll sort out our new home then. Is that all right?'

43

Aida looked scared and vulnerable. And Celine asked, 'But what will happen now? Where will we work?'

'C-c-can Teddy really blacklist us?' Nick was clearly worried.

Peter had no idea, but he had to pretend he did. 'Don't be worrying about that. Other theatre managers will fall over themselves to snap us up. We've already had plenty of offers.' Not strictly true, but then he hadn't been looking. 'I have enough in the kitty to tide us over, and I'll sort something out before the end of the month, definitely.' Though he had no idea how. All the West End had shows already running; they wouldn't just abandon them in favour of his. So yes, he probably could get them another venue, but not right away.

Relieved by his reassurance, and grateful at the prospect of a bit more rest, they all trudged back to bed, leaving just himself, May and Mrs Juddy in the hallway.

'Right then. I'll go and see if poor Mr Campbell was woken by all this awful carry-on,' said the landlady. 'And if he is, I'll take some breakfast up to him so he can stay in bed.'

'Thanks, Mrs Juddy. I'm sure that would help him.' Peter was touched by her kindness.

As Mrs Juddy bustled past May on the stairs, she asked her rather pointedly, 'Did you sleep all right, Miss Gallagher?'

May smiled back at her innocently. 'I did, thank you, Mrs Juddy. I was already up and dressed when Mr Hargreaves started banging on the door, and when you went to open it, I ran up the stairs to call for Peter to come and help you. I didn't think you saw me.'

'Of course, of course...' The landlady was easily mollified. As long as things looked respectable on the surface, she wasn't that bothered about the details. She disappeared on up the stairs, and they could hear her knocking gently on Two-Soups's door. 'Mr Baxter?' She had always refused to call Two-Soups by the name everyone else used.

At the foot of the stairs, Peter took May's hands in his. 'Thanks, May. You were magnificent.'

'I've no idea what criminal negligence is really, but I read it in one of my whodunits and thought it might sound frightening.' She giggled like a schoolgirl. 'Now we just need to find another theatre to perform in.'

He sighed, feeling the weight of the world descend upon his shoulders again. 'I know I told everyone it would be easy, but I don't think it will be.'

She squeezed his hands in hers. 'Don't you worry about that, Peter Cullen. You've got me helping you now, and together we're going to conquer the world.'

# CHAPTER 6

 ETER

THEY ALL ACCOMPANIED Two-Soups to Scotland with Betty's body and buried her in the churchyard in their village. The big red-headed Scotsman stayed behind with his sweetheart's heartbroken father. He promised Peter to come back to the show as soon as he was needed, as long as he could find someone else to help the old man with the farm, though Peter wondered if his grieving friend would ever laugh again.

On the train back to London, Peter sat staring out of the window at the passing countryside, the mountains of Scotland giving way to lakes and fields and then the smoking chimneys of the industrial north. Opposite him, Enzo and Ramon dozed while Celine and Millie Leybourne, who had become friendly with each other, read the papers. Nick had finally opened the long letter he'd received from his grandmother and was reading it with a deep frown on his face. Beside the window opposite him, Aida sat stitching up a tear in the pocket of her black coat. Peter's eyes drifted towards her, her little hand going to and fro, holding the delicate needle. There was a stillness to Aida despite her frenetic energy, and he found her intriguing.

'Peter?'

He tore his eyes away and turned to the girl sitting beside him. 'Yes, May?'

She handed him a notebook in which she'd done some neat calculations. She spoke quietly so only he could hear properly. 'I have it all written down for you. Full house every night for eight weeks at a shilling a seat in the main theatre and two bob for the boxes. The Acadia held two thousand people, so that's' – she showed him the calculation – 'two hundred pounds a night gross. So that's a bit more than fourteen hundred pounds a week, then multiply that by eight weeks – it's over eleven thousand pounds generated. And I have all the cuttings from the newspapers saying how you were the main draw at the Acadia, professionals among amateurs, so what theatre is going to argue with that? Money talks louder than anything.'

'Louder than Teddy Hargreaves?' he asked quietly.

'For sure. That awful man can blacken your name as much as he likes, but every theatre manager in London will know the Acadia was a deathtrap and the fire was caused by years of neglectful management, not you and your entourage. And with figures like these, there's nothing for us to worry about.'

He smiled at her gratefully. 'You're a genius, May, did I ever tell you that?'

'Yes, you did. And you're right, I am,' she replied primly.

It was true – she really had been invaluable these last few days. After sending a telegram, then a long letter to her parents to assure them of her safety, she had arranged everyone's travel to Scotland, managed to retrieve what was left of Enzo's props and any of the costumes that had survived and had persuaded Mrs Juddy to let her store them all in the downstairs parlour where May was still sleeping on the sofa, at least as far as her parents and Mrs Juddy were concerned. Luckily Peter had been putting aside five percent of what Teddy paid his troupe each week, so they were financially solvent for now at least. But that money would run out soon, and then they would be in trouble if they didn't sort something out.

At least lack of money and uncertain prospects gave him a good excuse to put his wedding to May on the long finger.

In Scotland he'd had a long conversation with Nick and Enzo about it all.

'I had no idea she was going to turn up out of the blue,' he'd told them, 'and I don't know what to do now. She's refusing to go home, says she wants us to get married here.'

'Well, just tell her you don't want to,' said Enzo. 'That's what I always do.'

'But that would hurt her, though, and I like her a lot.'

'I know you like her, but d-d-do you love her?' Nick looked very worried at the thought of Peter marrying someone he didn't love. For an aristocrat, he was a real romantic, though his adoration of the lovely Celine was totally unrequited, it seemed.

'I don't know, really. Not sure I even know what love is. Look, she's a nice girl, and good fun and all the rest, and she's from a good background, plenty of money there, and she's mad keen...'

'B-b-but you're not?'

'I don't know. I think maybe I'm just too busy to be married to anyone, houses, kids, all of that.'

'C-c-can't you t-t-tell her that?' asked Nick.

'I don't know if I can,' Peter said gloomily.

'She's not pregnant, is she?' asked Enzo.

'No.' Peter was horrified.

'Well then...'

'But look, she and I...we have...do...well, you know...and so I suppose I sort of have to marry her now, and I know it's the right thing to do. If some fella had...you know...done *that*...with my sister, he'd better bloody well marry her then. But I...'

'But you d-d-don't want to?'

'Not really,' he admitted.

'Then talk to her,' said Enzo, exasperated. 'Come on, mate, you've run up and down the lines under huge fire from the Germans, dodging snipers and landmines and all sorts, and you can't face down a young girl?'

Peter inhaled deeply as he thought about it, then blew out his breath. 'Facing the Hun is one thing, Enzo, but May Gallagher is a different prospect altogether.'

Besides, she was clearly not going anywhere, so he might as well get used to it. He knew Nick was still worried for him, but Enzo had stopped advising Peter to get rid of her after his good white shirt had got a lipstick mark on it somehow and, despite knowing nothing about laundry, May went and found out how to remove it. It involved a hot iron and some brown paper, but she got it good as new. After that, Enzo had realised she was very helpful and told Peter she was worth having on board as a permanent fixture. Nick had teased Enzo for being so shallow, though he admitted he liked May as well.

Peter smiled across the carriage at his best friends, thinking about the time they'd sworn that oath of undying loyalty to each other. And then he saw that Nick was brushing away tears as he read the long letter in his hand.

'Nick, what's the matter?'

'I...I...I...I...'

As Nick did his best to get the words out, Ramon stirred and woke up and the girls turned to see what was happening.

'Has something happened to your grandmother?' asked Celine anxiously.

'I...I...I...I...'

'It's his brother, Wally,' said Enzo flatly. 'Sorry, mate.'

Peter didn't even bother to ask how Enzo knew. 'Condolences, Nick,' he said quietly.

Celine moved away from Millie and closer to her singing partner and took his big hand in hers. 'Poor Nick,' she said in her French accent. 'I'm so sorry for this.'

Nick smiled at her, then finally found his voice, as he often did when she was with him. 'We weren't c-c-close, but still.' He shrugged and swallowed his tears. 'Brothers are b-b-brothers still.'

'What happened to him, Nick?' asked Millie, leaning across Celine.

49

'My grandmother says he d-d-died in a hunting accident. Banting-White, a viscount we know, he thought poor Wally was a d-d-deer or something and shot him in the b-b-back.'

'Will you go home for the funeral?' Peter asked. He posed the question out of genuine concern, but at the same time, his manager's brain was already calculating how they could audition for shows without Nick as well as without Two-Soups.

'It's already t-t-taken place. My grandmother d-d-didn't have my address to write to, until Florence reminded me to send it. Now I'm the heir to Brockleton if Father dies, and she thinks I should come home to see Father. But I can't. I d-d-don't want to...' Nick's big chest heaved. Celine smoothed his hand and patted it, while Millie rested her chin on Celine's shoulder, gazing at him with her big brown eyes. Aida came to sit on Nick's other side, putting her arm around him and murmuring to him in a mixture of Spanish, English and broken French.

'Peter? Peter? Peter!' whispered May in his ear.

Peter started and turned back to her, dragging his eyes away from the sight of Aida comforting his friend. 'Sorry, what –'

'What does Nick mean, he's the heir to Brockleton?'

'Ah...' Of course, half of them in the carriage wouldn't know what Nick was on about; the big fellow had only blurted out the stuff about Brockleton because he was so upset about his brother. It was hard to know what to do. He'd promised not to break Nick's confidence, but everyone had heard what was said. 'Mm, well...'

Then Millie asked the same question, only more loudly and directly than May had done. 'What do you mean, you're the heir to Brockleton, Nick? What does that mean?'

'I... Well...' Nick flushed, tear-stained, looking helplessly at Celine.

'What does Nick mean?' Millie asked Celine, and Peter wondered at the sharpness in her tone. He knew she and Nick and Celine knocked about a bit together; he thought Millie must be hurt at being left out of what was obviously some big secret between the other two.

'Millie, it's Nick's business who he tells about his past,' he said calmly.

'But I suppose *you* know, don't you?' complained May, rather cross herself.

Ramon also looked annoyed. 'Is there something important that some of us haven't been told?' He looked at Enzo, who by his innocent face was clearly in on the secret.

Only Aida, Peter noticed, wasn't making a fuss about being left out of the loop.

Poor Nick was getting redder and redder, horrified at the idea he'd hurt or offended anyone. 'N-n-no, this is m-m-my fault. I m-m-made Celine and P-P-Peter and Enzo p-p-promise not to t-t-tell anyone,' he began in halting, stammered sentences. Again, he looked pleadingly at the French girl. 'Celine, you t-t-tell them, p-p-please...'

She pressed his big hand tenderly. 'Only if you don't mind?'

'I d-d-don't mind.' He rested his head back against the seat, the weight of the world on his shoulders.

Celine turned to the others. 'It is not his fault, but Nick, he is not Nick Gerrity from Waterford. He is the son of a baron, and he come from a very, very...*aristocratique*... Um...Brockleton, it is a... um...chateau...'

Millie looked fascinated. 'Goodness. I take it you mean a very big house. I'm so sorry about Nick's brother, obviously, but are you saying he's due to inherit a mansion in the future, or is it just some draughty old ruin that nobody wants?'

'Oh...I...' The French girl wrinkled her pale forehead. 'I do not know the answer to this, Millie. Nick, *ne m'a pas dit*... Nick?'

Everyone in the carriage turned to Nick, who had opened his eyes again and was gazing miserably at his friends. To his shame, Peter found himself as interested in Nick's answer as the rest. He knew his friend was from the aristocracy, but he realised he didn't actually know what that meant in terms of his prospects. Lady Appleton, who had been so kind when they were starting out in London, had told him that lots of lords were as poor as church mice, having gambled away all their lands. Had Nick's da been that way? He'd sounded like a pretty awful man when Nick described him.

51

Nick looked humble. 'It's just a three-storey house in Cork, a bit gloomy-looking, though some of the rooms are nice.'

'Goodness.' exclaimed May, extremely impressed. 'That's bigger than my parents' house in Ranelagh. I bet it's worth even more.'

Millie's eyes had also widened. 'Oh my. So one day you're going to be a man of real substance.'

"E always was, Millie, money or no money,' said Enzo.

Peter heard the slight admonishment there and agreed with him.

He and Enzo were going to have to be extra protective of their gentle friend now and stick to the oath the three of them had taken back in the war, to always have each other's backs. Millie had quite a predatory expression on her sharp little face now that she'd heard about this big house in Cork Nick might inherit one day, and Peter wondered if she was planning to set about elbowing Celine aside, trying to take the French girl's place in Nick's heart. He was starting to have second thoughts about having her join the cabaret, but without Two-Soups for the foreseeable, she was a great fit and she'd jumped at the opportunity when he'd mentioned it last week.

*Good luck with that, Millie*, he thought, with an inward smile.

It was a shame Celine wasn't as shrewd as Millie, or maybe she would be more inclined to chase after Nick herself – or at least let him chase her.

# CHAPTER 7

AY

AS MAY GALLAGHER stretched out on the sofa, the sun streamed through the thin curtains of the guest house.

She wondered if she could risk sneaking up the stairs to Peter's room. It was probably safe, and if Mrs Juddy caught her, she'd just say she was on the way to the bathroom.

Peter would still be asleep. It had been another very late night, all of them sitting up worrying about never getting another job in the theatre because they'd been turned down by the Palladium and the Royal and the Lyceum already. Peter's assurances to everyone that theatres would be banging their door down had proved to be quite wide of the mark. Teddy had clearly been going around blackening their names, blaming them for the fire and taking credit for all the good reviews. Anti-Irish sentiment was very strong, and people didn't need much of an excuse to hate them and slam the door in the face of any act with 'Celtic' in the title.

She got up and checked the clock: 6 a.m. She pulled on her

dressing gown and slippers, opened her door quietly and crept up the stairs with her sponge bag in her hand in case she was intercepted, but no one seemed to be around. Peter's room was at the end of the landing on the right, so a straight run once she made the top of the stairs.

She slipped into his darkened room quietly. He was fast asleep, lying on his back, his bare chest gently rising and falling. He looked to her like a golden angel, muscular and lithe.

He stirred as she climbed in beside him, and his arms went around her. He moaned contentedly as she drew his head to her breasts, only a thin lace-and-silk nightdress between them. They made love quietly and sensually. She really did enjoy it, as he was so gentle and considerate, and afterwards she lay with her head on his sweat-dampened chest, listening to his heart thump back to an even pace.

She longed for them to marry, and she still wore the sparkling diamond she'd bought on his behalf, but there had been no mention of a wedding, which was very frustrating. She was sure he'd get there in the end, but in the meantime, she was taking precautions. She didn't want a rushed affair, like had happened to Cecily Fitzgibbon from the tennis club, who had had her baby only four months after the wedding.

So she'd gone to see a lady she found in an advertisement at the back of a magazine. The lady had an office near Liverpool Street station, and she supplied May with a Dutch cap and some jelly that would prevent her getting pregnant. Peter had been shocked at first, but May explained she wanted to be intimate with him and definitely didn't want a baby until after they were married, so for now, while he was too busy to think about marrying her, it was the best option. He'd blushed then, and offered to 'take care of things himself', by which she assumed he meant one of those awful-sounding rubber sheaths, but the woman she visited had been most forthright about such things, saying firmly, 'The woman is left carrying the baby in every sense of the word, my dear, so in my experience, it's best you take matters into your own hands. That way you can ensure it's done properly.'

So he'd accepted doing things her way. As he would everything in the end. Though she knew him well enough by now to know she had to play it clever. He didn't like being openly undermined or told what to do, and once or twice, he gave her a look, one that suggested she was overstepping the mark. She loved and respected him, of course, and he wasn't bossy or anything, but she knew she had to be careful to defer to him in all things, especially the business of the show. Make him think whatever it was, was his idea.

She was sure Peter was fond of her. He certainly enjoyed going to bed with her. He was gentle and passionate and always told her how beautiful she was. Her parents would be so appalled and horrified if they thought she was sleeping with him, but she wanted to, and she also felt she needed to lay her claim to him and not leave him free for any other woman to get her hooks into.

She would have loved if he'd taken the lead on the wedding, demanded they marry as soon as possible because he desperately wanted to make her his wife, but if wishes were horses, then beggars would ride, so she would, like in all other matters, take it into her own hands.

Peter woke, pushing himself up against the pillows, his hands behind his head. She put her hand on his chest, but as usual, as soon as he was properly awake, he started talking about the business.

'I'm thinking of going to York today,' he said. 'There's a place up there running a revue that's been getting terrible reviews. I'm going to see if they'll boot whoever that is out and put us in instead. I know it's probably another Teddy Hargreaves situation, with them taking most of the profit and paying us a pittance, but it's either that or unemployment and we all go our separate ways. I'm just hoping Teddy's poison won't have spread as far as York. I can't afford to waste another train fare on a wild goose chase, like when the two of us went to Dorset.' He sighed.

She ran her fingers over his chest. 'Imagine if we had our own theatre,' she purred, barely audibly, but he heard her and laughed cynically.

'You'd need a fairly powerful imagination, May, to imagine that right enough. We currently have enough money to do us about two weeks. After that we're all on the streets.'

'Well, maybe not a proper theatre, but while you were talking to the theatre manager in Dorset, I was speaking to his wife. She was telling me all about these things called fit-ups. They're touring theatre companies, and they have their own tent, like a circus but rectangular. She was with one for years before she got married and settled down. Some of the companies only travel in the summer when the weather is good, but if we had a really good tent, we could do it all year. Wouldn't it be great if we had something like that?'

'It would, surely,' he said vaguely, checking the small clock by his bed.

'Of course, it would cost a lot to set it up, not just the tent but having to get chairs, transport, costumes, props…and a way to transport everything and everyone, but if we could, we would make so much money and keep it all for ourselves. That's what the theatre manager's wife said to me.'

'It's an idea, May. Maybe some day, who knows?' He kissed her head absent-mindedly.

'So you'd like that?' she probed gently.

'Oh, I'd love it, who wouldn't? Our own business, our own show, we keep the door, we decide who, when, where. It's a pipe dream, but you never know. Some day maybe. Anyway, this man in York might take us, and he mightn't be the cheapskate misery Teddy Hargreaves was, so we might be able to start saving up if we are successful.'

He threw back the blankets and got out of bed, and she admired his slender body as he walked across to the chest of drawers to get his shaving things. He put on his dressing gown, covering himself before slipping out to the bathroom.

She rolled over onto his side of the bed and pressed his pillow to her face. The smell of him never bored her. He wore a faint tangy cologne, and the trace of it on the pillowcase set her pulse racing. Sighing, she sat up, waiting for him to return. On his bedside locker was the letter from his mother, which had come two weeks ago.

Bridie Cullen had written to say Peter's father had died in his sleep and the Guinness brewery had paid compensation because it was down to the head injury Kit Cullen had suffered a couple of years ago at work. Peter had been hardly sad at all; it seemed to be a relief to him to know his father was gone. But he had been talking about how he and May should go home for a visit soon, and that made her anxious. If they went back, there was the risk her father would talk Peter into leaving her in Dublin, and that was the last thing she wanted.

Perhaps it was time to put her whole plan into action, even if it meant pushing Peter along a little quicker than she'd been intending to.

A few minutes later, he was back.

'Urgh, freezing-cold water meant I didn't linger.' He got dressed rapidly. 'What have you on today while I'm off to York?'

She had hoped he'd ask her to go with him for support, but they were low on money, so of course it was better to save the rail fare. 'Just planning to write to Mother, and Aida needs some black lace for her dress, so I'll shop around for that. I found a nice photo of Two-Soups and Betty, so I thought I'd have it framed for him, so I'll do that too and post it back to him. And we need some more white grease-paint for the next audition.'

Hitching his braces over his shoulders, Peter crossed the room and bent down to kiss her cheek. Then shrugging into his jacket and straightening his tie, he stood back, striking a pose.

'Will I do for York?' he asked.

She laughed at him for even asking; as always, he looked amazing to her. His wing-tipped shirt was snow white and starched, and his emerald-green silk tie added a splash of colour to his beautifully cut charcoal suit, which he'd confessed to finding in a pawn shop in London.

'You'll do and well you know it. You're like a peacock preening.'

'Shh. A man's allowed a small bit of vanity, surely. Ye women can't have it all?' He winked.

'Ye are, I suppose, and at least you have something to be vain about. Now, anything else you need me to do today?'

'I can't think of anything, May, but we'd be lost only for you.' He glanced at his watch. 'The train isn't till nine, but I'll go downstairs and get a cup of tea. Want to join me?'

She nodded and got up. She could feel his eyes on her as she slowly pulled on her dressing gown. 'Check the corridor for me,' she instructed.

'Coast is clear. See you downstairs.'

Picking up her sponge bag once more, she slipped to the bathroom, where she washed, then back to the front room, where she supposedly slept on the sofa. She dressed carefully in front of the mirror, pinning her hair in the new modern style he liked and choosing her fuchsia skirt and baby-pink blouse. Peter always said it was so lovely to see girls in colours again after the drab war years.

He was reading the paper with a pot of tea in front of him when she entered the empty breakfast room. Mrs Juddy was so familiar with them all now, she let them look after themselves from the kitchen when they rose. She'd allowed them a bit of leeway with the bed and board payment too, knowing the situation.

He put the paper down and turned up a china cup, pouring her some tea.

'Look at you making the tea for the woman. How very modern.' She smiled.

'Well, that's about the extent of my cooking skills, so...' He winked at her as he added a splash of milk. He knew how she took her tea, and she loved that he cared enough to make it for her just how she liked it.

Somehow, this little act of affection convinced her the time was right.

'You know the thing we were talking about?' she asked, taking a sip.

'What thing?'

'The travelling theatre, with the tent and all of that?'

He chuckled. 'Oh yes, the thing I can't afford no more than the man on the moon?'

'You could if you had two thousand pounds, though?'

He buttered the toast he'd made for them and passed her a slice with the pot of marmalade. 'I could, that's true.' He pretended to take the question seriously for a second, and then his face cracked into that huge smile that made her catch her breath. 'And if I had two thousand pounds, I could also sail to New York City and take you to dinner on Broadway and buy you diamonds and furs, and we'd stay in a fancy hotel, sleeping and who knows what else, but you know I'm poor as a church mouse.' He paused, thinking about what he'd just said, then smiled at her. 'You know, if you're having second thoughts about me, May, I wouldn't blame you. No hard feelings. I once promised your father I wouldn't marry you until I could afford to keep you properly, and now I doubt I'll ever be able to give you the life your parents rightly expect for you, so…'

'Do you want me to leave you?' she asked, trying to keep her voice neutral.

He took her hand across the table. 'I don't, you know I don't. But I can understand why you'd want to. That's all I'm saying.'

'Do you love me, Peter?' she asked, her eyes locked with his.

'I do,' he answered with a smile.

No hesitation. That was good.

'Well then.' She lowered her eyes to the table and spoke slowly. 'I have two thousand pounds. My grandaunt left it to me in her will, and I can give it to you to set up our own theatre. And before you say anything, I don't need my father's permission. The money is in my name, and it will be mine when I'm twenty-one.'

His hand squeezed hers. 'That's so kind of you, so incredibly kind, but even if you could get it now and not for another year, I couldn't take your money, May. I do appreciate the gesture, but what kind of a charlatan would I be if I let my girlfriend promise her savings to me for a venture that might or might not work out?'

*Fiancé, not girlfriend*, she longed to say, but she restrained herself. Mrs Juddy's clock ticked on the wall, a tiny little cuckoo emerging from behind its door to tell them it was seven in the morning.

'There *is* a way I could get it now, though, and I would give it to you, not lend it or anything.'

'Ah, May, no… It's… Look, just no, all right? Thank you, but –'

'Marry me.' She lifted her eyes to him and held his gaze.

'What?' He blushed and half laughed. 'It's a bit early in the morning…'

'If you marry me, I can access the money right now.' She spoke as clearly as she could. 'The terms of the will were either when I got married or reached the age of twenty-one. So if we get married, we can have the money and use it to set us up properly, for life.'

'But, May, that's not a good reason for getting married –'

'So here are my terms.' She interrupted him before he could turn her down flat. Her heart couldn't take that kind of rejection. 'I want to marry you. And I know you don't want to marry me, or at least not now. And the reason you give is the instability of your lifestyle. So if I set us up in business, both of us, our family business, Cullen's Celtic Cabaret, and not just a bit of a stage act for someone else but our own show, that we control and we keep the profits, then we have stability. But you're right – I'd be a foolish girl to give it to a boy who might leave me. So I'll only give it to my husband.'

He swallowed. She'd never seen him lost for words before. She debated if she should say more or just let it lie. She couldn't help it; she had to keep pushing.

'So will we do it? Will we get married this week, or next, and set up our own company with my money?'

'May…' He looked totally nonplussed. 'I… May, you don't need to bribe me to marry you, but I… This feels wrong.'

'Which part?' She tried to keep the bitterness out of her voice but failed. 'The money or the marriage?'

'The money,' he answered quickly. 'Of course the money.'

'So you want to marry me?' She felt a sudden warmth in her heart, an ember of hope.

'We agreed to marry back in Dublin, didn't we? Before any money was on the table.' He looked so sincere, his words so heartfelt, she longed to take him in her arms, but she resisted.

'We did, but ever since…' She blinked back the tears that were pooling in her eyes; she swallowed the lump in her throat.

60

'Because I had nothing to offer you.' He ran his hand through his hair, messing up his carefully coiffed locks. 'Things are so uncertain. I've nothing to offer you.'

'So take the money and use it to set us up. Let's never be in this position again, relying on others. Let's be masters of our own fate. It's simple really.' She wiped a tear from her cheek.

'Oh, May...' He stood up then, came around the table and pulled her to her feet and into his embrace.

She clung to him, not knowing what this gesture meant. Was this the way her life was going to be from now on, Peter Cullen's arms wrapped around her forever as she'd always wanted? Or was he just hugging her goodbye?

They stood there together for a long, long time, neither speaking. If he refused her offer, she would return to Dublin today.

Then he kissed her. Not passionately as he'd done in the early hours of the morning, but gently, lovingly.

'Is that a yes?' she whispered, not daring to hope.

'That's a yes,' he murmured against her lips.

# CHAPTER 8

DUBLIN

 ETER

'Do I look nice, Peter?' Connie Cullen, normally full of the cheeky self-confidence of a working-class eleven-year-old, looked so vulnerable, Peter thought his heart would break with tenderness for his little sister.

The dress she was wearing was new, the first time Connie – or any of his sisters, for that matter – had a new off-the-peg dress from a shop, but May had insisted on bringing them all to the dress section in Arnotts, where she decked out his ma and his sisters, Kathleen, Maggie and Connie, not just with frocks but with shoes and stockings and even little hats to match. Flame-headed Maggie refused at first to have May spend money on her, but Kathleen had a staff discount that she'd never been able to afford to use, so May was able to say that Kathleen had paid for the clothes as well, and that meant Maggie was able to swallow her pride.

Connie was the first one ready on the wedding morning, and as she stood before Peter in the parlour in her pink velvet dress with tiny white flowers on it, her snow-white knee socks and black patent-leather shoes, he went down in front of her on his hunkers.

'No, Connie, you do not look nice,' he said quietly. Her face fell, and he beamed. 'Nice isn't the word. You look absolutely beautiful, the most beautiful girl in the whole of the Iveagh cottages – in fact the most beautiful girl in the whole of Dublin.'

The Iveagh cottages were some of the red-bricked terraces that Guinness had built for their workers behind the brewery, and the Cullen family had been given a house there as part of their compensation package for Kit Cullen suffering a fatal injury at work. It was a tiny two-up, two-down, but to the Cullens, after the slum in Henrietta Street, it was a palace. Bridie Cullen kept it like a new pin, and she and his sisters were forever making little cushion covers and curtains. It was like a little doll's house. There was even a bathroom, with a steel bath and a toilet and a sink. Peter was delighted for his ma. She'd had enough of the tenements and the cold and rats and overflowing sewers. She deserved a bit of peace and comfort at long last.

'Ya can't say I'm the most beautiful girl...' Connie giggled, her crooked front tooth more prominent now as she got older.

'And why can't I?' he demanded hotly.

"Cause May is gonna be the most beautiful, 'cause she's the bride. So you can't be sayin' that other girls are the most beautiful.'

'Fair enough.' Peter pretended to give it some thought, sitting down in the armchair and pulling her onto his knee. 'You are the most beautiful eleven-year-old in the whole of Ireland, or even the whole world. Is that better?'

'Yeah.' She giggled as he tickled her.

'Wrinkle that dress and I'll be dug outta the pair of ye!' Kathleen warned, popping her head into the parlour; she was still in her dressing gown, her hair in curlers.

'Ah, Ka, you look beautiful too,' Peter teased, and he jumped up to

63

pull his older sister into the room and waltz her around among the antimacassars and china shepherdesses, singing, 'If you were the only girl in the world, and I was the only boy,' trying to imitate the way Nick always sang the same song to Celine.

Connie laughed and clapped, and the merriment brought Bridie into the room. The sight of his mother made Peter stop dancing and just stare. He knew May had taken Bridie to the hair and beauty salon on Grafton Street this morning, but he'd been out getting his suit fitted when his mother got back, and this was the first time he'd seen her all day.

His whole life, he'd been used to Ma wearing nothing but a plain work dress, usually with the colour long washed out of it, a thread-bare cardigan and flat brown shoes that had been mended so often there was precious little leather left to fix, and always with her grey hair caught back in an elastic band and hidden under a headscarf. But now…

'Ma…' He was speechless.

Tears filled his mother's eyes. 'It's too much, I knew it was. I'll wash the colour out.' She turned away, her hand to her head, but Peter crossed the room behind her in two long strides.

'Stop right there, Bridie Cullen,' he commanded.

She turned anxiously, and he took her by her thin shoulders, gazing down into her usually careworn face. Her soft grey hair was coloured blond and set in gentle waves around her thin face. She wore a coral-pink dress and matching coat, ankle length, and on her feet a pair of kid button boots with a slight heel. She had powder on her face and a little rouge and lipstick, and she seemed twenty years younger – or she would if she'd only stop being so worried.

'Peter, I know May meant well, but 'tisn't for the likes of us to be –'

'Ma, you look so radiant, like a star. I'm the luckiest man in Ireland today to have my lovely family, so fine beside me on the day I wed. I just never saw you looking so…well, elegant before, and I got a surprise is all. But oh…' He was speechless again.

'You're like somethin' out of a story, Ma, like a lovely, kind queen or somethin', Connie filled in for him as she rushed over to hug her mother.

'Ah, Connie, thanks, pet.' Bridie was finally beginning to smile and relax. 'And look at you – isn't that the nicest frock I ever saw?'

Connie stood back so her mother could admire her, and as she did, Peter caught Kathleen's eye and gave her a wink. All the years of poverty, drunkenness, fear and violence when Kit was alive had melted away. His family still didn't have much, but they were all working and helped each other out, and nobody was pouring the money for bread or milk down their necks in the form of porter, so that was a definite improvement. There was coal for the range now, so it was warm, and food for their bellies, and it made Peter's heart sing to hear Connie and Maggie laughing and tricking about. That was an activity reserved for people with enough to eat and a warm bed and no fear of hurt or humiliation.

'Holy Mother of God, is tha' the time?' Kathleen glanced at the clock. It had been a wedding present for the young couple from some distant cousin of May's, but May, realising when she came for tea that the Cullens had no clock, had asked Peter's mother to 'please mind it for us until Peter and I have room for it'.

'Is Sean picking you up here?' Peter asked, and Kathleen flushed. The family's improved circumstances meant that Kathleen could consider herself for once, and she was doing a line with a friend of Eamonn's, a cobbler whose father had a shop on Exchequer Street.

'I'm meeting him at the church. I said I'd be busy getting everyone here ready and trying to keep this little flower girl clean.' She smoothed Connie's straight fair hair. 'Now' – she turned to Peter – 'have you everything? Clean handkerchief? Money for the priest? The altar boys?' She brushed his shoulders and fixed an imaginary stray hair on his temple.

'I have. Stop mithering me, woman – I'm grand. So let you and Ma and Connie head over to Ranelagh now, as soon as you're dressed yourself. Eamonn will be back in a few minutes – he just had to pop out for something – but we'll follow ye on.'

'You talk funny now, Peter, all posh or somethin', Connie observed.

'Well, I'd not get far over in London if I was all do bees and does-bees and howra head, now, would I?' he joked, putting on a strong working-class accent, even stronger than he had before he left.

His mother and Connie laughed, and Kathleen started ushering them out.

'Right, let's get going, Ma. We'll get the 9:50 tram if we're quick.'

Kathleen dashed upstairs to the girls' bedroom to get into her own dress.

Maggie was at the Gallaghers', getting ready with May, Celine and Aida, the other bridesmaids; May had made a point of inviting her so Peter's middle sister could feel grown up and special and different from Connie, who had always been the mollycoddled baby. Poor Maggie had been put out to work at age twelve, when Kit was very bad on the drink and they were on the edge of hunger, and Peter was delighted for his sister that May was purposefully making her feel so special. May had paid such attention to everything, even the colour of Maggie's dress. She had started off wanting all her bridesmaids to wear pink, like Bridie and Connie, but at Arnotts she'd realised pink would clash horribly with Maggie's copper curls, so she'd gone for pale blue instead for her feisty sister-in-law. It was common for all bridesmaids to be in the same colour but May wanted her wedding to stand out, to be unique, so the girls were all different pastels, they looked like a bouquet of flowers.

Maggie, once she'd got over her pride, had declared May to be the 'nicest lady on earth', and everyone in his family, even Eamonn, seemed to be of the same opinion.

His mother stood before him as they waited for Kathleen to come down. 'I'm so proud of ya, Peter, I really am. And May is a lovely girl, and she's so well got but no airs and graces. So mind you, be a good husband to her, look after her, and if the Lord grants ye babies, be good to them too. You didn't learn how to be a father or a husband in this family, God knows, but you're a good man, and I know you'll do me proud.'

'I will, Ma, I promise.' Peter swallowed. His mother wasn't one for flowery speeches, but he knew she was sincere. 'And I might not have learnt how to be a good father, but I had the best of mothers, so if I follow in your footsteps, I'll be doin' all right.'

She laid her hand on his cheek and nodded. Kit Cullen was never mentioned in this new house. It was as if they didn't want to taint the walls with him, and nobody missed him.

Kathleen, the maid of honour, came back down in her primrose-yellow dress and hat, perfect for her sandy tanned complexion. 'Come on, Ma, we'll miss the tram.'

Connie caught her mother's hand, and Kathleen had herself, her little sister and Ma out the door, and they were gone.

Peter was alone in the house for the first time. Moving out of the parlour into the back room, where the family gathered most evenings to eat the dinner that Ma cooked in the tiny scullery she was so proud of, he checked his hair in the cracked and spotted mirror over the range and straightened his lapels, admiring himself. He was wearing his charcoal suit from Savile Row, the one he'd found in the pawn shop – thanks no doubt to one of those feckless lords Lady Appleton had told him about. Today he was wearing a royal-blue silk tie that May had bought for him and that matched his eyes perfectly.

He hated that she was paying for everything, as well as her father hosting the wedding breakfast – in the Gresham Hotel even – but Peter's older brother had advised him to stop complaining about the cost of everything. The Gallaghers had it to spare, said Eamonn, and May was their only child now her brother, David, was dead – or at least missing, presumed dead, which was as good as – and if they wanted to make a splash to impress their own sort, then let them do as they pleased and Peter should just enjoy getting something back from the middle classes for a change.

Eamonn liked May, but he had a healthy disrespect for the class she came from, the Dublin bourgeoisie with their pro-British instincts and nervous, conservative ways.

The Gallaghers had invited the whole Cullen family to tea last Sunday, and thanks to Eamonn's harping on about middle-class this and bourgeois that, Ma had been in the horrors about what kind of people Peter's future in-laws were and what on earth she could say to them.

But it had all gone fine, because May Gallagher – soon to be May Cullen – was so clever with people.

Over the tea table, she'd started a conversation about the vigil in the local church for the exposition of the Blessed Sacrament and how poor Father O'Reilly was having trouble filling the 2 a.m. to 3 a.m. slots. Then Bridie had ventured that the priest in her inner-city church, poor Father McLoughlin, always asked the younger people to do the early shift, for fear the older ones might fall in the dark going home.

Well, that started a whole conversation between Olive Gallagher and Bridie on all matters evangelical, and May had shot Peter a triumphant glance. The two women might be from different classes, but they were united by religious devotion. It helped as well that poor Father McLoughlin was very bad with his knees, so Olive was able to match Bridie ailment for ailment with the weak chest of poor Father O'Reilly. Eamonn seemed to have suspended his dislike of the class the Gallaghers came from, because he really seemed to be very fond of May, and the girls loved the Gallagher house and May's bedroom, which looked like nothing they'd ever seen before. So common ground had been found, and now everyone was looking forward to the day.

Turning away from the mirror, Peter sat at the scrubbed deal table and considered his life to this point.

Had he always known things were going to be different for him? That a life in the brewery, a wife in a tenement, with a tribe of kids and not enough of anything to go around, were not on the cards for him?

He'd had aspirations, it was true, but they'd been vague and could easily have been turned aside. It was that night at the Gaiety that had been his turning point, when the actress who played Lady Macbeth had been rushed to hospital and the director made Peter play the part because he was such a good mimic. The roar of the crowd had enthralled him and convinced him the theatre was the life for him. And then his father had heard about him dressing up as a woman and tried to kill him. If it wasn't for that, he'd never have had to run, he'd never have joined the army, never met Enzo and Nick.

'Ah, would ya look at him, moonin' over his mott?' Eamonn teased him as he came in the door, all dressed and ready to stand by Peter's side as best man. He was wearing Michael Gallagher's second-best suit, and he looked very respectable. May had wanted to buy Eamonn his own suit for the wedding, but Peter's brother told her that while he didn't mind her spending on his sisters and it was lovely for her to treat them, a suit was a suit and he thought he looked just fine. 'I'm not a dandy like me brother,' he'd said, cuffing Peter fondly across the head.

Eamonn took after their father in his looks, swarthy and black-haired and handsome, with big strong shoulders and thick thighs, not slender and almost girlish like Peter, with his blond curls and Cupid's-bow mouth.

'Firstly, a mott is a young one from Henrietta Street, the type you knock around with, I suppose, but my May is no mott. She's a lady, and she'll be treated as one. And anyway, I wasn't thinking about her. I was thinking about the night you clattered Kit with the kettle actually.' Peter looked up at Eamonn with a rueful grin. They never called Kit 'Da' or 'Father' or anything – he was Kit Cullen.

'Well, less said about that, the better,' Eamonn replied, taking a cup from the hook and dunking it in the bucket of drinking water in the scullery. He gulped it down in one swallow.

'Nobody misses him, not one person. That's a failed life, isn't it? That not one person cares that he's dead?'

Eamonn shrugged. 'Ya reap what ya sow, I s'pose. He was a dirty, useless yoke, and we're well shot of him. If he wasn't liked, he'd no one to blame but himself.' Eamonn was very black and white about things, very sure of himself.

'Ma looks lovely. Wait till you see her.' Peter smiled as he moved the subject to a happier note. 'The girls too.'

'It's nice for them to have a day out, get dressed up, after everything they've been through.'

'Yeah.' Peter nodded. 'At least there's a bit of peace now and they can enjoy life a bit. And this new house is lovely. Hopefully now they'll just be able to get on with life and be happy.'

The look his brother gave him was quizzical. 'You think so?'

'Ah, Eamonn, no politics today, all right? I'm getting married. I don't want to talk about the fight for Irish freedom, all right? One day off.'

Peter knew Eamonn was a staunch supporter of his namesake, Éamon de Valera, who'd recently declared himself president of Dáil Éireann, the illegal government. Such was Eamonn Cullen's passion for a new Ireland that he'd even gone back into education, taking night classes to improve his Irish. He wrote to Peter in their native tongue often now, and the irony was that Peter had to get May, with her loyalist middle-class background, to translate his brother's letters; she'd been good at Irish in school, as she'd been good at every subject. He often apologised to her for making her read them, as Eamonn's prose could be very bloodthirsty, but she was lovely about it and insisted she found the letters interesting. She was learning a lot about what was really going on, not the sanitised version she'd picked up in her parents' drawing room.

'Well, we won't talk about it today, little brother, but there is only one authority in Ireland and that is of the elected government of the Irish Republic. But there's plenty above in Dublin Castle have something to say about it, so peace isn't on the cards for any of us. Not till this is done and they leave our country for once and for all.'

'And by "they", you do know you mean young lads like me and Enzo and Nick and Two-Soups, don't you?' He'd long ago guessed that Eamonn wasn't just interested in learning Irish; his brother was in the Volunteers and probably actively involved in protecting his famous namesake. 'I know your grievance with the British, and I agree they've no business here – enough is enough. And they promised Redmond that if we fought with them in the Great War, we'd get Home Rule, but that isn't going to happen, so I see why you and your gang are not happy. But killing soldiers, Eamonn, it could just as easily be me if I'd stayed in instead of getting demobbed.'

'You're right.' Eamonn smiled, his hand on Peter's shoulder. 'Today is not the day. We'll have this out, Peter, properly, sometime, and I'll make you understand why we have to do whatever it takes. But today let's get you hitched to that lovely girl and end your days of bachelor freedom.' He punched Peter playfully on the shoulder.

'And you've no notions in that direction yourself?' Peter asked. ''Tis time enough for you.' He knew all the girls fancied Eamonn; he was so typically tall, dark and handsome.

Eamonn shook his head. 'My life these days isn't exactly suited to romance. Besides, I haven't met the right girl, not like you.'

'Sure, there's plenty of "right girls" out there for everyone, I suppose,' answered Peter lightly.

Eamonn's demeanour changed, and he frowned. 'That's a strange thing to say on your wedding day, Peter. May *is* the right girl for you, isn't she?'

'May?' Peter smiled up at him. 'Yeah, course she is.'

'If you don't mind me saying, I've seen more excited bridegrooms.'

'I'm as excited as I need to be. Now we better go, I s'pose.' He started to get to his feet, but Eamonn, who still had his hand on Peter's shoulder, pressed him back down into his chair again.

'Hang on one minute, Peter.'

'Ah, will you stop. We're going to be late.'

'We've a few minutes.' Eamonn went around the table, took the chair opposite Peter and rested his forearms on the scrubbed deal. 'Peter, I'm serious now. As your older brother, I need to be sure this is the right thing for both of ye. May deserves the best. She's beautiful and bright as a button.'

Peter smiled and shrugged. 'I know it, that's why I'm with her. But it's not like anything important changes after today.'

'Aha.' Eamonn raised an eyebrow. 'So that's it, is it? You're not excited because the best bit of being married is a treat already had?'

Peter sighed inwardly. He knew that Eamonn, who had girlfriends galore, had been shocked to discover he and May were sleeping together. Apparently it wasn't the done thing with nice girls. He wished he could explain to his brother how May wasn't like other 'nice' girls. She knew what she wanted and took it, and woe betide anyone who stood in her way.

'Ah no, it's not that, and I'm happy to make it legal,' he said patiently. 'Look, I'm very fond of her and we're a great team. We've such plans for our future, she's great at organising, we work together really well and all of that.' He didn't mention about May funding the fit-up; Eamonn was already being critical enough without Peter giving him reason to think he was only marrying May for her money.

'But do you love her properly?' Eamonn asked, and Peter waited for the jeer or the joke about his and May's goings-on in the bedroom. Eamonn wasn't one to bring the word 'love' in the conversation in the emotional sense. And yet his brother looked deadly serious. Was Eamonn a secret romantic, despite his rebel ways?

'What are you on about, big brother? I'm just about to marry her, aren't I? Come on. We'll be late, and she'll murder me.' He got to his feet properly this time.

'Peter, you didn't answer me.' Eamonn also rose and stood before him, his bulk blocking Peter's path.

'Ah, will you stop and get outta me way. Goin' on like a schoolgirl about love and all that. I'm going to the church to marry May Gallagher, and we'll live happily ever after, all right?'

'And you're completely sure it's what you want? 'Cos there's no going back if you're not. She's a great girl and she's mad about you – the dogs on the street can see that – so it would be wrong of you to marry her if she wasn't the one for you. And' – he moved to stop Peter getting out the door – 'it will end in tears if you don't marry for love. Now I know she's got money and she's been very generous to you and your big plans, but if she was poor as a church mouse, would you still be doing this?'

Peter was about to make a joke and dodge the question, say something about how he wouldn't be marrying her if she looked like the back of a bus either, or had only one leg, but he knew his brother and he knew Eamonn wasn't going to let it go. For someone who often came across as easy-going and a bit of a joker, Eamonn could be quite intense about things. And clearly this was bothering him.

Peter decided to reply as truthfully as he dared. 'In all honesty, probably not, not now. I feel I'm a bit young for it, truth be told. But she wants to draw down her inheritance so we can move ahead faster with our plans, and the only way to do that is for us to get married now.'

'I see.'

Peter felt a stab of irritation. 'No, Eamonn, don't look at me like that. You don't get it. This was all May's idea, not mine. She knows what she wants, and she goes for it. And why shouldn't I marry her? If I'm going to settle with anyone, I could do a hell of a lot worse. Look, May's beautiful and she's great fun. She wants the life on stage the same as I do, she's not afraid of going on the road, she gets along with my friends, and they all love her and so does my family. And she wants me. Where else will I ever find someone as perfect as her, even if I do hold off until I'm older?'

'And what about when someone really does steal your heart, what then?'

Peter hooted with laughter. 'Ah, would you listen to himself, with his heart stealing and love talk. That soppy old stuff won't get you far in the fight against the Crown, brother, so you get on with your job and I'll get on with mine.'

Yet Eamonn looked so sad still, Peter felt a stab of guilt. His big brother was only trying to look out for him as he'd always done, and make sure he didn't ruin his life. The thing was to reassure him. 'Look, every day I survived in France was a miracle – you've no idea the carnage. But I got out, and so did Enzo and Nick and Two-Soups and Ramon, and then the girls came with us and the show took off, and then May... Eamonn, I'm living on borrowed time, and who knows what's coming next, for either of us. So we just live for now and let the future bring what it will bring. I'm happy now, May is great, and I'll do right by her. Fair enough?'

Eamonn shrugged and sighed, finally stepping aside and letting Peter to the door. 'I suppose 'twill have to be.'

* * *

THE CEREMONY WAS LOVELY, more simple than May's mother had wanted, Peter knew, but May had curbed the worst of Olive Gallagher's excesses, and it was really nice.

He stood at the top of the aisle, Eamonn by his side and all his gang from the cabaret decked out in their finery in the seats behind the family. They'd all spent their own money to come over to Ireland. He hadn't expected that, but it was lovely to have them there. Even Mrs Juddy came, and she was so excited, she was practically fizzing. His ma was glad to claim them on the Cullen side to balance it out. An only remaining child of deceased parents, she didn't have any relatives to ask. She'd moved too recently to know her new neighbours, and her old neighbours from Henrietta Street were far from respectable. So the cast filled out the Cullen side nicely.

May wore a stunning dress, silk and sheer, with a long veil of lace, and she took his breath away, she was so pretty. Her priest spoke of how he'd baptised her and given her First Holy Communion, then confirmation, in this very church, and now he was celebrating her marriage. He said how he was so happy that May was marrying into such a fine family and how Father McLoughlin, the Cullens' parish priest, had nothing but praise for the Cullen family.

Peter didn't dare catch his ma's or any of his sibling's eyes at that piece of news. Father McLoughlin was their new priest, after the move, and he'd not known Kit Cullen. Just as well.

There were prayers for David, May's missing brother, and Peter knew the Gallaghers had been touched when his ma had a Mass said for David's safe return last week.

The whole thing went off well. The breakfast in the Gresham was delicious – cold meats, breads, salads and a big bowl of trifle that Connie almost single-handedly devoured. The ladies even had a few sherries, and the men had a few pints of Guinness, paid for by the brewery where Eamonn still worked and where Peter used to be a messenger boy, though Peter himself stuck to lemonade as usual.

Eamonn and Michael Gallagher had a cordial if differing conver-

74

sation on Irish independence, and May led Peter around to meet all of her friends from school and the tennis club and assured him afterwards they were green with envy because her husband was the handsomest man in all of Dublin.

The evening finished up with a sing-song, where the manager of the hotel, reluctantly at first and then with delight, allowed Nick to play and Celine and Millie to sing, and it was well after midnight before everyone left.

# CHAPTER 9

# *N*ICK

BEWLEY'S CAFÉ WAS BUSY, and almost every table was occupied, but the nice waitress in her black and white uniform had managed to find him a spare one at the back. He didn't mind being tucked out of sight; he was nervous at being out and about in Dublin, in case he was seen by someone who knew his parents. Luckily it seemed like everyone here was too busy with their own business to bother about him.

Another advantage of this seat was that he was sitting by the door to the toilets. He would bolt in there and hide if anyone he recognised appeared. Except for darling Floss, of course.

After his grandmother had written to tell him about Wally's death, he had written back expressing his sorrow but also saying that he had no intention of coming home and to please not mention him to his parents. He wrote that he would be in the Irish capital for the wedding of his best friend on the sixth of August, and that on the seventh, he would be in Bewley's café on Westmoreland Street all morning, before getting the ferry back to England that afternoon, so would she come and meet him there instead?

He'd had no reply from her by the time he'd left London for Dublin, but he did hope she would make it; Floss was the only person he missed from his old life.

The Dowager Baroness Alicia Shaw, whom he'd called Floss since he was a toddler, wasn't a long-standing member of the Anglo-Irish aristocracy in Cork. She was in fact a cool, elegant American woman from New England high society. The fourth baron de Simpré had married her for her money, thus restoring the family fortune after a disastrous gambling episode. She was smart, witty and very musical, and she'd always had a soft spot for Nick, which was just as well, because his parents had no interest in him at all.

His oldest brother, Roger, had been the apple of his mother's eye: a swashbuckling, handsome, romantic boy. Harriet Shaw had been furious when her husband, Walter, the fifth baron de Simpré, encouraged Roger to join the British Navy – and nearly lost her mind when he was killed in the war. Nick's next brother, Wally, was his father's favourite, a 'chip off the old block'. Like Nick, he was big and broad-chested, with a round, blunt face, but unlike Nick, he was incapable of honesty or loyalty.

Now it was just Nick. But he was certain nothing had changed at home. Just because he was the only son left to carry on the Shaw name, it didn't mean his parents were suddenly going to start loving him or thinking he was any use. If anything, they'd probably despise him even more for turning up still alive when his brothers were dead. No, whatever his grandmother said today, he was not willing to give up the life he had built for himself, with dear friends and a career doing what he loved, to return to the cold, dour mansion that was Brockleton.

The nice waitress, who had strawberry-blond hair and pale-green eyes, served him a second pot of tea and a third currant bun as he waited. It was 11:10 and there was no sign of anyone.

Maybe he was asking too much of Floss. She was seventy-four years old now and had bad arthritis. But surely if she was too infirm to travel, she'd send someone with a message? Perhaps one of the gardeners – there was a man called Liam Doherty who was very fond of Floss, and he grew all sorts of roses for her. Or his son Billy. Every time Nick heard boots on the stairs, he half expected to see one or the other of them. But still no one came.

He sipped his tea, a profound sense of disappointment in his heart. Maybe this was about him refusing to accept his position as heir to the estate. He'd thought his grandmother, as an American, would be less rigid in her beliefs about inheritance. Among the English and Anglo-Irish aristocracy, the eldest son was the only important person in the family, even if he was stupid and dull. It was his duty as heir to inherit all the land and wealth, marry another member of the aristocracy – some hare-brained, horse-faced girl from his social circle – then pass all that wealth on to his own oldest son.

But Nick didn't want to be that person, someone who only existed to own money and land and pass it on to his heir, the next little baron. Nick wanted to be loved for himself. He wanted to be respected for having talent and working hard and being loyal to his pals. He didn't just want to be the sixth baron de Simpré, with everyone bowing and scraping to him, however badly he behaved, however many poor girls he got pregnant, however much money he squandered or however many Irish tenants he bullied off their land. Everyone telling him how wonderful he was even if he was an arrogant daredevil like Roger or a pathetic letch like Wally.

It was difficult to explain to people, though. He'd had a conversation with Celine about it only last night.

'I do not see why you are not happy, Nick, to have this three-storey chateau. It will one day be yours – why don't you want it?' she'd asked, her thin forehead wrinkled.

'It's just… Well, it's hard t-t-to explain. I wasn't happy when I lived there, and now I am, and I have the show and my friends and…' He longed to say 'you' but resisted. 'Certain expectations exist when you're an aristocrat, and I like my life better now.'

'But if you marry someone, would you not want your child to have all this big house?'

As always, when Celine 'forgot' she and he were engaged to be married, it felt like a stab to his heart. He didn't blame her. He knew it was just a pretend engagement to placate her father, but it still hurt to be reminded that she didn't love him.

And the trouble was, the only person in the whole wide world he would ever want to have a child with was Celine. If he couldn't have her as his wife and mother to his children, then he didn't want anyone. And that was another good reason – maybe the best reason – he couldn't be the heir to Brockleton. His parents would just have to leave it to some distant cousin – there was always a distant cousin somewhere in the background, some lad who had been packed off to New Zealand or America to make their fortune and would be only delighted to be let home again – and that cousin could do the marrying and have the next baron.

He drained the cup and took a small nibble of the third bun. Even for him, with his enormous appetite, three buns were too much. He would just leave it. It was 12:20, and Floss wasn't coming.

He stood, and then he saw, coming up the stairs, being helped by two liveried waiters, his darling grandmother, an arm linked in each, all three of them laughing. At the top of the stairs, the men placed her carefully on her feet and handed her back the ivory-topped cane she always used. As Nick went to meet her, he saw her slip them each a half crown for their troubles.

'Nicholas, darling.' A tall, elegant woman, beautiful still, she wore a floor-length dress of crushed black velvet, with lace at the cuffs and neckline. Her long hair was pulled back in her signature bun, and she had pearls at her throat, in her ears and on her tiny hands. She looked every inch a part of the Irish aristocracy these days, despite her American upbringing. Slowly and painfully, she came towards him. He opened his arms and they hugged, and he kissed her powdery cheek and inhaled the smell of rosewater that he forever associated with her.

When she finally released him, she placed her hand on his face. 'I'm so glad you're home from the war at last, Nicholas. I lit many a candle and said many a prayer since we last met here in Dublin.'

'And how is everyone at home?' he asked. He guided her to the

79

table, pulled out a chair for her and called to the waitress for Earl Grey tea and cucumber sandwiches with the crusts cut off, which was all his grandmother ever took for elevenses.

'Your mama was in Brighton with her family, but I believe now she's on the French Riviera. She has not come back to Brockleton since Wally died.'

'And Father?' he asked, not even wanting to know the answer.

Floss made a face. He'd forgotten she had such an expressive, movable face. She used to make him laugh at the dinner table by pulling faces when his father was boring them all to tears with some diatribe; she'd never had much time for her boorish, pompous son. But now she looked genuinely sad. 'He's crushed, Nicholas, as any man in his position would be. He believes he has no sons left to him.'

'You mean Roger and Wally?' Nick could hear the hurt bitterness in his own voice.

Floss leant over and placed her bony, elegant hand on his. 'He's crushed because all his sons are dead, or so he believes. He finds life hard. Your mother blames him still for her darling Roger's death, and then you, Nicholas, never came back from the war, and after that, when Walter died in the hunting accident, it broke his heart.'

Nick noticed Floss didn't say anything about his mother's or father's feelings about his own disappearance. But he didn't need her to articulate the truth. He knew his parents didn't care about him. 'I'm sorry that Father has no son and heir, but what can I do about it, Floss?'

'You can come home, Nicholas. You are his son. You are his heir. You can let him know you're alive.'

'He doesn't want me, Floss.'

'That's not true.'

'It is.'

Nick pictured that terrible last scene at Brockleton. His mother screaming at his father, 'So if Wally dies, you want Nicholas to be your heir?' And his father, looking horrified, as if this awful possibility hadn't crossed his mind. 'God would not punish me that way, Harriet.' he'd boomed.

'You're wrong, Nicholas,' murmured Floss, stroking his big strong fingers with her long thin ones. 'Walter is a softer man now his heart is broken. A kinder one. Even I have come to like him a little.'

He smiled slightly. 'Floss, please don't ask me to go back to face more rejection.'

The waitress returned with a pot of Earl Grey tea and a plate of cucumber sandwiches. She apologised for taking so long; she'd had to pop out to the shop for the cucumber.

'And it's not just that, Nicholas,' said his grandmother, taking a tiny bite of the sandwich and shuddering because he knew from experience that it was cut far too thick for her tastes. 'If you don't come home, Walter's dreadful cousin Harvey Bathhurst will be the heir.'

'Harvey?' Nick felt his jaw drop.

'Yes, Harvey.' She took a sip of the tea and wrinkled her nose. 'Far too strong, and no lemon.'

*Harvey Bathhurst?* Nick found himself horrified and flabbergasted. He'd never even thought of that man as a relation. He was such an appalling fellow, a manipulative cretin who hated the Irish, denied his own Irish ancestry and sucked up to the British at every turn. Even among the Anglo-Irish aristocracy in Cork, nobody liked him; everyone in their social circle tried to avoid him. 'B-b-but surely there's a closer relative, Floss? He's not a first c-c-cousin. He can't be more than a second c-c-cousin –' Nick didn't know why exactly, but he was experiencing an emotion horribly like jealousy. But why would he be jealous of Harvey for being the heir? He'd left that life; he didn't want it.

Floss cut across him, with distaste for the man in her voice. 'He's a second cousin once removed. Yet legally he's still the next in line, whether your father wants it or not. So if you don't come home to Brockleton, Nicholas, and claim what's yours, then when Walter dies, Harvey will inherit the lot.'

'Well, that's...' Nick searched for the word.

'Ridiculous?' his grandmother suggested silkily. And then she drew herself up, stiff-backed in her chair, and fixed her cool grey eyes upon him. 'My sentiments exactly. I may be American, and not in favour of the aristocracy, which is why we threw off the English yoke ourselves over a century ago. But I still understand the importance of wealth and power. And, Nicholas Shaw, that estate and house and all those who work there and rely on it for their living need for you to come home. I understand from your letter how much you prefer this new life you have, and I'm not blaming you for being angry with your parents – you have every justification – but, my darling boy, don't be foolish. And please, don't put everyone at Brockleton at the mercy of that idiot Harvey.'

Nick fell silent, processing this latest development. He'd never thought of Harvey Bathhurst as family, however distant.

Harvey was known on the scene in London as a letch, a million times worse than poor Wally had ever been. Women steered clear of him, and Nick had heard some upsetting stories about Harvey being forceful, even violent, in his advances on very young girls. And not just girls either. Nick himself had a very odd encounter with the older man when he was about fifteen. Harvey had cornered him during a Christmas ball at one of the big houses and tried to kiss him. The older man had been very, very drunk, and Nick was big for his age and had easily pushed him away, but the encounter had left him shaken. Had Harvey mistaken him for a girl? Somehow he doubted it.

'Is there really n-n-nobody else?' was all he could manage.

Floss raised her eyebrows, straight dark lines that shot up to her remarkably smooth forehead. 'No. The war, it changed everything, Nicholas. Your first cousins, second cousins – all of them dead. So many of our young men lost, from all the big houses. Such a stupid waste of their expensive public-school educations. People like your father, left with their big houses empty and nobody to carry on the name. Except the likes of Harvey, who were too cowardly to fight.'

'But I just can't go back to that life, just because...' Nick was having trouble processing this.

'I know you don't want to, Nicholas.' Floss's old face was troubled and sympathetic. She was clearly torn between wanting him to be happy and wanting to save their estate. 'I know you love your life now, your friends, your music, and I don't blame you. But what are we to do? The tenant farmers are terrified for their future. Harvey has no loyalty or sense of tradition. Roger was arrogant and Wally was an idiot who would have done well to think with the organ between his ears rather than another part of his anatomy, but, God rest their souls, neither one was bad. Harvey is rotten to the core. He just sees the wealth of your father's estate and titles as his to use for his own pleasure. He cares nothing for the people who work for us, or the land – he's made that quite clear. I wish for your sake that there was someone else between him and Brockleton, but there just isn't.'

Nick found himself fuming. 'He'll be awful. The tenants are right to be worried.'

Floss nodded, clearly approving of her grandson's indignation. But then she shrugged her elegant shoulders and said, 'Look, darling, maybe it doesn't matter. Soon the likes of the de Simpré barons will be *persona non grata* in this country. Irish independence, like American independence, is just a matter of time, so perhaps who owns what is a moot point anyway. So many of the aristocracy in Cork have either gone back to England or are considering it.'

Nick surprised himself by feeling a burst of defensiveness about Brockleton. 'I don't think our family have anything to fear from the rebels. We've always been g-g-good to those in our employ, and we've been fair and honest in our dealings. My father might be a b-b-buffoon, but he's not the worst landlord – everyone says it. He never threw anyone off their land or raised their rents b-b-beyond what they could afford.'

Floss paused, gathering her thoughts. 'That's true, Nicholas, and there's a good reason for that. I come from rebel stock myself. In Boston we threw all the English tea into the sea rather than pay taxes to the Crown. My husband, the fourth baron, was a bad landlord in Cork and a drunkard and gambler, and so I drummed it into Walter from when he was a child at my knee that if he wanted to survive the coming rebellion – because it will come whether we like it or not – he had to treat his tenants with respect and compassion. But that dreadful Harvey doesn't give a hoot about the tenants. He doesn't think of himself as Irish at all. He despises this country and its people

– he thinks they're subhuman. You can see the greed in his eyes each time he visits. As soon as your poor father dies, I know he plans to raise the rents sky-high and force the Irish tenants off the land that by rights belongs to them.'

Nick felt sick. 'I d-d-don't know what to do, Floss. I never thought… Harvey, it's a d-d-dreadful prospect.'

'Everything is different now, Nicholas – *everything*. If you come home, your father will welcome you with open arms.'

'Because I'm less likely to get Brockleton burnt to the ground by the rebels than Harvey is?'

Floss sighed. 'Because you are his own flesh and blood, Nicholas. You look so like him, just as Wally did. You're his son.'

'I really don't want to be.'

His grandmother patted his large hand, hers tiny by comparison. 'Shaw blood runs in your veins, my boy, nothing you can do about it. You might feel differently once you've had time to think. Now' – she poured herself more tea and took another bite of her cucumber sandwich – 'enough of this. How is your exciting life in the theatre? Tell me everything.'

So he told her about the theatre, about Peter and his friends, about their plans to go on tour with Cullen's Celtic Cabaret. And about Celine, how she was so wonderful to sing with and play for, and so beautiful and talented…

'Do you love her?' the old lady cut in suddenly, her cool grey eyes fixed on his.

'N-n-no. N-n-nothing like that.' He could feel the tips of his ears redden under his hair. It had been one of the main awful things about the army, when his hair had been cut short; his flaming-red ears were like beacons when he blushed. They were almost hidden now, but his grandmother wasn't fooled.

'Have you told her you love her?' she persisted quietly.

'Floss, it's not like that. She's b-b-brilliant, b-b-beautiful. Everyone loves her, not just me, and she sings like a lark. But we are just friends – it can't be more.'

'Nicholas, if you want to marry her, bring her to Brockleton. Show her what she'd have if she becomes your wife.'

'I can't d-d-do that.' He was horrified by the suggestion of bribery, and besides, Floss didn't understand. Celine was too lacking in guile to marry for money. 'If I ever d-d-did ask her to marry me, I want her to marry me for myself, not b-b-because of a house. And anyway, she knows about it. I told her it has three storeys, and she was very impressed but didn't suddenly throw herself into my arms or anything.'

To his surprise, Floss pealed with laughter. 'Nicholas, you are so naive sometimes. What do you think ordinary people hear when you say a three-storey house? They think of the three-storey houses they know, which might have four or five bedrooms. Did you tell her that *your* three-storey house has thirty bedrooms, and stables for twenty horses, and a domestic staff of twenty-five, and it's on eighteen thousand acres, with many tenant farmers? And that you inherit several more properties in England, including a townhouse in Mayfair and a Scottish hunting lodge? Nicholas, you're the heir to a barony. You will sit in the House of Lords, and even more than that, you have connections to the cream of New England society from my side. And you're a thoroughly nice chap to boot. And handsome too.'

He rolled his eyes with a groan. 'Now we both know you're lying.'

'Stop that this instant.' She was still smiling, but her voice was sharp. 'I mean it, Nicholas, stop it. Only stupid or ill-bred people give into such self-doubt. You are a fine catch, so show her who you are, and if this girl has a modicum of intelligence, she will see it and snap you up.'

'But she doesn't love me, Floss, she just doesn't,' Nick answered miserably. 'She's very fond of me, and she says she trusts me and likes me, but it's not enough.'

'And why isn't it enough?' Floss arched a sophisticated eyebrow.

'I want to marry for love,' he said simply.

Floss sighed. 'Oh, Nicholas, you have sung too many romantic songs. Love is a luxury for the working classes. Do you think I married your grandfather for love? Or your mother married your father for love? That's not how it works in the aristocracy, I'm afraid, my dear, and whether you like it or not, you're one of them, as I am. Things are different for us, always were and always will be. And besides, *you* love *her*, and she'll love the house and the money and the titles – what girl wouldn't? And then she will give you an heir, and that will make her very happy too.'

'And I should be content with that?' He sighed.

'I should think so. I know of several very successful unions that had nothing whatsoever to do with love.'

'Floss, I d-d-don't…well, I d-d-don't think it can be like that.'

'It can be if you bring her to Brockleton,' Floss insisted.

Nick shook his head. 'It's hard to explain, but no, it's not for me. She's not for me.'

Floss sighed and squeezed his hand again. 'I tried.'

'You did.' He smiled. It wasn't that he wasn't touched by her concern. When Peter had taken him to meet his family, Nick had to hide his envy despite their impoverished circumstances. Seeing Bridie Cullen fuss over Peter, her love for him and his siblings clear, made him feel such loss. For all the fine houses and money and titles, his own mother had never displayed anything like the love this very poor woman showed for her children. But Floss had stepped into the gap, and even now, here she was, making the long journey to Dublin just to see him.

He would always adore his grandmother, but he couldn't take her advice to bribe Celine with Brockleton. But maybe one day he would get to introduce Celine to Floss. It would be so lovely to see them together, his grandmother and the love of his life, the two women he worshipped most in all the world.

# CHAPTER 10

*ETER*

PETER COULDN'T BELIEVE how fast things had moved.

As soon as he married her, May Gallagher – now Cullen – had stuck to her word and drawn down her inheritance of two thousand pounds. Five hundred pounds of that money, to her parents' silent horror, was now in the hands of a swarthy man in County Limerick called Eugene Stakelum, who smelled of grease and porter, and he was constructing a tent for them that they would be able to take around the country. It would be heavy, with a wooden frame to be constructed first and the canvas draped over and pegged down, and they would need a truck to transport it and another vehicle for the cast, not to mention all the costumes and props. But May was determined, and it would be done.

Peter had come around more and more to the idea of the travelling fit-up show since May had first sprung it on him as the solution to all their problems. It was increasingly clear that no theatre in England would have anything to do with them, plus anti-Irish feeling was getting so strong in London, whipped up by the rapidly growing rebel activity here in Ireland and the likes of Teddy Hargreaves over there, that Peter was quite happy at the thought of returning to his home country.

But he was so worried his friends would refuse to come with him, he put off mentioning May's idea until she told him she had the tent ordered. They were all in London at the time, and everyone was still staying at Mrs Juddy's, waiting for the next move. As each week passed and they were no closer to finding a home for their show, the tension was palpable. Nobody wanted to be the one to call it, to say it was time to go their separate ways, but it was looking more like that every day.

Peter had called a meeting in the breakfast room, outlined his idea, explained how they were proposing to make it happen, and to his relief, everyone – even poor broken-hearted Two-Soups – agreed they would prefer a life on the road with him in Ireland rather than stay in England to work for dodgy types like Teddy. Even Mrs Juddy wanted to come, and she had to be dissuaded by her husband, Stanley.

Over the next few days, as the news spread in the theatre world, a lot of Teddy's former acts decided they wanted to join Cullen's Celtic Cabaret as well.

That handsome American guy, Magus Magicus, was in. He hadn't wanted to go back to America after the war because of something to do with his Cherokee family, he didn't go into details and he wasn't a man who invited confidences. May said he gave her the creeps, not in a lecherous way but just that he seemed to look at you and could read your mind or something. She was right, he was disconcerting, but audiences picked up on it too and found him frighteningly compelling.

Nobody wanted Cecily Duffy and her Maltese terrier because Sparky was so vicious. He'd had a chomp out of almost everyone at one time or another and had once eaten one of Aida's shoes, a crime that saw the ferrety dog lucky to escape with his life. And the chap who did mime, Alfred Cox, just wasn't good enough, even though he begged and begged and nearly cried when Peter turned him down, which made Peter feel heartless and mean.

Peter would have taken the Chinese contortionists from Limehouse, but they were too settled with their families and had already found a new venue over a pub in the West End.

A few days after he'd turned down Alfred Cox, he received a surprise visit from a delegation of Teddy's chorus girls. He hardly recognised them when they turned up at Mrs Juddy's; they looked downtrodden and half-starved when they weren't wearing their sparkling costumes and the padded tights that gave their legs such a nice shape.

Wondering what they could possibly want, he ushered all ten of them into the breakfast room, where May was still sitting, drinking her morning tea and buttering a piece of toast. 'May, look who's here. It's the girls.'

'Hello, Mrs Cullen,' said several of them, dropping curtsies.

'Good morning,' said May quietly, raising an eyebrow at Peter.

He turned to them, smiling. 'So, what can we do for ye, girls? Can we get you a cuppa and a bite?'

'No thank you, Mr Cullen, Mrs Cullen.'

He was tempted to say 'call me Peter', but May had told him that anyone junior to him in life should refer to him as Mr Cullen and her as Mrs Cullen, not call them Peter and May. Going by their proper titles gave them an air of authority, she'd said, and that was important if you wanted people to treat you with respect. Peter had accused her of having ideas above their station, that most grievous of Irish sins, but he went along with it.

'Well, sit down then and tell us what ye want,' he said kindly.

The girls perched uncomfortably on the edges of their chairs, and after much blushing and squirming and poking each other with their elbows, they explained in fits and starts and with much interrupting of each other how they'd heard he was going to put on this amazing show in Ireland and please could they come because their families had disowned them for running off to be chorus girls and now that the Acadia had burnt down, they had nowhere to go.

Peter's heart went out to them. As well as that, he could see pound signs. Chorus girls, in Ireland. That would bring the crowds, and crowds meant money. 'Of course, girls –'

'Peter, come and talk to me in the parlour, please,' said May, getting to her feet.

In Mrs Juddy's front room, she stood on the hearthrug with her arms folded. 'We can't take them, Peter. They're too young and wild, and they've no chaperones – they'll cause havoc. You know that a lot of them have another business going after the shows, and that sort of thing is *not* something we want to be associated with.'

His heart sank. He'd suspected some of the girls were prostitutes of course, but what they did when they weren't on stage wasn't his business. Besides, they worked for Teddy, not him. He didn't like to go against May – she was so kind, and she was paying all the bills now that the troupe's savings had run out – but chorus girls still seemed like a good idea to him.

'Look, May, that's not our business. They'll bring in the men, and any money we spend bringing them over, they'll pay us back double in no time,' he pointed out. 'Which is more than you can say for anyone else.'

'That's as may be.' May said crossly. 'But the priests will *hate* it. If we're too racy, you know the Church will shut us down in a heartbeat, preaching from the pulpits about how we're the work of the devil. Besides, it will only be a matter of time before one of them finds themselves pregnant and no man in sight to take responsibility, and then what will we do? Leave her by the side of the road?'

Peter sighed. He was so grateful to May. She had been wonderful about the cabaret, very helpful and supportive, even though what she really wanted was to make enough money for her and Peter to buy their own theatre, where they would put on plays by Shakespeare and stuff like that. She was always saying how Peter was such a talented actor and how it was such a waste for him not to do what he was best at. But he knew it was really so she could prove to her parents and the girls from the tennis club that she and Peter were respectable.

And of course nothing was less respectable than chorus girls.

He decided to appeal to her softer side. 'But you see, it's not their fault, May. They've been so badly brought up. They need a firm motherly hand to guide them.'

'You want me to become their mother now, as well as everything else I'm doing for the show?'

'I just meant –'

'Please don't make it my job to rescue every silly girl from the street.'

'But you're *good* at rescuing people, May. You rescued me, didn't you? And you've been so kind to my sisters, helping them learn how to use the right cutlery and wear the right clothes and everything – they could never have learnt that stuff in Henrietta Street. Couldn't you do the same for these poor girls, who've been so badly brought up but just want to make something of themselves?'

May looked torn. She really was a kind-hearted girl even though she hated upsetting her middle-class parents. 'I don't know, Peter...'

He redoubled his attack. 'The girls think you're wonderful, and they'll look to you for guidance. Think how much better they'd be with you looking after them.'

She sighed. 'Looking after them? Peter, they're a law unto themselves. They won't do as I say.'

'They will if I put the fear of God in them, that one toe astray and they're out and they can find their own way back here.'

'They do add a bit of glamour, I suppose.'

'Exactly.' He made sure not to look too triumphant.

'But at the same time, I mean, all that high kicking and showing off their bloomers... I'm not against a bit of dancing, but people in Ireland would be mortified by that sort of carry-on.'

He didn't think May was right about that. He knew from Teddy that it wasn't about the dancing. To be honest none of the chorus girls Teddy had chosen at the audition were much good at anything but kicking their legs as high as they could go. It was more about whether they looked pretty and flirty, with faces and bodies that would draw the men in, men who might otherwise not want to come to the shows. He could see women flocking to their tent, but getting men in was a different story, and barely dressed young women leaping around would do just that. Irish or English, men were men. But that line of persuasion he would keep to himself.

'Well, what about if they tone it down a bit?' he suggested, his hands in his pockets and head to one side.

May thought about it, frowning. 'I don't know... It's possible, I suppose. Maybe some ballroom dancing, in nice dresses? The new ones show your ankles, so that's quite risqué enough for the country towns. Mother nearly had a fit when I bought one like that for myself. And our boys could dance with the girls as part of the show. Enzo can do ballroom – Lady Florence showed him how – and Ramon could learn it in a second, and that American fellow you've brought on board is so handsome, it doesn't matter if he can dance or not. Nick had a dancing master at that posh school of his, and maybe even Two-Soups could help out, once he gets over Betty.'

'Hmm. Maybe.' It was hard to imagine the big Scotsman ever dancing again.

But May's imagination had taken off; she was back in control of the situation. 'We could do a dance show one of the nights in every town we stay in, and the girls and Enzo and everyone can show the audience how it's done. And afterwards we can stack the chairs and benches and teach everyone in the audience some basic ballroom steps. The ladies will be delighted at the chance to spin around with Magus, Nick, Ramon and Enzo – they're all so handsome. And at least Two-Soups is tall. They can lead the women around to the music, and everyone will be happy. The country men will be shy at first, but if we can get the girls behaving nicely, like they were their sisters or cousins, then I'm sure they'd be happy to get up and practice a few foxtrots and waltzes.'

'So...' He wasn't sure. 'Is this a yes?'

She smiled and shook her head. 'It's a maybe. Now let's go back in and talk to them, lay it all out clearly. They do as we tell them, no company-keeping of any kind, and if they step out of line, they're out, no second chances. Let's see how they react, and then I'll...I mean, *we'll* decide.'

As Peter opened the door into the breakfast room again, ten hungry pairs of eyes looked at him nervously. They were all so young, poor things. He understood in a way May never could what it was like to come up from nothing. They had to do what they had to do to survive. Sure, they were cheeky and raunchy in their way of going on, but underneath it they were just kids. They were supposed to be eighteen at the audition, but Peter knew some of them had lied about their ages and were only fifteen or sixteen, and Teddy had known it when he employed them.

'Ladies, may we have your attention please?' He made sure to look very serious, his demeanour giving no indication he was anything but stern. 'If we're going to work together, this is very important. My wife and I are very concerned that there might be members of this chorus who will behave in a way in Ireland that brings our production into disrepute, and indeed into conflict with the clergy.'

He gazed from one to the next, to much blushing and a few smirks. They knew exactly what he was talking about.

'Now, this show is very important to us all, and we need to be accepted and welcomed into the Irish communities we visit. And therefore it is vital that nobody does anything that would jeopardise that. Morals and acceptable behaviour are different there, and everyone is expected to conform without question.'

Now they had the grace to look embarrassed.

He frowned and deepened his voice. 'Many of you are under the age of majority, and I need to be very clear here. If you come with us to Ireland, my wife, May, is going to be your chaperone and will oversee your lives off stage. One word from her to me about your behaviour being even remotely suspect, and I will give that person the sack, without any discussion and with immediate effect.'

'So wha' are we not allowed to do?' a cheeky dark-haired girl called Eliza asked. She was sultry-looking, boldly announcing to all and sundry that her father was an Indian sailor her mother entertained one night down the East End docks, explaining her exotic look.

Eliza was trying to embarrass him, and Peter met the challenge head-on.

'You rehearse, you perform, and we'll talk about that later. It will be a different sort of dancing from now on, so you will rehearse during the day and perform each night. In addition, you will do whatever jobs my wife asks you to do, because this will be the sort of outfit where everyone mucks in and does everything – cleaning, cooking, sewing, selling tickets, washing costumes, whatever is necessary.'

'Ah now, Peter –' began Eliza.

'Mr Cullen,' he said sharply. He was beginning to think May was right; maybe it didn't do to let people like Eliza get ideas above their station.

'Mr Cullen, then,' Eliza said, with a toss of her head. 'D'you mean you're not going to let us do nuffin' at all, and we'll spend every day dancin' and every night on stage, and if we're not doin' that, we'll be sewin' and washin' and about a million other things if May – Mrs Cullen – want us to, and we'll be so worn out, we won't have an ounce of energy for anything else?'

Peter caught May's eye; she looked quite amused. The unspoken sentence passed between them: *That's the idea.* He gave her an almost imperceptible smile. 'Well, if you're not happy about it, Eliza, then I suppose you won't be coming with us. How about the rest of you?'

'Oh, we want to come, Mr Cullen. We'll do anything...' cried the others, who had been looking more and more horrified at Eliza's carry-on.

Eliza went a bit pale. 'Nah, I want to come, like, but we do need time off too – that's all I'm sayin', Mr Cullen.'

'And you will have it,' Peter said with a flourish, 'but what you won't do is behave in a way that draws the parish priest down on my head. Are we clear?'

Eliza made one more attempt to fight back. 'Ah here, we're not kids, and what we do in our own time is our own business. You're not my old man...'

'No,' Peter replied calmly. Eliza was the most bolshy of the lot and could be a troublemaker, but she was also the most attractive, with curves in all the right places, whereas some of the others were only scraps of girls. But for that fact, he would have dismissed her out of hand. 'This is my cabaret. The rest of my acts have worked very hard to earn their place, and I will not allow you or anyone else to destroy what they've achieved.' Peter faced the girl down, and slowly she dropped her eyes.

'So yes, you can have fun,' he said more gently, 'but only within reason. In your down time, you may attend the cinema, but not with men. You can of course go to church –'

Eliza suppressed a titter but kept her eyes downcast.

'And you can spend time with each other, in lodgings which you will share. But there is to be no company-keeping of any kind with men while you are with this show. Is that crystal clear?'

His blue-eyed gaze went from one girl to the next, each of them mumbling, 'Yes, Mr Cullen,' as his eyes rested on them. Point made.

'They're all yours now,' he said to May with a wink as he turned to leave the room. 'You can explain to them about the dancing.'

'Thank you, Mr Cullen,' May replied, with a very slight roll of her eyes.

# CHAPTER 11

A FIELD IN DUNDALK, WEEKS LATER

*A*IDA

'ARGH! It would be easier to train pigs to dance...' hissed Aida.

'We're trying our best, Miss Gonzalez!' protested several of the girls.

'And this is your best? You stupid little girls have no idea what "trying your best" means. Dancing is an art, one that requires constant work and diligence. We're opening in a week, and people will want to get their money's worth and actually learn steps from you, but you girls are still not good enough to dance ballroom yourselves, let alone teach anybody anything.'

She was relieved her grasp of English now meant she was mostly correct. She'd studied every minute she wasn't rehearsing or on stage since arriving, and those long weeks in Mrs Juddy's gave her ample opportunity to learn. She read books in English and even took a class at the local library, unbeknownst to anyone. She would not be made a fool of, and not knowing the nuances of English meant she could be, so she set her mind to mastering this infuriatingly complicated language.

'Mr Cullen says it's about making sure the punters are having fun?' piped up the most annoying of the girls, the one who challenged Peter before, called Eliza.

Aida inhaled, then forced herself to calm down. She couldn't believe May had dumped this horror show on her, like it was her job to sort it all out just because she danced flamenco. Did Peter not understand she was an artist? She hadn't come here to sit in a field in Ireland to teach ballroom dancing to elephants. She wasn't supposed to be a teacher – she was a star. She wasn't supposed to end up like her mother.

The image of Gabriella Gonzalez flashed before her eyes. Her darling mother, who had been so kind and lovely with all the little children who came to her for lessons in flamenco, hardly charging their parents a penny even though she and Aida hadn't enough to feed themselves. Her beautiful, talented mother, whose heart had been crushed by her careless lover, Rafael Narro. Poor Gabriella, who had been nothing more than a dockside dalliance for the arrogant Spanish admiral, who kept his wife and children in a beautiful villa in Madrid, not on the fourth floor of a run-down tenement in Valencia, like his mistress and the daughter he didn't even acknowledge as his own.

'Why do you let him treat you like this?' Aida had demanded of her mother, after the rich, devilishly handsome *villano* had as usual thrown a few coins on the table – 'to treat yourselves' – before walking out on them without a backwards glance.

'Because I love him, Aida. He's the only man I've ever loved, or will ever love. And I know it seems terrible to you, but I'll take whatever he gives me, because I can't be without him,' Gabriella had said sadly.

That was the day Aida had decided. That very day. Never in her life would a man have that power over her.

The tent protected them from the howling rain and wind outside. It was supposed to be summer, but nobody in this damp green place seemed to think it amiss that the weather was atrocious. Did they not know Spain existed? That there they could bask in sunshine and eat oranges off the trees? It seemed they loved this place, and she couldn't understand it.

She cast a glance at Nick, sitting at the second-hand piano Peter had bought at an auction. Apparently the political situation here meant a lot of the rich families who saw themselves as English were leaving and going back to England. She didn't blame them. But they were selling a lot of their stuff, so Peter was picking up all sorts of things all over the country.

Nick had been providing accompaniment for the so-called dancing and was now studiously examining the keys. He had sensibly decided not to get involved in her admonishment of the girls.

She noticed the dancers – and that term did not, in her opinion, describe them – were looking to him to back them up and maybe say they weren't that awful, but even though Nick had a kind heart, he was a very musical man and clearly couldn't bring himself to lie. Still, he cast her a pleading glance, as if to say, *Don't be too hard on them – they're trying.*

She shuddered and took a deep breath. 'Very well. Again. Remember to hold the frame, elbows high, chins up, backs arched. And off we go...' She nodded to Nick to begin 'The Blue Danube' on the piano once more.

As the girls thundered around the stage, breaking her heart, Peter appeared at the back of the tent and beckoned her.

'Keep going,' she ordered them sharply, then turned and stalked across the floor to him. The tent had arrived last week, its canvas striped green, white and orange. Apparently this look was very patriotic, reminiscent of the Irish flag that had been adopted as the national flag after the rebellion of 1916. Aida disliked the plywood floor; it was flimsy and not well sprung for dancing. But Peter said at least it would stop the field from becoming a quagmire if it rained.

'Yes?' She stopped in front of him, glaring at him. She was still seething at what he and May were putting her through.

'How's it all going?' he asked, pretending not to notice her fury.

'Truth?' She raised an eyebrow.

'Go on.' He smiled very slightly.

'Terrible.'

'Mm…' He grimaced. 'Oh well, as long it is good fun for the men dancing with them.'

'Fun? With these girls?'

'Well, they're all very pretty…'

'They might be pretty and good with the make-up and with men' – *the silly little fools*, she wanted to say, but stopped herself – 'but there are twenty left feet up there.' She knew he probably found her austere manner off-putting, but right then, the perfectionist in her didn't care.

'Can you fix them?' he asked quietly.

'You've given me a bunch of silly, skittery girls with no modicum of dedication, absolutely no rhythm, who look like chickens running around a farmyard with their heads cut off, so what do you think?'

'But can you fix them?'

'I'm a dancer, not a magician, you know,' she answered fiercely.

'But you will try?'

'I *am* trying.'

'Thank you. Now there's something else.'

'What is it now? Teach Two-Soups ballet?' She could almost have scratched his eyes out for speaking so calmly.

'Aida, this is an operation where everyone pitches in, and there's no room for prima donnas.'

She looked at him, suddenly alert. Was he accusing her of being a prima donna?

'I was wondering if you would mind doing a demonstration of ballroom dancing with Magus Magic's on the fourth night of the show,' he said.

'Magus? Why?' She didn't like him; there was something dark about him.

'I was thinking – as well as encouraging the men to have fun with the girls, and their wives to dance with the boys, it would be nice if the audience could see a demonstration by a true professional. What do you think?'

She didn't know what to think. 'I wasn't expecting you to ask me to do this, Peter. It's true I can do anything, ballroom, foxtrot, waltz, tango, also some Latin, merengue, rumba, salsa… But with Magus? No. He is so withdrawn, Peter. To dance like a professional, you need not just perfection but passion. Passion even more than perfection perhaps.'

His eyes were shadowed. 'I don't know about the passion side of things, Aida, but May thinks you two would look wonderful together, and I have to agree.'

It was strange, though, the way he said it; he looked like he'd swallowed a lemon, as if he didn't agree with May's opinion at all.

'So you wish me to…*pitch in*…by dancing with the magician? Who has never danced ballroom in his life?'

'Well, in a nutshell, yes.'

'Nutshell? What is this?'

He laughed then, that hearty laugh he had where he threw his head back and his eyes sparkled.

'Another mistake for me?' She sighed wearily, but in reality she didn't mind. They all helped her with English and reassured her that her command of their language was much better than their command of hers.

'No, not at all. It's just a phrase. It means "yes, that's about all of it." So will you give Magus a try?'

She shrugged. 'I don't know. Ramon would be better.'

'Except he will be doing the piece with Enzo and the cannon after that and is needed for accompanying Millie too, and Magus has time,' Peter explained. 'Besides, he looks the part. He's taller than you and dark, so you'll make a very dramatic-looking pair.'

She knew it wasn't a request, it was an instruction, but Peter was nice enough to make it sound like she had a choice. She could try, she supposed.

'I will go and find him later today and see how he is at his foxtrot, waltz, and tango. I will let you know.'

'That's my girl.' Peter winked.

Aida held his gaze. Something about this man, his drive, his energy, matched hers, and she found herself drawn to him. He looked away first, and she admonished herself – she shouldn't do that, hold gazes of married men. Besides, she had no interest in any man and never would.

\* \* \*

SEVERAL NIGHTS LATER, she was dancing on her board, a piece of mahogany that Ramon had found for her to practice on. The soft pine of the stage was put over the flimsy plywood floor of the tent, but she had placed her hardwood board on top of the pine; it was the only way to get good sound from her heels. She liked to dance in the dark; it internalised the movement, the rhythm, and she wouldn't be disturbed.

She knew the chorus girls laughed at how much she practised, but she didn't care. Gabriella Gonzalez and Conchita Suarez – her mother and her mother's best friend, Ramon's mother, the two women she most admired as dancers – practised every single day of their lives. Until they got ill and died in poverty, Conchita a widow and Gabriella abandoned by that devil, Rafael Narro.

If you didn't practice, you got rusty, and though it was true that nobody here would notice if her *planta* and her *tacón* were incorrect, *she* would know and Ramon would know and it would not be good enough. And her *vuelta quebrada* needed some work, so she would get it right or die trying.

She didn't notice anyone watching her until she'd completed several of the broken turns, and then she saw Peter, leaning on an upright pole at stage left. Everyone else had gone back to the boarding house for dinner, which was probably a rather thin stew with hardly any meat. The Ireland's Eye Guest House was not as nice as Mrs Juddy's, but it would have to do for now, when they had so little money.

'Don't let me stop you.' Peter smiled as she spun to a halt.

'I am finished anyway,' she said, wiping her brow with a towel she'd brought with her. She was dressed in just a leotard and tights;

her dresses were all hanging up at the guest house, being aired. The hard heels and soles of her sandals echoed as she walked across the pine boards of the stage.

She joined him and sat opposite him at a trestle table they used for props. He was dressed in just a shirt and trousers, no tie or jacket, and he looked younger, more boyish than he did in the top hat and tails he wore on stage. There was a faint stubble of fair hair on his chin, and his sandy-blond hair was swept back from his forehead, the length giving him a rakish look.

He handed her a cup of water, which she gulped down greedily. She wiped her mouth and handed it back. '*Gracias.*'

'You work harder than anyone else, Aida. And yet you are the most talented,' he said quietly, putting the cup aside.

She shrugged. He was right. She was the only professional in the cabaret, and there was no point in false modesty. Even Ramon didn't practise enough. Celine had a lovely voice, but it was untrained, same with Nick, and Two-Soups was making it up as he went along. Enzo was naturally athletic, but he put very little effort into his work, though the audiences loved his antics. Even Peter himself was only feeling his way.

'You can't ever stop if you wish perfection. My mother and Ramon's mother danced together, and they practised every day. I have done it too, since I was a little girl.'

'How little?' he asked, his dark-blue eyes smiling at her.

'Since I could walk.' And it was true. Dancing was to her like walking; she'd always done it.

He looked around. 'Where is Ramon? Don't you need his guitar music to practice?'

She brushed back a strand of her long black hair, which had escaped her tight bun. 'No, I hear music in my head. I don't need it, not for this. For performing, of course then yes, but' – she shrugged – 'for so long, the music is in my head, in my heart.'

He rested his smooth forearms on the table. 'It's amazing, watching you, the music and the rhythm, so graceful and controlled.'

'Thank you. Do the gypsies here dance?' She'd been meaning to ask him this question. Ireland had never featured in her experience of life before now, but being here in the damp, mystical country that was growing on her, she found herself interested.

He seemed surprised. 'Do you mean the tinkers? I don't know. I don't think so. Why?'

'Well, flamenco is the dance of the *gitanos*, the Spanish gypsies, from Andalucía originally, but later it was adapted to other regions. But we are the – I don't know the word –*las personas moviéndose por el mundo* "moving about the place" people.'

'Well, here I suppose you could call them travelling people, but mainly we say tinkers because they work with tin and fix pots and pans and things like that. But I honestly don't know if they have special dances. There's Irish dancing, but that's different. But again, I'm no expert. Not much in the way of dancing classes where I grew up.'

'Did May learn this Irish dancing as a little girl?' she asked, interested.

He shrugged, smiling. 'I've no idea. I never asked her.'

'Where *is* May anyway? You've been so busy together, arranging everything for the rest of us. Not much of a honeymoon, eh?' She smiled and cast him a roguish glance.

He chuckled. 'I suppose not, but we wanted to get the tent sorted as quickly as possible. They're saying it will be fine until Halloween, so we wanted to get cracking before the weather turns and see what it's like in the good months, before we have to do it in the driving rain and snow. It will take a while to learn how to fit up and strike every few days.'

'And this is the life you want? Going from town to town, doing our show?'

'Of course it is. I thought we all wanted that?' He cast her a quizzical glance.

She shrugged. 'For me, yes, I think I will like it. Though the teaching of these girls...'

He raised a sceptical eyebrow.

'All I've ever wanted to do is dance, to be paid. Seeing new places, it's good for me. But you're a newly married man. Don't you want to start – what do they say in English, Two-Soups told me – em…feathering the next?'

'Nest?' He laughed.

'Yes, this. Where birds live. You don't want this? To have babies and a garden and all of that?'

Peter laughed again, his eyes sparkling, shaking his head. 'Definitely not.'

'And May, she doesn't either?'

'May knew what she was getting when she married me. I'm not one for that kind of thing.'

'Aha…I see.' Aida smirked.

'What do you see?' he asked, leaning closer, gazing into her face.

'Nothing.' She suppressed a smile.

'Tell me.'

Aida found herself making a gesture that was reminiscent of her mother, a kind of shrug but with palms outstretched. 'Just that I think women say they don't care about this to get the man to marry, but they don't mean it.'

'And you think May is like that?' He frowned slightly.

'Not May alone, just women. It's in them to want that thing, a home, babies, flowers in the garden…'

'And that's what you want?' His eyes were fixed on hers.

She dropped her gaze. 'I'm not a usual type of woman.'

'Well, that's certainly true. But you never know. Maybe one day you and Ramon will stop fighting long enough to get married, and then the place will be full of little señoritas and señors running around, playing music and dancing and arguing…'

She laughed, shaking her head.

'What?' he replied. 'It's not an outrageous suggestion?'

'It is, and you know you don't believe that. Ramon and me are like brother and sister. We grew up beside each other. We could never think like that about each other.'

'So if not Ramon…' Peter raised an eyebrow quizzically.

'Look at you, just married, and now you can't wait to see the rest of us tied up like farm dogs too.' She laughed mockingly. 'Single people never say this thing, just married people, and the more miserable they are, the more they want to see others in marriages.'

'Maybe you're right,' he answered, suddenly serious.

'But *ai-ai-ai*.' She flapped her hands, ashamed of herself for poking fun. 'I am just joking. I know you and May are happy, but maybe so am I – you think of that?'

He pushed back from the table, folded his arms across his chest and just sat there, looking at her. She looked right back at him. His eyes were an intense navy blue; his mouth reminded her of that bow, the one Cupid always held in paintings and statues. Cupid, the messenger of love.

'And are you happy, Aida?'

'Of course I am,' she said, with a slight defensive movement of her chin.

He continued to hold her gaze for a long moment, then smiled and broke eye contact, saying lightly, 'And did you catch up with Magus?'

'I did, and he knows nothing about dancing. And he certainly has no passion. He is such a strange man. So I'm afraid your wife's idea is not going to work.' She had been dreading telling him this, in case he accused her of being a prima donna again, but he just shrugged, like he wasn't surprised.

'But you would be happy with someone who could dance?' he asked, still not looking at her. 'It's not that you don't want to dance ballroom at all?'

'Of course I would dance ballroom, if I could find a partner.' She hated that he would think of her as unhelpful. She wanted this travelling cabaret to work – surely he realised that? Even those silly girls – she was working night and day to knock them into shape for him.

'So you don't mind this life?' He glanced at her sideways from under his long lashes, a very slight smile on his mouth.

'I love it.' She almost surprised herself by saying it, but it was true; she did love this life. For the first time since her mother died, she felt that she had a family, and she knew she would do whatever it took to help Peter – and May, of course – make their show a huge success.

'I know I rejected the idea of Ramon, but if I move things around a bit, maybe it would work with you two?'

'No. I thought about it. He can't bear for me to criticise his steps when he practices with the girls. We would fight and kill each other.'

'You're right,' he agreed, with a rueful smile. 'Enzo?'

'Enzo is too flighty. He makes everything funny. His trapeze act is wonderful and crowds love him, but it is all freestyle, while dancing is about precision and control.'

'But also passion?' He gave her a wry grin. She knew she used this word a lot, but it was important, the essence of dance.

She could see his mind whirring as he thought about what she'd said. He was always plotting, thinking and planning.

'Controlled passion. Unspoken passion. It's no good if the passion is free – it has to be held in the heart, like steam in a sealed pot. It has to drive the movement... See, like this.'

Jumping up, she performed a few steps of the tango, quivering, taut. When she stopped and looked at him, he applauded softly. 'More,' he said, and watched her intently as she did a few more steps.

This time when she'd finished, he stood up, moved back his chair and joined her on the plywood floor. 'Like this?' He performed a few steps, exactly as she had done.

She stared at him in amazement. Of course, she had forgotten – Peter Cullen could mimic anyone, their voice, their actions. Night after night in the Acadia, he'd had the audience in stitches when he introduced the different acts in the guise of Charlie Chaplin, and Laurel and Hardy, and even that Russian revolutionary Lenin with his pointy beard. And now he was imitating her few steps of tango, exactly as she had shown him.

'Yes...but...' Then amusement bubbled up inside her, and she pealed with laughter.

Peter smiled awkwardly, looking almost as awkward as Magus Magicus had when she asked him to dance. 'Was I that bad?' he asked.

'No, it is perfect! It is just, that is the woman's part.'

'Oh...' He blushed.

'This part is the man's.' Still smiling, she showed it to him, and once more he copied it to perfection.

'Peter, you can do this,' she said seriously. 'You have it.'

'Ah, but do I have the passion, Aida?' he asked, with that same cheeky smile, spreading his hands.

'I don't know until we try it together. Let's see.' She took his slender hands and placed one on her shoulder and the other on her waist. She was wearing her heels, and he wasn't much taller than her. 'Now...'

At first she was genuinely curious to see if he could partner her at all. It wasn't as if he had ever expressed any interest in dancing before; he was only imitating her. But as he looked into her eyes as they danced together – slowly at first – she thought to her surprise that there was something inside him after all, some passion for the dance in his heart, tightly controlled, suppressed, unseen, exciting. Faster they danced, and faster...

'Peter?'

Instantly he dropped his hold on her and stepped back, looking around him for the source of his wife's voice.

'Peter?' It was coming from outside in the dark.

'I'm coming, May!' he called, and without even a look at Aida, he picked up a tilly lamp from one of the tables and went quickly to the flap of the tent, beyond which stars were pricking through the dark night.

Left alone, Aida stood, sweating and shivering, slowly becoming aware she was wearing only her leotard and tights. She took her long black coat from the back of the chair where she'd left it and wrapped it around her, then moved her mahogany board safely out of the way behind the stage, closed the lid of Nick's piano, which he had left open earlier, and picked up one of the other tilly lamps to light her way home, turning down the wick until it was just a flicker.

As she moved to the opening in the tent, she could see Peter's own much brighter light swinging from side to side as he moved across the field, throwing the shadows of two figures across the grass. For a while she stood there, watching until Peter and May had disappeared and the light was gone.

# CHAPTER 12

DUNDALK, TWO WEEKS LATER

ICK

NICK WAS the happiest he'd ever been in his life. He was so proud of himself, of everyone in the show and most of all of his best friend, Peter Cullen. And of Peter's lovely wife, May. It was so brave of May Cullen to invest in her husband's dreams, spending all of her inheritance on keeping his show on the road after the Acadia burnt down, and so imaginative of her to suggest reinventing Cullen's Celtic Cabaret as a touring company.

And it had all gone wonderfully.

The rain had held off all week, by a miracle, and Cullen's Celtic Cabaret five-day show had filled the tent in Dundalk on the east coast every single night. May had come up with the ingenious idea of offering a discount on five-consecutive-night tickets, so there was never an empty seat, and the audience were happy to keep coming back every night because every act was perfect. Even the chorus girls had their timing down to a tee, and on the dancing night, Nick had spotted Aida looking happy for once, laughing with Peter.

Two-Soups had opened the first night, and Peter had been right to stick with him. He had the audiences wiping their eyes with his act; he seemed to have become funnier if anything since the tragedy. Though once he was off stage, he just went home to his lodgings in the Ireland's Eye Guest House. Since Betty died, he'd been so quiet and sad. Celine, who was usually so good with wounded men, had tried to reach him, but even she said it was impossible.

Enzo was on the same night as Two-Soups. He had replaced the cannon Betty had made him – it had been destroyed with the theatre – and combined with the trapezes and a tightrope hanging from the roof of the tent, he had the audiences gasping at his daring. He loved the fit-up, saying how he felt much more at home in this environment because of all the circus work he'd done with his Italian aunts and uncles before the war.

He had a trapeze partner as well now. The cheeky little chorus girl Eliza had spent so long hanging around watching him practice flying through the air, her mouth wide open, that he had decided to recruit her into his act, dressed in a pink sparkly leotard that Aida had embroidered for her.

Eliza was so crazy about Enzo that she let him fling her around all over the place, and even managed to smile while he was doing it. On that first night, Enzo was his usual incredible self, lithe and fearless, twirling and somersaulting across the heads of the crowd, half man, half bird. He had the whole place breathless at his audacity, making them laugh and scream as he pretended to teeter on the edge of falling, then dropping poor Eliza, only to swing underneath her and catch her again. Eliza had been terrified of doing this particular stunt at first, but like all girls, she found Enzo too hard to refuse.

Nick wished he had the same problem.

Millie had opened the second night, and Peter's secret worry that rural Ireland might not be ready for a male impersonator had turned out to be unfounded. She strutted on and off as a dandy, a soldier, even a priest – which had everybody gasping in shock through their laughter – and she sang all those great comic songs by Vesta Tilley that everyone loved. Nick accompanied her on piano because Millie's accompanist hadn't wanted to come to Ireland, and he was happy to do it. He liked Millie, not in the same way he loved Celine, of course, but because he thought she was a true professional. For instance, during her act, the tilly lamp was fading on stage, going lower and lower, and Millie had calmly gone over and pumped away as she was doing one of her funny monologues, making it look like it was part of the comic routine.

Sometimes Nick thought he liked Millie so much that he almost wished it was her he was in love with rather than Celine. She was older than the innocent French girl, older than Nick as well, and much more worldly-wise than either of them. She wouldn't have been out of place in the Anglo-Irish aristocracy, which was full of shrewd, well-groomed women who knew which side their bread was buttered, in the same way Millie had known right away that Cullen's Cabaret was the way to go if she was ever going to make money and a name for herself. He suspected if he dangled Brockleton in front of Millie as a bribe, then unlike the pure-hearted Celine, she would snap it up.

But loving Millie was not possible. Nick's heart belonged to the innocent French girl, and only to her.

The American magician followed Millie on the second night and performed a stream of magic tricks, shaking doves out of handkerchiefs, discovering rabbits in his hat and swallowing fire. After the interval, he sawed one of the chorus girls in half and threw knives at another pinned to a wheel that rotated slowly. The little kids in the front row shrieked and clutched each other with excited fear. May had let all the kids in for half price, and those under five were free, but they were all put on low benches at the front so as not to block the view of the adults.

Finally Magus dragged a metal box with chains around it onto the stage and invited a man and his wife to lock him inside it by securing the chains with a huge padlock. After a long wait, Ramon jumped up

110

on stage and suggested the worried-looking couple unlock it again, in case poor Magus had suffocated in there.

When they did, with Ramon's help, the box was empty. While everyone stared in astonishment – and some of the children even ran up on the stage to search around – Magus sauntered in through the back of the tent, eating an ice cream from the hut outside and grinning. The crowd had gone wild.

The ice cream hut had been Enzo's idea. His Italian father was an ice cream maker, and he'd persuaded May to invest in a hand-cranked freezer with which he produced the most delicious ice cream from the local cows, and it went down a storm with adults and children alike.

Nick marvelled at all the unexpected skills his mates kept demonstrating. Ramon could make these amazing Spanish biscuits – his mother had taught him – that May sold at the interval. Two-Soups had learnt welding from Betty and was working on making Enzo a more transportable and elaborate cannon, in Betty's memory. May knitted everyone jumpers and hats to keep out the cold when they were waiting around behind the scenes, and Aida could embroider beautifully.

Celine kept saying she was no good at anything, but it wasn't true; she was wonderful in the intervals. She was so used to serving crowds of clamouring soldiers in her father's drinking establishment that she had no problem serving the audience tea and biscuits at the interval, taking orders from several people at once, never forgetting who wanted what and getting the right money from everyone.

The third night was kicked off by Peter, mimicking the politicians of the day, and Two-Soups made another appearance, this time doing a set piece with Millie, who played the straight man in all of them, like when he was a drunk who thought the lamppost was a policeman and she was the actual policeman who stood watching him.

But after that, the night belonged to Nick and Celine. They had lengthened their set from the early days and could keep the audience enthralled for well over an hour. Nick's grandmother, who still wanted him to come home, had sent him some of her favourite sheet music, which she'd sourced from America, and he and Celine had been expanding their repertoire with Tin Pan Alley songs and tunes. Nick, though classically trained, loved playing ragtime piano, and as always, Celine's alto was a surprise to people who hadn't heard her before and who might expect a sweet soprano. She was almost gravelly on the lower register, and it still gave him goosebumps. The combination of romantic ballads, operetta, folk songs and a few comedy songs went down a storm.

They had finished their set with 'Let me Call You Sweetheart', exiting the stage to huge applause. Everyone was on their feet, and it was exhilarating. People started shouting 'Encore, encore,' so Celine grabbed his hand and they ran back on to sing 'If You Were the Only Girl in the World', which also went down a treat.

Nick loved the encore because it allowed him even more time with Celine, and he loved singing that particular duet with her because it gave him a chance to gaze into her eyes. And she in turn gazed at him so soulfully, it made him feel she might love him too.

The fourth night was the dancing night. Aida and Ramon came on to perform a thrilling twenty minutes of flamenco, but it was the appearance of the chorus girls that got the tent buzzing. They didn't do anything nearly as risqué as they had in London, but there were still a fair number of flirty glances at the men in the audience as they twirled around the tent poles. Then Aida and Peter demonstrated a few ballroom numbers – they danced very well together – and after that Nick went up with Two-Soups, Ramon, Enzo and Magus, and they took the various girls for a spin about the stage – with nothing like the elegance of Aida and Peter together but with plenty of enthusiasm. Nick would rather have been dancing with Celine than Eliza, who kept 'accidentally' standing on his feet, but it was still good fun.

The second part of the night was dancing with the audience, which was a huge hit.

The final night was everyone performing, each doing a little bit, so at the end of the week-long show, the whole audience went home happy.

Now it was the end of the last show, and Nick, Enzo and Ramon had stayed behind to move the chairs out of the tent into one of the lorries. They would have a day's rest before a group of local men came in to help dismantle the tent and pack it into the second truck so they could move on to the next location.

Everyone else had gone home to their digs, exhausted. Even the chorus girls, despite their protests, had been rounded up, counted and escorted by May and Peter to their lodgings, where they slept in bunk beds. Celine, Aida, Millie, Magus and Two-Soups had gone back to the Ireland's Eye Guest House.

When they'd finished stacking the chairs in the van, Enzo got three cups from the tea counter, pulled a naggin of whiskey out of his back pocket and led the way behind the stage.

The tent was constructed in such a way that there was a small space back there for storing costumes and props and getting changed. Peter and May had had to put up with a lot of complaining from the girls that it was too small, and it was, but May said every inch that wasn't a seat was money lost, and so they had to make do.

The men tried to be discreet, leaving one half of the backstage for the girls and taking the other for themselves, but in reality the ladies had most of it and squashed the men into a corner. It was a common sight to see a girl in her underwear – and an odd time not even that – as they changed costumes, and as a boy who had grown up with only brothers and attended a male boarding school, Nick had to become used to seeing ladies in various states of undress and not blush or flinch.

Now he, Ramon and Enzo sat around the table at the men's end, beside the rail for their costumes. The costumes weren't hanging up at the moment – they were in a pile waiting to be laundered by the girls tomorrow – and the cramped place smelled of greasepaint and sweat.

'Some bloke was 'angin' about outside trying to ask Celine to go to the pub with him or something,' Enzo told them as he splashed out whiskey into the cups.

'What did she say?' Nick asked, trying to keep his voice light.

'That 'e was wastin' 'is time, that she wasn't that sort of girl and that 'e was barkin' up the wrong tree.' Enzo chuckled as he helped himself to a homemade bun from a tin handed in by a local lady who had enjoyed the show.

Nick inwardly heaved a sigh of relief.

'Just tell her. Put us all out of our misery,' Ramon said, picking out a soft, complicated tune on his guitar. The instrument and the man were never apart; it was as if the guitar were a part of him.

'Tell her what?' Nick asked, helping himself to a bun as well, though he probably shouldn't. He'd had to start using a different hole on his belt of late as his girth widened back to his pre-war weight. Aida had said a nice thing when she was teaching them to dance, that he had the body of a man, that women love a strong, tall, well-built man, not thin, wiry chaps like Enzo. It wasn't true, of course. Enzo had women eating out of his hand and Nick was mortifyingly inexperienced, but it was nice of her to say it.

Peter had told him so many times to respond to the chorus girls that he thought were flirting with him, but Peter was just being kind, like the girls were. They said nice things to him, like he was kind and funny and they could listen to him sing all day, and one of the chorus girls, Dora, said she loved being in his arms when they were dancing, that he made her feel safe. But that wasn't the same as fancying someone. His friends wanted him to get some experience; they knew he had absolutely none, and they'd made a pact to stay away from the brothels on the front because of what you could catch. Nick was glad of that, because even without the risk, the very idea of being naked with a woman, any woman but especially one who knew what she was doing, left him puce in the face.

He knew his friends were probably right, that he should get it over with, do it once with someone willing, but he just couldn't. He was destined for lifelong virginity, it would seem.

'That you love her, of course. Everybody can see it, like the little puppy after her every day. Tell her and get it over with,' Ramon teased.

'I d-d-don't.' Nick felt his face flush.

Ramon raised an eyebrow, and Enzo started whistling 'If You Were the Only Girl in the World'.

'I d-d-don't,' he protested, harder now. 'We're c-c-close, we're friends, but she has no interest in me like that, and I d-d-don't have any interest in her.'

'The first part might be true.' Ramon laughed. 'But the second part certainly is not.'

'Nick,' Enzo reasoned, 'you ain't got nothin' to lose, mate. Tell 'er. She agreed to come out with me and the Lady Florence that time in London, didn't she? If it wasn't for poor Betty, God rest 'er soul, you might have 'ad your chance that night. Give it another go. If she says she is cracked for you too, then 'appy days, and if not, you ain't no worse off than you are now, are ya?'

There was no point pretending not to know what they were talking about; they knew him far too well. 'I c-c-can't,' he said simply.

'Why not?' Ramon asked. 'She is very fond of you – we can see that. Maybe she's just waiting?'

'She isn't.'

'And how do you know that?' He lit one of his pungent Spanish cigarettes. Ramon was less public about his love life than Enzo, but he had plenty of interest from the ladies too and took advantage of it when it suited him. Unlike Enzo, however, he seemed to have no trouble shaking them off afterwards. It wasn't a nice way to be, Nick thought, but it was Ramon's own business, he supposed. They were all friends, but there was a darkness inside Ramon that nobody could reach, whereas Enzo was an open book.

'I d-d-don't know. Anyway, I c-c-can't. I wouldn't know what to say.'

Enzo chuckled. 'Just ask 'er out, mate, like you did before.'

'B-b-but that was just for fun. We were going with you and Florence.'

'Well, ask her out for fun again. Nobody's telling you to jump on top of 'er.'

'I would never…' Nick said, flushing again.

'That's what I'm sayin', mate.' Enzo was getting exasperated now. 'Look, you're a gentleman, and ladies like that, so just tell Celine that you really like her and you'd like to take her out for a nice meal sometime when we're back in civilisation.' He rolled his eyes. Rural Ireland was not to the taste of this East End London boy. 'Tell her you want to get to know 'er better.'

'She'd think I was m-m-mad. I do know her.' Nick knew he sounded stupid, but he genuinely had no idea.

'Well, maybe not get to know 'er, just that you'd like to court 'er, what about that?'

Ramon laughed. 'Is that what *you* say, eh? I'd like to court you?'

'Nah, but I'm different. I'm just an old alley cat, but Nick 'ere is a gentleman, and he wants to behave like one.' He nudged his friend. 'The birds I knock about with aren't exactly...ladylike, if you know what I mean.'

Nick did. He was astonished at how many women, from all strata of society, were willing to risk their reputations by being seen to behave improperly with Enzo, a man who had no intention of marrying them.

Nick decided to throw himself on his friends' mercy. They were good men, and he trusted them, though they teased each other all the time. They knew more about this than he did.

'So what sh-sh-should I say?' He felt foolish and innocent. It was all right for Enzo and Ramon, thought Nick sadly. They were both so confident around women. All the chorus girls were in love with them, and half the women who came to the show as well. But Nick was just a big lump, who'd never even kissed a girl.

Ramon played another string of pearly notes on his guitar. 'Nick, tell her the truth. That you are fond of her, you think she's beautiful, and you'd love to court her. She'll either say yes or no, and as Enzo says, if it's a no, you're no worse off.'

'Except she'll know,' he replied miserably. He saw them exchange a glance and was so embarrassed. It told him that she knew already, everyone did, that he was like a lovesick fool after her.

Feeling like a terrified five-year-old at a birthday party but desperate to know, he asked, 'What are my chances, d-d-do you think? Not that I'm going to t-t-try...'

There was an unspoken conversation between his friends.

'I'd give it fifty-fifty,' Enzo said eventually.

'Really?' Nick was amazed.

'Maybe thirty-seventy,' said the more brutal Ramon, rinsing his cup in the basin of water on the table before getting to his feet with a yawn.

'Thirty-seventy? For or against?' asked Nick, his heart sinking again.

'What does it matter if you're not going to take the risk anyway? If you're not in, you can't win, my friend.'

\* \* \*

WALKING HOME ACROSS THE FIELDS, warm from the whiskey, Nick thought about his friends' advice but decided they were wrong. It wasn't like he was miserable with the way things were. He got to sing with Celine all the time, gaze into her eyes, even hold her hand when they were taking their bows. Celine often said he was her best friend, even more than Millie, and that would have to do, because he was never going to risk what he had with her now by pushing for anything more.

# CHAPTER 13

A COUPLE OF MONTHS LATER

*M*AY

MAY SAT with a pot of tea and a plate of toast in the dining car of the train as it pulled out of Cork station on its way to Dublin. She had the account book for Cullen's Celtic Cabaret at her elbow and the chequebook open in front of her, and she was writing her signature over and over, on cheque after cheque.

*May Cullen, May Cullen, May Cullen...*

There were so many expenses to be paid. Repairs to the trucks. Oil for the tilly lamps. A local landowner had charged them a ridiculous amount for the use of his land and also for his farm labourers to bring the tent up and then down again – and that was a wasted expense. She wished they had more men in the troupe instead of so many girls. On top of the rest, it was essential for morale to pay wages in full and on time to all the performers, as well as cover the cost of their digs in the lodging houses, meals and all the rest of it, often not taking anything for herself and Peter when weeks were tight. There had been so much outlay in the beginning; the costumes and props, not to mention the tent, had eaten up all her capital, and there was no margin to play with. Audiences were enthusiastic and in plentiful supply, and Cullen's Celtic Cabaret would, in time, be very lucrative, she was sure of it, but in the meantime, cash flow was a constant headache.

*May Cullen, May Cullen, May Cullen...*

It took her back to when she was an innocent girl, so excited to have a sweetheart in the army, practising her future signature at the dressing table in her bedroom, experimenting with swirling the M or, at other times, a big curly C for her surname. She couldn't believe it when the love of her life had finally married her, when she was finally the wife of Peter Cullen and he was her husband.

*May Cullen, May Cullen, May Cullen...*

But she wasn't getting the same thrill from writing her married name today. And not just because every time she wrote it that meant money gone. She didn't even mind about the money. She knew it had to be spent, and she was proud of the cabaret and all everyone had achieved.

No. The thrill was gone because of her.

Aida Gonzalez.

When Aida and Peter danced the tango for the audience on dance night, swirling around the floor in perfect time, it made May feel sick with fear and anger. Why couldn't the bad-tempered Spanish woman dance with Ramon, or Enzo, or Magus Magicus? Why did it have to be Peter?

Yet when she'd asked this simple question, Peter had given her one of those looks, the one that said she was overstepping, allowing her petty feminine jealousy to interfere with the cold work of business. So what if he was the best man to dance with Aida, he'd said. People paid to see a good show, and anything he could do to facilitate that, he would. Wasn't May always worried about paying the bills, and wasn't the dance night always the best attended? People left their children at home, so every seat was paid for at full price. And others crowded in to stand at the back, and that was extra money in the bank.

Anyway, what was she on about, he'd added dismissively. Aida was made for Ramon.

May thought that was utter nonsense about Ramon. Peter knew it too; she could tell when he lied. The flamenco guitarist and the dancer mainly spoke in Spanish to each other, so it was hard to tell exactly, but they fought like cats half the time, and that didn't look like love to her.

Still, she tried to accept that it was all about the show, and she made a big effort to put the Spanish girl to the back of her mind. And most of the time, she managed to do so.

Except for that one night in the week. Dance night. It wasn't just the tango, or the way they gazed into each other's eyes as they performed it, so precise and passionate. It was how they laughed so easily together afterwards. Aida was not one for laughing, God knew, but it was as if she and Peter had a connection that the Spanish girl didn't have with anyone else.

As the train puffed through the green countryside, May twisted the wedding ring on her finger. The ring she'd paid for. At least Peter had married her after he met Aida, she reassured herself, so it wasn't like he got hitched to May and then found out that the Spanish beauty was in the world and realised he'd made a terrible mistake.

Unless he'd known it was a mistake and done it anyway, because of the money…

No, she refused to believe that. Her love life with her husband was passionate, even if in the last couple of weeks it had been nonexistent, but that was only because they were both so tired. Anyway, even out of bed they had so much in common. Both of them loved everything about the theatre; both of them were ambitious and driven to succeed. He listened to her advice, and nine times out of ten, he acted on it. Time after time, he told her he couldn't have done all this without her, and she knew it was true.

He'd been so proud of her when a magazine invited her to do a feature article on women in business. It was a big two-page spread with a lovely photo of them both, but the article focused on her: her family, her upbringing and how she'd come to be the force behind Cullen's Celtic Cabaret. It had made her sound like a tycoon, and even if it wasn't strictly true, she'd loved it. The journalist told her it was going to be published in several magazines and even translated into other languages.

She slipped all the cheques into different envelopes, stamped and addressed them and put everything away into the lockable leather bag that travelled with her everywhere these days. She poured herself another cup of tea and sat gazing at the countryside chugging past.

Something she'd overheard Millie say to Celine a few days ago bubbled up into her mind. Millie and Celine were changing behind a screen and didn't know she was there. They had been talking about Nick, and how it wasn't a bad idea for Celine to hang back. Letting men think you liked them gave them too much power, and according to Millie, men had too much power as it was. Even though they were talking about Nick – poor lovestruck Nick – Millie's advice had been niggling at May ever since.

She herself was always fussing over Peter, trying to get him to love her more. Maybe she should pull back a little, make him chase her a bit. She was going to see her mother today, and maybe she'd stay for a week instead of for one night. If she wasn't there to do his bidding, then maybe he'd miss her and realise how much he needed her.

She hoped so.

The other obvious strategy was to get pregnant. If she was carrying his child, then he'd have to give his wife all of his attention, and that would stop all the silly laughing and joking and hanging around with his mates, with Aida always there.

She wasn't pregnant, though, and she didn't understand why. Without telling Peter, she'd stopped using the Dutch cap on their wedding night. That sort of thing was necessary when she was an unmarried girl sleeping with her boyfriend, but not for a married woman. But every month she was disappointed when her period came, as it had ten days ago. What was the matter with her? Was there something wrong with her body?

Without telling him she was trying, she'd broached the idea of a child with him.

'Wouldn't you like us to make a baby together?' she'd asked, after a particularly passionate night. She refused to blush at raising such a topic, as other wives might. He was her husband, and she was a married woman; she would not feel ashamed about her body.

He'd laughed – actually laughed – at her. He'd been sitting up in bed, reading a piece in the paper about a Scottish fit-up that were going to America to perform, and he was already plotting about America for themselves; she could see it.

'Sure, what business have we with making a baby? Living like this, so busy, no stability, so many places to go, all these foreign sights to see... Why would we spoil it?'

She'd hidden her hurt as well as she could. She wanted them to be a family, to buy a house some day and settle down in one place, own their own theatre made of bricks and mortar. This life was fine, and it was fun when she wasn't worried about money or upset about Aida, but surely he didn't plan for this to be their lives forever?

'So you don't want to have a family at all, is that what you're saying?' She'd failed to suppress the quiver in her voice, but he was so absorbed in the story about the vaudeville touring shows in America, he didn't notice.

'Sometime maybe...' he said vaguely. Then smiled at her. 'But not now, definitely. You just keep using that thing, you know, the thing you got in England.'

The Dutch cap was what he meant.

She couldn't find the words to respond to that, it stung so sharply.

He must have taken her silence for agreement, because he'd jumped up then, pecked her cheek and was dressed and out the door to speak to a carpenter about fixing the coffin for Magus because he was always sawing them in half.

As the train puffed on towards Dublin, May blinked back tears. Peter loved her. He said he did – he swore it. He did. She was just being paranoid. And maybe he didn't want her to get pregnant because he wanted her all to himself, and available all day every day to help him and the business, which she wouldn't be able to do as much if she had an infant to care for.

Anyway, she had to get on with things now. She had a lot to do today, including a visit to her parents, where she had nearly made up her mind to stay for the week.

In Dublin, she caught the tram to Ranelagh and alighted. The streets around her middle-class home seemed smaller, more provincial, now that she was a woman of the world, a married woman who had spent time in London, who had travelled all over the south coast of Ireland in the last few months, running a business, paying bills, employing tradesmen, looking after a bunch of actors, organising the flighty chorus girls – which was the hardest thing of all. Getting those flighty girls to behave was like herding cats.

She was an adult now, no longer May Gallagher, who had once been an impulsive girl herself. As she approached her parents' front gate, she tried to infuse her being with confidence, but with each step she took up the garden path to the front door, she felt more and more like a little girl, and more defensive about her life and marriage.

It wasn't that Olive Gallagher ever said one word against Peter, but May knew that her parents had hoped for better than a boy from Henrietta Street. Peter had insisted on being honest about his background much to May's disapproval. And they were horrified when she drew down all her inheritance to invest in a travelling theatre. They hadn't dared try to stop her from doing as she wanted, though. When they'd tried to prevent her leaving home last year, she'd terrified them by upping sticks for England, and now they were so glad to have her back in Ireland, they never complained.

She knocked on the door, and after a lot of rustling and bustling behind it, it opened.

'May, darling.' Mother, soft and shapeless in her pearls and a taupe velvet day dress, was delighted to see her, and May felt a pang of guilt. She knew she was her mother's world now that David was gone, and she really should visit more often.

'Hello, Mother, you look well. I love your dress.' She kissed her mother's cheek as she removed her hat and coat.

'Thank you, dear.' Olive beamed as she led the way down the hall to the kitchen. 'I bought it in Arnotts. I met Peter's sister Kathleen in there actually – she serves behind the counter now – and she was telling me that she'd got engaged.'

'Yes, we heard. She and Sean are a great match. He's a lovely gentle fellow, a cobbler, and he's mad about her.'

'I must send them a little something as an engagement gift, perhaps a piece of Belleek?'

May suppressed a smile as Olive fussed around the bright sunny kitchen, the low winter sunshine making a rare appearance, putting the kettle on and taking a porter cake from the tin. Her mother gave a Belleek china teapot to every couple who'd ever got engaged. 'I'm sure she'd love it.'

'Oh, and Eamonn called last week. Remember at the meal we had before the wedding, he said he'd clear the gutters for us when autumn came. I don't like your father going up the ladder – I'm afraid he'll fall – but Eamonn promised he'd call and do it in a few minutes, and true to his word, as soon as the leaves were falling off the trees, he did. He's such a nice man, and that whole family, really…'

May smiled and felt a rush of love for her mother. Olive could have dug her heels in about the Cullens being 'not their sort of people', but she had embraced them and so had her father, and now here her mother was having Eamonn around to do odd jobs and buying gifts for Kathleen as if they really were family.

'Yes, Eamonn is really nice. He called down to see us at the show last week. Peter was so busy with dance night – he has to partner with the professional dancer we've employed. He doesn't really like doing it, but no one else is good enough. So anyway, Eamonn danced with me himself, which was nice.'

It had been more than nice. It had been lovely actually. May really enjoyed dancing, but Peter never seemed to think about that; she was always relegated to the refreshments counter or the ice cream hut outside or taking money from latecomers at the door. So when Eamonn insisted on paying for a dance, but only if May would stand up with him, it had been a huge treat for her. He was good at it too, waltzing and foxtrotting with the best of them. It was the first time she hadn't spent dance night just standing on the sidelines, feeling physically sick at the sight of Peter and Aida and hoping nobody could tell what she was thinking and be sorry for her. A couple of weeks ago, she'd caught Nick looking at her anxiously, and she had glared at him. She never wanted anyone to see the cracks in her marriage, her loneliness, her fear over Aida; she would never accept anyone's pity.

'It's nice for you, having a brother-in-law. He won't replace your brother, but it's nice…' The sadness in her mother's voice broke May's heart. Poor Olive missed David now just as much as the day he'd left for the war. He'd never been found; he was missing, presumed dead, one of the countless nameless men who died in France and Belgium – and for what?

It was hard to tell now. It had seemed so much clearer before. King and country and all of that – it had all seemed romantic and gallant and somehow worth doing, but nobody thought that now. The men who'd been there, Peter, Enzo, Nick, Ramon, Magus and Two-Soups, never ever mentioned it. Occasionally they'd share a memory or joke about this fellow or that officer, but never a mention of the actual war.

Things were different here to England as well. The Easter Rising of 1916 was not, as people like her father hoped, a flash in the pan. It seemed to have steeled the rebels to organisation and action, and there was a menacing air in the city that had not been there before. British barracks were being targeted, and even policemen who were Irish but worked for the Crown were left under no illusion that their continued association with the forces of occupation, as the English were now being called, would no longer be tolerated.

May was weary of it all. Would men ever give over their endless need to bash each other's heads in? One of the many things she enjoyed about Peter was that he cared not a jot for any of it. He was obsessed with making Cullen's Celtic Cabaret a huge success, and that was his only thought.

'How is Peter?' asked Olive.

May caught the surreptitious glance at her flat abdomen. Her mother would adore being a grandmother if she ever got the chance. 'Peter's wonderful, and he wants us to start a family as soon as we can, but we need to be on an even keel first. He's making so much money, but it will take a lot to build a proper theatre. So obviously if God sends us a baby, we'll be thrilled, but in the meantime –'

'That's lovely, dear.' Olive quickly changed the subject. May knew she'd love a grandchild, but any discussion on how such an eventuality would come to pass would be toe-curlingly embarrassing. May and her mother had never had a conversation about anything to do with bodies, and they never would.

Her mother joined her at the table, and they sat and chatted easily about motherhood and babies, the post-birth part. Olive got out the family album, and they looked at pictures of May and David when they were little children, and Olive smiled and sighed and wiped away a tear.

Madge, the housekeeper, arrived back from the shops then, so May took the opportunity to get going. Her appointment was at 2 p.m., and she didn't want to be late. She wanted to see Peter's mother and would maybe stay the night with her in-laws, but she promised Olive she'd come again tomorrow and stay a few days, and she hugged her mother tightly.

In the hall she took her hat and coat and gloves from the neat little hallstand and checked the mirror before she left. She looked as good as the day she'd married, and that made her happy. She would not be one of those pretty girls who became frumpy old matrons overnight once a ring was on their finger and there was a baby in the pram.

\* \* \*

Dr de Vries was a specialist. May had read an advertisement on the back of a women's magazine that explained discreetly what he did. She'd written for an appointment and got one by return of post, which she'd had to hide from Peter. The speed of the reply either meant Dr de Vries was very efficient or he was a total charlatan desperate to take her money.

Either way, she was going to see him. She had nobody to confide in, and she needed some answers.

Walking through the city centre, she found it subdued but not especially threatening. There was a lot of activity down the country at the moment, RIC barracks being attacked, policemen being shot, but here in Dublin, she knew from reading the newspapers that the focus was political. The republicans had managed to gain control of all the major city councils, so every day they were growing in strength.

Like Peter, May wasn't a big fan of politics, but unlike him, she could see that keeping up to date about what was going on in Ireland was unavoidable these days, especially for a theatre company on tour. When Eamonn came down to see them, she'd quizzed him about what parts of the country they should avoid in case of violence, because everyone knew Eamonn was in the Volunteers.

Instead of being helpful, Eamonn had started talking to May about all the brave young men he knew who were prepared to lay down their lives for their country.

'Well, I wish your brave young men would stop running around with guns and turn their hand to helping us put the tent up and down every week. That would be a lot more useful as far as I'm concerned,' she'd said rather tartly, and Eamonn had thrown his head back and laughed and said he'd see what he could do.

Dr de Vries's consulting rooms on Bachelors Walk beside the River Liffey had a discreet brass plaque set into the wall outside. Inside, the waiting room was reasonably well decorated and smelled hygienic, but there was nobody else sitting on the chairs and no receptionist. Surprised, she took a seat and hoped someone would come for her soon.

She was beginning to worry she had the wrong day or time when a man appeared. He looked slightly comical, a bit like a mad professor in a storybook: tall and very thin, with a halo of fair hair sticking out at odd angles around a bald pate. He wore a white coat, though, which made him seem legitimate, if a little eccentric.

'Mrs Cullen?' he asked, his accent slightly foreign like his name.

127

'Er...yes, that's me.' She stood and smoothed down her dress, feeling very foolish and self-conscious.

'Follow me, please.'

He led the way upstairs, and she climbed behind him, her heart pounding. If this man was a scoundrel, nobody knew she was here. He could murder her and nobody would even know where to look, but the thought of explaining her problem to old Dr O'Riordan who'd cared for her family all her life was so blood-curdlingly embarrassing, she couldn't do it. It would have to be this oddball.

The room he showed her into looked reassuringly like a doctor's office. A cabinet with a lot of brown glass bottles, a weighing scale and an examination table on one side, a desk with a chair either side of it on the other. She took a seat as he gestured she should before sitting down himself.

On his desk was a thing that looked like a small wooden trumpet. She must have looked perplexed, because he said, 'It is called a Pinard, after French doctor Adolphe Pinard. It allows us to hear the baby's heartbeat in the mother's womb.' He passed it to her, and she examined it. It had a small hole through the centre. Not sure what to do next, she replaced it on his desk.

'Now then, Mrs Cullen, how may I be of assistance?' He steepled his long fingers in front of his face.

The rumble of traffic and the sounds of voices floated up from the quayside below, the familiar smell of the river wafting through the open window.

'I...' She swallowed. She'd practised this over and over. 'I've been married six months and I'm not pregnant yet, and I am worried something is wrong.' She knew it sounded garbled, but at least she got the words out.

He nodded and didn't seem in the least bit shocked.

'And you and your husband engage in normal intercourse regularly?' he asked, entirely unfazed, as if he was discussing the weather.

She knew her face was blazing, but she'd come this far; she might as well get the job done. There was not one single other person she could ask. She'd even thought of trying to talk to Bridie Cullen, but the idea of bringing up her and Peter's sex life with his mother...well, she couldn't do that either. No, it was this man or nothing.

'Yes, well, usually yes...' She swallowed and licked her dry lips. This was excruciating.

'And you understand that your husband must provide his seed into your body in order for the conception to take place?'

May nodded. She knew that much.

'That is good.' She caught the hint of a smile on the doctor's face before he stopped himself. 'Some women in this country do not know the basics of human reproduction. Forgive me for asking, but it is important to clarify, I have found.'

She could well believe it. She'd only picked up what little she knew from hearing the more racy girls talking on the factory floor where she worked in the office, and even among the middle-class girls in the tennis club. The war had made girls much bolder, and so not everyone she knew was a virgin. But no teacher, parent or medical person had ever so much as hinted to her at how anyone got here.

'And you have regular menstrual periods?'

'Yes.'

'How long does your period last?'

May swallowed again. She'd never discussed this with anyone, even her mother. 'Between four and five days.'

He nodded. 'And not too much cramping or heavy bleeding?'

'No.' She remembered girls at school being pale and even fainting. There was never anything said, but she knew it was to do with the 'time of the month'. But she'd never had anything like that.

'Mrs Cullen, are you familiar with the work of Theodoor Hendrik van de Velde?'

'No?' She was grateful to be off the subject of periods.

'Well, he is a countryman of mine, and in 1905 he was able to discover – or at least prove – what civilisations had only anecdotal knowledge of before this.'

'Which is?' She was more intrigued than intimidated now.

'That women only ovulate once in each monthly cycle. Therefore a woman can only get pregnant at certain times of the month, when the egg is released. If you have intercourse at that time, and assuming all is well medically with your husband, then that is the time you will become pregnant, not any other time.'

His calm, scientific way of speaking was serving to dissipate her discomfort a little.

'And how would I know when that time I might conceive is likely to be?' She flushed but not as much as previously.

He smiled, a real smile this time. 'Well, this is not an exact science, but based on my research with my patients and that of colleagues, I believe it to be in the middle of your cycle. So roughly ten days after the start of your monthly bleed. It is not one moment, however. The following days, three, maybe four or even five, are all your most fertile days, so you should have sexual relations often during that time.'

May tried to process this information. She was pretty sure barely a night had gone by in the early days of their marriage without herself and Peter having 'sexual relations'. Things were different now, but she felt too embarrassed to tell the doctor that.

'So if I were you, Mrs Cullen, I would just count the days from when your next cycle begins. It might take a few months to work, but if you have had sex with your husband at the appropriate time each month, and some days either side of it, and you still have not conceived in another six months, then return to me and we can see if there is something to be done.'

He stood; clearly the consultation was over.

She was still dressed, mercifully. She had been sure he would want to examine her, but she wasn't sure she had what she came for. From what he was saying, she and Peter had been doing everything right for the last six months anyway, so despite what this Dr de Vries said, something clearly was wrong. 'Maybe I need a supplement, a tincture or something?'

He placed his hand on her shoulder in a fatherly gesture. 'No, Mrs Cullen. As far as I'm concerned, I think you are a healthy young woman, and I assume your husband is a healthy young man. Though of course that may not be the case. The issue may be with him – some men are infertile and their seed does not grow. But that's something we can look at further down the road if necessary. So try my suggestion first. We can investigate further after six months if you have not conceived.'

Men could be the cause of a woman not having a baby? This was the first May had ever heard of such a thing. Any time there was a couple with no family, it was always assumed it was the woman's fault, that she was barren. It had never occurred to her that it could be something wrong with the man. Surely not Peter, though? He was so manly, and so…well, active…in bed.

Her mind in a whirl, she nodded and opened her purse. 'What do I owe you?'

'Nothing this time. That was just friendly advice – there is no charge. If you need me in the future, we can discuss my fees.' His pale-blue eyes were kind, and from nowhere she felt herself well up, even though she wasn't here for sympathy.

He put his hand on her shoulder. 'Relax, Mrs Cullen, just relax. It will happen, I think, and in the meantime, enjoy your time as newly-weds without somebody screaming at you in the middle of the night.' He chuckled, and she gave him a watery smile.

'Thank you, Dr de Vries,' she said, though she had to choke out the words.

'You're welcome. Good luck.'

She walked back downstairs, careful not to fall as her eyes were still blurred with tears. Why couldn't anything be simple?

She was married to Peter, had his ring on her finger, even if she had paid for it, but it just didn't feel like he was really hers. She'd felt him pull away, time and again, not in bed but when she talked about the future, settling down, getting a house… But a baby would draw them back together. It would make him see there were more important things than travelling the world. He would be a wonderful father, so much better than his own had been. And then they could be a proper family, and everyone would see her not just as Mrs Cullen, Peter's wife, but as the mother of his child.

But what if she and Peter never had that baby? Maybe then Aida would take him from her. The Spanish girl was so attractive, in a way that May just wasn't. She knew she was a pretty girl – Peter assured her she was beautiful – but she didn't exude that sultry, sensuous appeal.

It all felt so hopeless, like everything she'd worked so hard to achieve was slipping through her fingers.

Outside, the biting wind rushed up the Liffey. Soldiers gathered in groups on street corners, and people scurried rather than dawdled along. The Dáil, the unofficial Irish parliament set up by the rebels, was sitting, and though they were a thorn in the side of the authorities, her father said they were reluctant to do too much to rock the boat.

She walked on towards the tram, intending to go and visit Bridie Cullen in the Iveagh cottages. The wind was now carrying snatches of misty rain, the earlier sun forgotten, and she had her head down against the cold when she heard someone call her name.

'May, there you are. I was waiting for ya.' It was Eamonn, Peter's brother, and he kissed her cheek and tucked her arm into his very fondly; he seemed overly effusive.

'Goodness, Eamonn, I wasn't expecting to see you here?' She was glad he hadn't caught her coming out of the doctor's consulting rooms, but she was also puzzled as to why he was waiting for her at all. They had made no plan to meet.

'Of course I'm here. You're my wife, aren't you?' he murmured. 'And now we're on our way to Doyle's Hotel for tea.'

'What? I...' But then she understood. There was a checkpoint up ahead. A barrier had just been erected, and people were being filtered through a gap flanked either side by an armed British soldier. She looked over her shoulder, and there was another checkpoint in the process of being assembled further down the street.

'Please, May, I need you to help me here. Can you do the talking?' There was an urgency to his voice, and she knew what he meant – her middle-class accent was safer for them than his working-class one, which unlike Peter, he had never changed. The soldiers ahead of them were less than fifteen feet away, so she would just have to bluff their way through it.

The soldier eyeballed them as they approached the gap.

'Name?' he barked.

'May Cullen,' she heard herself say imperiously. 'And this is my husband, Peter.'

'Address?'

'Twenty-three Northbrook Road.'

'And where are you going now?'

'Doyle's Hotel. We're meeting my father there for dinner.'

'So we need to get goin'. Don't want to keep the father-in-law waitin'...' Eamonn tried to joke with the young soldier as they walked through, but at the sound of Eamonn's accent, the soldier frowned and placed his rifle across the gap.

'You'll be going when I say you'll be going. Where were you both this afternoon?' He glanced at May and held a hand up to silence her. 'You' – he nodded at Eamonn – 'where is Northbrook Road?'

'Ranelagh,' said Eamonn, without hesitation.

'What number Northbrook Road was that again?'

'Twenty-three.'

May blessed her mother for making Eamonn welcome, so that he knew the address of her house off by heart, even though it was in an area of Dublin he'd never otherwise have set foot in.

'And now we're off to Doyle's for dinner,' May said imperiously, 'to see my father, Michael Gallagher, who is a banker. Is there a problem?'

The soldier gazed at them both for a moment, murmured something to the other soldier and then stood aside. 'You can go.'

'Thank you.' May smiled, and Eamonn linked her once more. As soon as they were out of sight of the checkpoint, she turned and hissed, 'What on earth was that about?'

But before he could answer, a skinny, ragged young man came racing around the corner of the next side street, chased by two English soldiers with their guns out. As soon as the boy had passed them, his eyes wide with terror, Eamonn pulled May into the middle of the pavement, and before she knew it, he had put his arms around her and was kissing her deeply, his large arms holding her tightly.

Eamonn was such a big man that they were blocking the pavement, and the soldiers had to slow down to move around them. She could hear them grumbling because they'd lost their man.

After a full minute of kissing her, he finally released her.

'Eamonn, what…' She was stunned and shaken. She looked nervously up and down the street, fearful of being seen by someone who knew her. They weren't that far from Arnotts, what if Kathleen…

He grabbed her hand and pulled her along the street then, forcing her to walk faster than was comfortable to keep up with him, ducking in and out of the shadows. He turned down an alleyway and then another, and eventually they reached Doyle's, a Georgian house converted into a hotel.

There was nobody on the front desk, and he led her up the stairs. 'I'll explain up here. Just trust me, all right?' His eyes locked with hers, and she gave a tiny nod, allowing him to go on and open a bedroom door with a key from his pocket.

Once the door was closed, she asked, 'What on earth?'

'Thanks, May, and sorry about that. I… Look, I was in a bit of a tight spot. It was so handy you came along. I don't know what I would have done otherwise. I needed not to be searched.'

'Why not? What are you carrying?'

'And as for kissing ya,' he went on, without answering her question, 'well, I was trying to give yer man a hand in getting away, and it takes a right eejit of a Tommy altogether to interrupt a fella kissin' his mott.'

She had to laugh at the audacity of him then, and also it was funny being called a moth. Peter used to call her his moth too, in the early days, when his adopted middle-class accent slipped. It was such an odd term of endearment, and pronounced in that inner-city accent, it sounded like 'mohh'.

'Well, the whole thing was outrageous, but I forgive you.' She ran her tongue over her lips, recalling the sensation of his mouth on hers. She couldn't help feeling a bit excited, putting one over on those British soldiers; it had made her heart race and her knees tremble.

He shrugged and grinned. 'Drink?' he asked, waving a bottle of whiskey that he'd picked up off the sideboard. There were clothes and papers lying around the room, as if he lived here – though how a Guinness worker could afford to live in a hotel was a mystery to her.

'All right, I will.' She barely drank these days, because Peter didn't, but the fright of the checkpoint and the soldiers made her think maybe a drink was exactly what she needed.

Eamonn poured two glasses and added a drop of water to each. He pulled out the dressing table chair for her, then sat on the edge of the bed.

She tasted her whiskey, holding the glass in both hands; it stung a little but it warmed her, and after the first few sips, she found she liked it.

'Eamonn,' she asked, as she'd never dared ask before, 'are you really in the Volunteers?'

He looked at her for a long moment, then said, 'Would you mind if I was?'

'I don't know.' She was so sick of men dying. She'd already lost a brother, and the thought of losing Eamonn as well…

He shrugged, and shutters came down across his eyes. 'I know you probably don't understand, with your brother and husband, my own brother, having been in the British army and all.'

'No, I do, I do understand.' Somehow being questioned at the checkpoint so rudely, then seeing that ragged young man running in terror through the streets, chased by soldiers, had focused her mind on things she'd been trying not to think about. It came back in a rush the way Teddy had treated the troupe in England, and getting black-balled by all the theatres, and accused of trying to blow things up with gunpowder when it was all pure nonsense. 'I saw it in England, the hatred just because we're Irish. That's why we had to leave. And then the way the English soldiers treat us here, the way they speak to us even on our own streets…'

He smiled at her again then, his eyes crinkling. It struck May that he was a different man from Peter. Not a planner, always trying to figure out the best way forwards, plotting how to slide around the obstacles in his way without battering them down. Eamonn was simpler. More direct. Passionate. In the way she was herself, always going straight after what she wanted.

'I worry about you. We all do,' she said truthfully. 'But I agree with you – we have to drive them out, however long it takes, whatever we need to do.'

He winked at her as he stubbed out his cigarette in a tin ashtray. 'Ah, a divil a bit of good it will do worryin' about me, May. And I wouldn't want ya to. I'll die for this country if I have to. I want to live to drive them out, but I don't expect to. I've a target on me back, so...' He shrugged. 'Don't go wastin' any worry on me.'

A deep sadness settled over her at the thought of this lovely young man dying. 'If there's anything I can ever do to help you...'

He lit another cigarette and looked at her with his eyes half closed against the smoke, the cigarette drooping from his mouth. His shoulders were big and strong and his thighs thick. 'Are you serious about that? Would you ever do something for the cause?'

She shivered a little, excited but suddenly afraid. 'I suppose that depends what it is.'

He took something from his coat pocket and held it on his knee. It was a revolver. She stared at it with round eyes.

'This is why I couldn't afford to get searched at the checkpoint. Possession of a weapon is a capital offence now, so if I'm caught with this... They'll be searchin' everyone tonight, but I can't leave it here either.' He shrugged.

She stood up, crossed the room with her leather bag, which she placed on the bed beside him, took the gun, unlocked the bag, removed the accounts ledger and chequebook, then her purse, headscarf and compact, placed the weapon in the bottom with the scarf tucked around it and piled everything else on top. 'I'll take this, and I'll leave it under the hedge beside the shed door in my parents' garden. You can send someone for it later.'

He watched her do it, without stopping her. 'Are you sure, May? It's dangerous, even for a woman.'

'Don't worry. They'll never search a snobby bourgeois lady like me. And I know that's what you think of me.'

'That's not true,' he protested.

'Yes it is.' She leant forwards then and kissed his stubbled cheek to soften her words.

He smiled up at her, a sad, slow thing that broke her heart. 'If only things were different, May…'

'But they're not.' She straightened up and stood back. She hadn't even been sure what he was about to say. If what was different? If Ireland wasn't at war? If she wasn't married?

She went back to her chair and sat down again, placing the bag on the floor beside her. Her heart pounded with excitement again, and she told herself it was because she was finally striking a blow for Ireland.

'I suppose you're right.' He stood up to refill her glass. 'So how's the show? Are ye making millions yet?'

She laughed as she held out her glass for another drop of water. 'Well, not millions, but breaking even anyway, providing me and Peter don't always pay ourselves. I'm hoping the winter won't treat us too badly. I'm busy knitting blankets for the seats – I think that will help – and we'll put the hand-cranked freezer in storage and do popcorn instead. The magician is American, so he loves making it, and I think it will be cheaper to produce than ice cream, but we can charge more because it's a novelty. If we could get cheaper labourers, it would help, but the landowners don't like us employing their tenants directly, and they're the ones with the big enough fields, so we have to keep in with them and let them take their cut…' She heard herself rattling on, Olive-style, trying to cover over any awkwardness. She stopped herself, laughing. 'Goodness, Eamonn, this drink is too strong. Listen to me babbling. You're not interested in any of this.'

'I am interested,' he said, laughing as well. 'And maybe I can help you out the same time as you help the cause.'

'Ah, everything's wonderful with Cullen's Celtic Cabaret. We don't need any help.' Peter would be mortified if he thought she was talking about their business to his older brother this way.

'Of course. How's married life suiting you?' asked Eamonn, smiling at her, returning to sit on the bed.

She smiled across the room at him. 'Wonderful.'

'Is that brother of mine treating you right?'

'Of course he is.' She smiled tightly.

'I'm glad to hear it, because he's a nice lad. But he can be too smart for his own good, always with an eye to the main chance, thinkin' and plottin' ahead and maybe not seein' what needs looking after right under his nose.'

She heard the warning there.

'We're fine, really.' She hoped she sounded convincing.

'How do you get on with his friends? Are they good to you? You've done them a great favour, the women as well as the men, keepin' them all in jobs and paying them well. They should be very grateful to you.'

'I don't want anyone to be grateful to me. Everything's fine, it really is, Eamonn...'

'Then why are you cryin'?'

She fixed her eyes on him, astonished. 'What? I'm not...' But then she realised she was, a tiny, slow trickle of hot tears, leaking unbidden from the corners of her eyes down the soft slope of her jaw. Where were they coming from?

'Ah, May, what? Is everythin' all right?' He came over, went down on his hunkers and took her hands.

And to her horror, she burst into real tears. As he pressed her hands and made soothing noises, everything that had been building up in her like steam in a pressure cooker came tumbling out. She'd not had a single soul to confide in for months, so it was like opening a floodgate: all her worries, the terrible feeling that she was not enough, not a good enough daughter to make up for the loss of David, not beautiful enough to keep Peter happy and out of the arms of Aida Gonzalez, not clever enough at business to make the show work and now not woman enough to ever be a mother.

He pulled her to her feet and held her as she cried, and his body felt so different to Peter's, big and broad where Peter was slim and elegant. She could feel the heat of him, and he rubbed her back with large strong hands as she buried her face in his chest.

After a while, she looked up and their eyes met. He wiped her cheeks with his rough thumbs. Her breath was ragged from the tears.

Slowly he lowered his big dark head to hers, and somehow kissing him was unavoidable. Tentatively for a moment but then deeper, and as her mouth opened beneath his and she felt his tongue on hers and his strong arms crushing her to his powerful body, she couldn't have stopped, no matter what.

'May, we shouldn't…' he murmured, in the few brief seconds when his mouth wasn't on hers.

She didn't answer, but she couldn't help herself. She unbuttoned his shirt, running her hands over the thick hair on his chest. She didn't know what was going on, but she knew that right now what she needed was this man, and she knew that he needed her too.

The day became night, and sometimes it was passionate, almost violent, in the need they shared, and then later they treated each other more gently, tenderly, slowly. He traced kisses on her collarbone, along her abdomen, down her legs. He did things to her that Peter never had, made her body react in ways she'd never thought possible, and the ardent need in him, the way he made her feel like she was the most desirable woman on earth, was heady and addictive. It was wrong, of course it was, but she couldn't stop it, and neither could he.

Eventually they fell asleep, spent and exhausted, tangled in each other's arms.

When she woke, her clothes had been left neatly folded on the chair and there was a jug and glass of water by her bed. But Eamonn was gone, too ashamed to be in the same room as her, now he realised what he had done, sleeping with his brother's wife.

And she had allowed it, sought it out, made it happen. From that kiss in the street to following him back here to drinking whiskey with him in a hotel bedroom like a loose woman. What must he think of her? The shame made her cheeks burn.

What kind of a person was she? Was she so loose in morals that she slept with Peter without even a ring on her finger, and now that she had the ring, she'd been with his brother? Waves of sweat, nausea and self-loathing washed over her. She grabbed her clothes and bolted for the bathroom, slammed the door and just made it to the toilet when she vomited. Afterwards she sat slumped against the porcelain. What had she done? How could she have done this with Eamonn, the very thing she'd been fearing about Aida? Peter would never be unfaithful, of course he wouldn't, and yet she had been, with his brother of all people. It was unforgivable, she knew. How could she just go back to her husband, having done what she did?

Oh God, would he tell Peter? Please, please, no…

Gasping and trembling, she washed her face and got dressed, then crept back down the mercifully empty corridor to the room for her bag.

Pushed into the top of the bag was a letter, addressed to her in Irish, the language he always wrote in now and which she had to translate for Peter. With shaking hands, she unfolded it.

*My dearest May,*

*I feared to wake you for what I would see in your eyes. I know I took cruel advantage of your misery. My only excuse is that I have adored you from the first moment I set eyes on you. I regret only that showing you my feelings must have caused you pain and confusion.*

*Darling May, you have nothing to fear from me. I know you love my brother, and I will never tell him a word of what passed between us this night.*

*I will not survive this war. I'm a marked man. They know who I am and what I do, and I'm not sorry about that either, no more than I am about the brief beauty we created here together. I should regret it, I know I should, but I can't and I won't. May, my love, when I die, it will be your name upon my lips, and I will carry you with me in my heart to my grave.*

*And darling May, I'm so sorry that I put you in danger at the checkpoint, and then asked you to dispose of the gun for me. I should never have put my love for my country ahead of my love for you. Please leave the weapon under the bed when you go. I will retrieve it later and take my chances.*

*May, please don't hate me. Please don't think too badly of me.*

*Eamonn Cullen*

With a groan she threw it into the empty fireplace, took a box of matches from the mantelpiece and knelt to burn it. Match after match failed to strike; the box was damp. In exasperation, she tucked the letter into the book of accounts. She'd burn it later. Tearing it up was too risky.

Under the book was his gun, still wrapped in her headscarf.

Tearing a sheet out of the back of the book, she wrote on it hastily in Irish.

*A Eamonn, táim as mo bheabhair... I am filled with shame about last night. It was a terrible, sinful mistake, and the only thing we can do is put it out of our minds and live the rest of our lives as if it never happened. But I also love my country and will do as promised. May.*

She nearly finished it there, but then she thought about how he had written about having a target on his back. She knew it was true; it was unlikely he would survive this war. A wave of misery rushed over her at the thought, and she pushed it back fiercely. *I don't love him. I love Peter.* She hesitated over the letter with the pen in her hand, then scribbled quickly.

*I don't hate you. I never could.*

That would have to do.

* * *

SHE WAS terrified walking with that thing in her bag, but she couldn't be the reason he was picked up and searched. They'd execute him, and she'd have his death on her conscience. Something had definitely happened; the place was swarming with police, soldiers and armoured cars. The tram was packed, and she squeezed on, her bag wedged against a man in a heavy greatcoat, damp and smelly. If only he knew what was at such close quarters to him.

On the journey home, she heard the conversations among the commuters. A high ranking officer in Dublin Castle had been shot dead yesterday morning. IRA were taking the credit. The city would pay a high price for such treachery, someone said. Just wait – they'd find whoever had done it. They always did.

And May, in her troubled heart, knew for a sure and certain fact that the murder weapon was in her handbag right this minute.

# CHAPTER 14

ETER

PETER CULLEN CAME SLOWLY AWAKE. A slender arm was draped across his chest, and for a moment, he thought May was back from Dublin early. But then he remembered he was sharing a bed with Enzo in St Philomena's Lodging House outside Newry. On Monday night he'd had the double bed to himself, because Enzo had been messing about with some woman from Belfast who, as usual, almost certainly had a husband, but last night the Londoner had come back to the lodging house 'for a rest', as he put it, and now he was lying curled into Peter, dead to the world, sleeping off his amorous adventures.

Peter jabbed him hard in the ribs with his elbow. 'Get off of me,' he hissed.

'Hey, wha'…' Enzo protested sleepily.

'Don't be spooning me. I'm not your latest fancy woman.'

'Oh, it's you… 'Ow about I wear a blond wig, like May, give you something to think about, eh?' The Londoner grinned without opening his eyes.

'No thanks. You stink and your skin is like sandpaper.'

'Well, you're no beauty either, mate. Dunno what May sees in ya.' And with a mighty yawn, Enzo turned over and fell straight back to sleep.

Unable to do the same, Peter got out of bed and pulled on his shirt and trousers. In the other bed, Nick was sprawled on his back, snoring gently, his broad chest rising and falling. Peter's two old friends often bunked in together when they stopped in a town; it saved money, and often there was a dearth of lodgings. After sleeping practically on top of each other in the trenches, they didn't care. For the last two nights, Peter had joined them while May was away in Dublin. Nick, being the tallest and biggest, had got the single bed, and so Peter was sharing the double with Enzo. He didn't mind; dugout life meant anything other than a damp, rat-infested hole was luxury.

He tiptoed downstairs in his bare feet and found four letters waiting for him on the table in the hall; the woman of the house must be up already. He recognised May's writing on one of them and hoped it was going to say she was coming back soon and not staying in Dublin more than a couple of days. He missed her, of course, but also she was such an asset to the company; she was brilliant at all the organising, and he really needed that.

He brought the letters into the breakfast room with him and placed them beside his plate. He could hear Mrs Collins already moving around in the kitchen, preparing the porridge. Apart from that, the house was quiet, and he hoped none of the other performers would join him for a while; he liked to have time to himself, to think.

Growing up in Henrietta Street had been chaotic, his family's tiny apartment crammed with the seven of them, and there were people everywhere in the rest of the house, children screaming and women bawling and men fighting on the stairs and drunks roaring in the streets. Solitude was in very short supply, so he loved it when he could find it.

The woman of the house came into the room at that point, looked taken aback to find him there and asked briskly if he'd like his breakfast. He nodded and smiled. She withdrew sharply and a few minutes later returned with some porridge, a boiled egg, some soda bread and a cup of tea. She put it down without a word. She was a hard-faced individual who made it obvious she did not approve of theatrical folk and only took them in because she needed the money. The whole house was full of holy pictures and statues, so Peter assumed she saw actors and their ways as godless. It was a common enough accusation, but it was water off a duck's back to him.

May was doing a great job of keeping everyone out of trouble. The chorus girls moaned that they were like nuns these days, but they knew May was not joking when she said they'd be out on their ears for blackguarding, and they loved the life so wouldn't risk it. Even Enzo was being very discreet with his romantic escapades. So they weren't being denounced from the altar, and that was enough.

Anyway, he liked that Mrs Collins didn't talk to him; he was glad of the peace and quiet. And the house was clean, and the sheets were changed, and though the food was simple fare, it was hearty and filling.

One of the jobs May had given to the chorus girls, whenever the cabaret arrived in a new place, was to go and find digs for all the performers at the boarding houses, or sometimes domestic houses would give them a bed for a few shillings if there was no guesthouse in the town. May had taught the girls all the tricks: putting a cosmetic mirror between the sheets to check for damp, and asking for a drink of water to see if a clean glass could be found. Still, in the smaller places, there wasn't a lot of choice, and the quantity and quality of the beds the girls found were almost always short on luxury. Last week in Donegal, the beds had been damp, the landlord snored like a bull and could be heard through the paper-thin walls, and breakfast was soggy toast with a scrape of jam. Compared to that place, St Philomena's Lodging House was bliss.

Saving May's letter until last, he began reading his post.

The first letter was from his sister Kathleen. All was well at home. They'd had a nice visit from May, but apparently the boy Maggie had been knocking around with had been beaten up very badly and put on the boat to England with warnings never to return. Peter knew the family weren't keen on him, but the poor lad probably didn't deserve that.

Peter sighed, wondering if Eamonn had anything to do with it. He'd apparently forbidden Maggie to see this fella, but knowing his feisty sister, she'd have ignored him. Things were complicated these days politically. Maybe Eamonn took a set against him because he was an informer or something; it was hard to imagine it was any other reason. Eamonn was too caught up in the republican cause to be worried about who Maggie was doing a line with. Instinct told Peter his brother thought the boy was a risk. He hoped Maggie wasn't too upset. She'd begged him to be allowed to join the cabaret the last time he was at home, but his mother thought her too young and wild, so he'd refused. She would be good on stage, though, so maybe sometime.

The second letter was a bill for fabric for the chorus outfits, and he put it aside for May to deal with when she got back. He knew she found keeping the funds in balance to be the biggest problem; the costumes and props, not to mention the tent, had eaten up all of her capital, and he was grateful that she managed their finances so well he could pay wages in full and on time to all the performers. He'd always promised himself he was not going to be like Teddy Hargreaves, feathering his own nest while the people he was responsible for went hungry.

It helped that May had lots of ways of making every penny count.

She'd invested some of her inheritance in a camera, for instance, and it had made them a fortune. Before each show there was a booth where people could go and have a snap taken. Celine took the photos, and May took them to be developed. People could come back at the end of the run and buy their photograph. May had even sourced cheapish frames that looked nice, and people often bought the photo and a frame, which doubled the profit.

There was a raffle each night as well, and it was a great money spinner. At first they'd offered a cash prize, but then May had decided that was a waste of money – they needed every shilling – so the prize would be a free special photograph. Several of the chorus girls were expert at make-up and hair, so they could offer a makeover to a lady – and a gentleman too, if the lady wished to bring one – and then Celine would take a photograph of the winning couple and they got to keep it. That was a huge success, and raffle tickets went like hot cakes, and it didn't cost the show a penny.

The third letter had a Belfast address in the top corner; he didn't recognise it.

*Dear Mr Cullen,*

*I am writing to you because I would like to join your ensemble. We have met before, in London, when we both performed at the Acadia. You've seen my act and were very complimentary about it at the time, for which I thank you.*

*I am the ventriloquist whose dummy, Timothy, was set on fire in the dressing room the first time the Acadia nearly burnt down. It caused me great pain and suffering, as I think of Timothy as my own child, but thankfully my son is now fully restored to his former health and is back to his old cheeky ways.*

*Since I last saw you, I have performed at a large number of music hall venues as well as doing the vaudeville circuit in the United States.*

*I understand your show is of the 'fit-up' variety, and I would like to assure you that I am a 'pitch in and do everything' kind of person, so I understand the nature of the work should you be in a position to consider adding me to the bill.*

*Yours faithfully,*

*Clive Stephens (and Timothy)*

Peter remembered the ventriloquist well. He'd been a great hit with the audiences. He was a very polite man who looked like an English vicar, while his 'son', Timothy, was a big schoolboy puppet with a freckled nose and sticking-out ears and a very naughty sense of humour. They would go down a storm in rural Ireland, though Timothy's language might have to be toned down a bit.

He'd ask May what she thought. Although he knew what she'd say. That there was no point in paying another salary when their budget was already stretched to the breaking point. But if they added another act, they could lengthen the stay in each place and cut the costs of all the travel.

May's determination to keep costs under control drove him mad sometimes. She was great at managing what they had, but she just didn't think big enough. She hadn't shown any interest in taking the show to America; instead she'd started going on about having a baby. As if there was time for that. He could think of nothing worse than a bawling baby taking May's attention away from the show. Everyone depended on him, and he needed to pay attention constantly; there was no time for a family. If he and May were going to make a go of this, Cullen's Celtic Cabaret needed to get a lot bigger. They couldn't afford to let things go stale. Finding new acts, trying to expand and keep it all fresh was always on his mind.

This ventriloquist could be a great asset. Maybe he should reply and invite him anyway. Easier to ask forgiveness than permission had become his motto, and it worked for the most part.

He poured himself another cup of tea from the brown earthenware pot the landlady had silently refilled for him and wondered how to persuade his wife that they needed to expand, even more than just one new act, even if it meant borrowing the money. He picked up her letter. It felt thinner than the big long missives she usually sent him if she was away.

The door to the breakfast room opened, and Nick came in as Peter was using his butter knife to slice open the envelope.

'Morning, boss!' he said cheerfully.

'Morning, Nick.'

The landlady appeared again with more porridge and another boiled egg and soda bread, which she plopped down in front of Nick.

'Thank you, Mrs C-C-Collins. That looks really lovely.'

'Harrumph!' With a disapproving sniff, she flounced back into the kitchen.

Grinning, Nick poured himself a cup of tea and topped up Peter's cup as well. 'So, you must be feeling p-p-pretty pleased with yourself, p-p-playing to a full house every night.'

'Yeah, I suppose so.' Peter frowned as he scanned the letter from

May, which was unusually short for her, just a paragraph to say she'd decided to stay in Dublin for a whole week and not to forget to talk to Magus about the popcorn.

'What's up?' Nick sounded concerned.

Peter shook his head, folding the letter back into its envelope. 'Ah...nothing. May's away until the end of the week, and I wanted to talk to her about taking on that ventriloquist, Clive Stephens – remember him?'

'I do. He'd be great to have on b-b-board.' Nick nodded enthusiastically as he sliced open his egg.

'I think so too. I just hope I can persuade May.'

'Why wouldn't she agree? He's a nice man, and the audiences love him.'

Peter sighed. 'Trouble is, May will probably say we're playing to a full house already, so taking on any extra performers would just reduce the profits. As it is, sometimes when the week ends, there's nothing left for her to pay herself or me. Not that she complains – she's great like that – but it makes it hard to suggest going into debt.'

'Oh d-d-dear...' Nick looked absolutely horrified. He put down his egg spoon. 'I d-d-didn't realise. It must be very expensive having so many of us in the show?' He was blushing all the way up his neck and face.

Peter felt bad for having even mentioned money; it was only it was so much on his mind. Normally he hated worrying his performers. It did no good, just put them under stress. 'Oh, don't worry, you all earn your keep. And maybe with even more performers, we could extend our stay in each location. Do six nights instead of five. That would reduce transportation costs, wouldn't it?'

'I suppose it would.' Nick was still rather red in the face but looked a bit happier.

'I really should sit down with a pen and pencil and try and work all the figures out to show May, though to be honest, she's much better than I am at the money side of things. All I have are these big mad plans. Tour the UK maybe, put it up to all those theatres that black-listed us, and then America...'

'That's a fantastic idea.' Nick's eyes lit up. 'Let's do it.'

Peter relaxed and smiled, and his mood lifted. It was nice to have an appreciative audience, someone who thought his plans were a good idea and didn't keep telling him how this or that wasn't possible because they didn't have enough money yet. He started telling Nick all about the Scottish fit-up that was going to America to perform, and the more he talked about it, the more it seemed possible. The Americans would flock to see Cullen's Celtic Cabaret by the thousands. It was going to be the greatest show on earth. All he had to do was find the money to expand, and surely the banks would agree they were the perfect company to invest in.

Of course he knew it was all a pipe dream – the banks were never going to invest in a ragtag bunch of actors with a tent – but it was nice to paint the vision and have Nick join in the enthusiasm. In a way, he was glad that May was going to be away for the rest of the week. It would give him some time to dream, before his practical wife brought him crashing back down to earth.

# CHAPTER 15

ICK

NICK WALKED the streets of Newry, his overcoat buttoned against the winter chill. He thought about Peter and his vision for turning Cullen's Celtic Cabaret into the greatest show on earth. And he thought about how selfish he had been not to have realised his friend was struggling.

Peter Cullen was such an inspiration. Unlike Nick, who had been born into wealth and tutored in piano and singing by professionals, Peter had had to teach himself all he knew, relying on his natural talents to turn himself into the person he was today. And he'd not only dragged himself up; he had brought Nick along with him, right from that first night in the Aigle d'Or, always organising, planning, working out the next best thing to do, for both of them.

Nick owed Peter an enormous debt.

Cullen's Celtic Cabaret had given him a life when he'd thought he had none worth living. He'd been ready to throw it away in the war. As a child, he'd felt so insignificant and unloved by his parents and brothers. Now, at twenty years old, he was applauded wherever he went. Every time the troupe arrived in a town or village, it was such a thrill to see people so excited to welcome them. Celine had said it felt like they were stars from Hollywood, and to see the faces of the crowd every night, lit up with glee and merriment, made him feel so loved.

More than that, he was spending all his days and evenings with Celine Ducat. Maybe he would never spend a night with her – though that was his true heart's desire, to spend every night with her in his arms – but at least he was in her life. He was important to her; she cared for him. Not in the way he adored her, but it was something. And it wasn't just Celine who made him happy; he had friends, real friends, for the first time in his life, who liked him for who he was, not what he had.

Peter Cullen had made Nick's dreams come true. Yet until that long talk this morning over breakfast, he hadn't even thought about the fact that Peter had dreams as well. Bigger and more wonderful dreams than Nick could ever have imagined. Dreams so big, they needed thousands of pounds to put into action.

The thing was, Peter Cullen didn't have that sort of money, and Nick was pretty sure no bank would ever lend it to him, a boy from the slums of Henrietta Street. Bank managers were only courteous to the likes of Nick.

Because Nick Gerrity had money. Or at least Vivian Nicholas Shaw, heir to the barony of Simpré, had. Vivian Nicholas Shaw didn't even have to wait until he'd inherited Brockleton to put his hands on a lot of cash.

Back at the estate, there were several acres of mixed deciduous woodland that had been planted by his grandfather long before Nick was even born, and which Nick would be allowed to sell when he was twenty-one. That woodland must be worth about ten thousand pounds now the trees were all fully grown. It would be a shame to fell them – the steep field where they were planted was one side of a suntrap valley, and the way the light dappled the leaves was a delight to anyone who saw it – but they would be felled undoubtedly.

He could hear his father's booming voice in his head as he thought about the ash and copper beech.

'The barony didn't achieve its huge wealth by unnecessary sentimentality about trees.'

Then there was a whole corner of the extensive wine cellar, where fifty bottles of port had been laid down for him at birth, also for him to inherit on his next birthday. Another small fortune. On top of that, ever since poor Wally died, Nick had the right to claim his own allowance from the estate as his father's heir.

So why was he taking money from his best friend, and letting Peter pay for his bed and board, when he had no need of it? Peter had given him a life, and in return Nick was forcing him to scrimp and scrape and go without.

He checked his watch. It was nine thirty in the morning, and at home in Brockleton, breakfast would be being served, if everything was as it used to be. But then, maybe it wasn't. He'd not set foot there since that day in 1917 when he'd heard his father and mother bewail how God had punished them with a stammering idiot for their third son.

His oldest brother, Roger, had been raised to be the heir, Wally the spare. Nick had never been a part of his parents' reckoning. But Roger would never see Brockleton again; he had bled to death in a lifeboat in the North Sea. Poor old Wally too, killed in a hunting accident. So here Nick was, the heir to the barony. Once his father died, he would de facto inherit everything as his only son. The title, the seat in the House of Lords, the estates in Ireland and Britain – all of it would go to him. It was a horrible prospect.

He walked glumly along the riverfront, imagining leaving the cabaret, his friends, Celine, to go back to that dark, cold place. As he turned uphill past the church, Floss's words rang in his ears. Harvey Bathhurst was just a distant cousin by marriage, but Nick was Walter Shaw's son. The Shaw blood ran thickly in his veins. Even if he was mere Nick Gerrity now, that was merely a costume, a persona. His true self was Vivian Nicholas Shaw, heir to the barony of Simpré.

Or maybe he could be both of those people?

That awful day in 1917, when he'd realised how much his parents despised him, he'd sworn never to return home. But things were different then. He was different. Back then he'd been younger, more naive, softer. He was a stronger person now. War had changed him. Life had changed him. If he took this leap, and if his father welcomed him – and it was a big if, despite what Floss said – then he would need to be strong and tell him he was not giving up the cabaret, he would not live full time at Brockleton, he would not come home to manage the estate, but he would be his son and he would not be a stranger, and when the time came – and hopefully it would be many years from now – he would knuckle down and accept his responsibilities.

Nick's heart sank once more at the thought of that future. He wasn't cut out to be an heir.

But he could hardly turn up, looking for his rights and his money, without first giving a commitment to care for the estate when the time came. And he should do this. Even his staunchly republican American grandmother thought he had a duty to the tenant farmers. Harvey Bathhurst must not be allowed to inherit. He was an awful man and would treat the tenants horribly. And it wasn't just that. There was something even more, something Nick couldn't explain, an instinct deep inside him, urging him to reclaim his destiny, however much the thought frightened him.

Up ahead, two women came out of another guest house, St Claire's Guest House, a tall, grey, terraced house with rusty railings. One of them was slender and dark and dressed in boyish clothes that made her look younger than her thirty years, and the other was a sweet little French girl of eighteen with a throaty voice.

Nick's heart lifted as the two women saw him and waved, then came quickly towards him, Celine almost skipping, wearing her smart dark-blue coat with the fur collar.

'Nick! Nick!' He loved the way she said his name in her soft French accent. 'Why are you out walking so early?'

Any time before midday was early for the actors. They were always up so late doing the show and then packing everything away afterwards, they often lay in until the early afternoon. Mrs Collins at

St Philomena's boarding house thought it was the most ungodly thing about them, although she hadn't seemed to like Peter and Nick being up early that morning either. With some people you just couldn't win.

'I d-d-don't know. I had some things to think about,' he said as the girls fell into step on either side of him. 'How about you t-t-two?'

'Ah, we woke, and the sun so lovely and birds singing...'

'Something on your mind, Nick?' asked Millie. She was a shrewd cookie, the English woman, always interested in what was going on in other people's heads and wondering what they were up to. Nick didn't mind, because he didn't think she was a gossip, just interested in others. And he liked the way she seemed to approve of his friendship with Celine, always telling Celine what a nice, talented, clever young man he was, which made him blush and stammer but feel good about himself at the same time.

'Just...this and th-that.' He wasn't sure he was ready to talk about Brockleton yet, or admit that it wasn't any old three-storey house but something much, much more magnificent. Maybe they'd be angry with him for keeping this secret from them? Celine was the first person he'd confessed to about his aristocratic background, but she was just impressed. She'd grown up on stories of the French aristocracy who had been dispossessed in the French Revolution, over a hundred years ago, and who had lost most of their money and power.

'Sounds mysterious?' Millie was grinning at him now, her dark-brown eyes gleaming, and Celine was smiling up at him as well, getting curious because Millie was curious.

'What is this thought that makes you look so sad, Nick?'

He sighed. Fighting the pair of them was futile, and it was going to have to come out sooner or later. 'Well, to t-t-tell you the truth, I was thinking of g-g-going home.'

'Nick, no.' Celine looked very alarmed, and for a moment, Nick thought with delight that she really didn't want him to be a baron or anything, but then he realised she thought he was planning to go home that day, and they were supposed to be performing together that evening.

'No, no, I d-d-didn't mean right now. Just for a w-w-weekend or something, as soon as I can get the time off.'

Celine still looked worried. 'But you'll be back? I can't sing without you.'

It warmed his heart that she needed him. 'Don't worry,' he said, tucking her little hand under his arm – a daring move on his part, though she didn't seem to mind. 'Nick G-G-G-Gerrity is going nowhere. I won't ever let you down.'

'Thank you.' She smiled up at him gratefully.

'But you are going to see your parents, in this big house of yours?' asked Millie, taking his other arm. 'Tell us what it's like?'

'Well...' He took a deep breath. 'It's a bit of a g-g-g-gloomy old pile from the outside, but the rooms are beautifully decorated.'

'How many rooms?'

'Mm...thirty?'

'Thirty?' gasped the girls in unison.

'Well, thirty bedrooms. There's about twenty other rooms as well.'

'Fifty rooms?' Millie came to a halt, pulling him to a stop as well, staring at him in astonishment.

'But what do you... All these...*salons*...*pour quoi*...' Celine had lost her English, she was so flabbergasted.

'Oh, you know, one of them is for b-b-b-breakfast. It's a lovely sunny room first thing in the morning. And then there's a-a-another for lunch and one for dinner, facing west, and there's the ladies' drawing room, and' – he began to count on his fingers – 'a c-c-couple of libraries, and the billiards room, and the music room of course...'

'You have a special room for music?' Celine asked faintly. 'Does it have a piano?'

'Oh yes, a Steinway c-c-concert grand and lots and lots of music books.'

'I would love to see this room, Nick,' she breathed.

'I'd l-l-love you to see it too, Celine.' He was embarrassed, stumbling, fearful she realised it was because he loved her, but he felt thrilled at the thought that she wanted to go there. He'd not even dreamed of bringing her to Brockleton with him, but of course, why wouldn't he? As far as her own father was concerned, she was his fiancé, so it was perfectly proper for her to travel there with him alone. Celine had never spoken and certainly never acted as if they were engaged, but she wore the ring they'd bought to persuade Monsieur Ducat to allow her to come on tour with the cabaret, and everyone in every town and village they stopped at seemed to think they were a couple because of the way they sang love duets together.

Sometimes Nick felt guilty that he was getting in Celine's way. If some fine farmer's son had his eye on her, he might be holding back because he thought she was spoken for. It had even crossed Nick's mind to suggest she remove the ring so that men wouldn't be afraid to ask her out. But he hadn't managed to bring himself to do it, and she'd never raised it herself.

'So what else does this house have? It sounds beautiful, doesn't it, Celine?' Millie smiled.

'Yes, it is hard to believe our Nick comes from such a place.'

'Well...stables for fifteen or twenty horses...'

'Twenty? Who rides them all?' Celine gasped.

'Well, the family does, or f-f-f-friends that come hunting.'

'And who cares for them?' Millie was all agog.

'The yard manager and the g-g-grooms and stable b-b-boys, of course.'

'And who does all the cleaning in the house?' asked Celine, her eyes wide. In her father's establishment, she'd been the one doing everything. 'So many rooms – it must be exhausting?'

Nick smiled at her. 'It's fine. We don't have to do anything ourselves. There's a d-d-domestic staff of twenty-f-f-five to look after everything.'

'You have that many people to clean for you?' She was clearly having difficulty getting her head around it.

'Yes, there's such a lot to do. They lay the fires and brush the floors, and make up the beds and puff up the feather pillows, and leave fresh towels in the bathrooms, and put flowers in all the rooms that are being used.' It felt odd to boast about a place he'd eschewed so vehemently, but he could see how much Celine liked hearing about it.

'And we have several cooks as well. Mrs Mulcair and her d-d-daughters make delicious food, and Alistair and John, the footmen, serve it up.'

'It sounds like a fairy tale...' Her amber eyes were shining, the gold flecks reflecting the morning sunlight. She looked like an angel.

'I suppose it is p-p-pretty good.' Despite having told his darling grandmother that he wanted Celine to love him for himself, he couldn't help but enjoy the way she was looking at him now, as if Nick Gerrity, the frog, had literally turned into a prince before her eyes. Maybe Floss was right that he should play to his strengths and use Brockleton the way Enzo used his own natural assets – his face and body – to impress the women.

'So if you have horses, do you have land as well?' asked Millie, more practical than Celine.

'We do. It's on eighteen thousand acres, mostly rented to tenant farmers, though. And there's a lot of woodland. And' – he might as well be hung for a sheep as a lamb – 'it's not the only house I'm going to inherit, to be honest. There's several more p-p-properties in England, and a seven-bedroomed townhouse in Mayfair, a Scottish hunting lodge...' his voice trailed off, he didn't want to sound like he was showing off.

'Mayfair...' Millie's jaw dropped at the mention of the exclusive London address.

He turned to Celine. 'So would you like to come to B-B-Brockleton with me, just for a day or two?'

She gazed up at him anxiously. 'But would your father and mother allow someone like me into this magnificent chateau?'

'Someone like you?' It horrified him that his beautiful, talented Celine would think herself not good enough for Brockleton. His father was a drunken boor, his mother a neurotic witch – neither of them were fit to lick Celine's little button-up boots. Anyway, his grandmother would adore her, because Nick adored her. It was Floss who had suggested bringing Celine home in the first place, back when he was still determined to have the French girl love him for himself or not at all. 'Celine, if they know what's good for them, they'll welcome you with open arms. You're not a common girl – you're my actual fiancé.'

'Oh...' She laughed and blushed, and her eyes flicked sideways to Millie, who nodded at her encouragingly. 'Yes...of course. I suppose I am. Though not...'

His heart ached a little, as it always did when she reminded him their engagement was just for show, but he forced a smile. 'I know, I know. B-b-but it will make things easier.'

'Well, I think it's a wonderful idea, the two of you going there together as an engaged couple,' said Millie encouragingly. She took Nick's arm again, and the three of them walked on in the direction the girls had been walking, back down to the river, where the low morning sun gilded the fast-running ripples with gold.

# CHAPTER 16

ICK

THEY DROVE to Brockleton in Millie's new two-seater car, which she'd acquired for a song off some poor young infatuated car mechanic in Athlone. The young man's father had come roaring and shouting to the lodging house, saying she'd tricked the poor boy with her feminine wiles, but Millie had been unrepentant. She had the bill of sale, it was all above board, and if the boy had got the wrong idea, it wasn't her fault. And anyone could see that was true; Millie was not one for feminine wiles.

She was driving the car now, whizzing along with her foot to the floor.

Nick was squashed into the passenger seat with his knees nearly up to his chin, Celine was sitting sideways in the place for luggage behind the front two seats, and the luggage itself was strapped to the top of the car.

It was Celine who'd suggested that Millie come with them to Brockleton, murmuring about the 'need for a chaperone', which upset

Nick a bit, as if he couldn't be trusted. But then he thought maybe it wasn't such a bad idea. Celine could be quite shy sometimes, but Millie, who had a rather haughty manner, would fit very well into Anglo-Irish society; sometimes he thought she was like a nicer version of his mother.

Peter had been very easy-going about the three of them taking time off together. After all his fears, May had been perfectly happy about hiring the ventriloquist, so Clive and his dummy-son, Timothy, could cover Millie's slot. Magus Magicus was a good enough dancer now to take over for Nick on dance night. And Peter, while not a singer per se – he couldn't hold a candle to Nick – did a good enough job of belting out music hall stage songs, funny ones like 'Burlington Bertie' and 'Delaney's Donkey', and one of the chorus, a girl called Peggy, had a sweet soprano and could duet with him, enough to keep the crowd happy and get them singing along.

And it was nice to get a break as well. As much as they loved the cabaret, they'd all been working very, very hard these past few months.

'Turn right at the sign to Blarney up ahead. And then just keep going.' Nick directed Millie through the nearest small village to Brockleton, and then along a narrow lane between rich fields, then over the brow of the hill. The wide expanse of the River Lee glinted to their right, and everything looked so stark, the trees bare, but the land was green and beautiful, Nick felt a surge of pride.

Millie drove slowly through the massive iron gates and down the long oak-lined avenue, both girls looking in amazement from side to side as he pointed out the different lakes and woodlands.

Both girls gasped as Brockleton came into view, down across the rolling green valley, huge, imposing, built of iron-grey stone. The demesne was first built in medieval times, but the old house was destroyed by fire in 1730 and this was the one built in its place. Its long upper windows glinted in the weak winter sun, but a grey mist drifted down from the hills behind, giving it a mystical look.

'C'est incroyable,' whispered Celine, her lips close to his ear as she craned to see between him and Millie.

Nick had always thought the place looked a bit dreary, but now, seeing it through the eyes of the girl he loved, he had to admit it was pretty impressive.

A stag observed them from a grassy meadow, from behind a HaHa, and the River Awbeg, a tributary of the Lee, he explained, bubbled merrily under the bridge, heavy with trout.

'What is this Haha?' Celine asked.

'It's a way of k..keeping animals off the lawn, a sort of dyke that they c..can't traverse and it means there are no unsightly fences or walls interrupting the view. The story g..goes that whoever invented it was trying to find an aesthetically pleasing way of protecting his flowers, and when he hit on the idea he said 'aha.'

'I think in French we call it a *saut de soup*.' Celine replied, charmed.

The pleasure gardens, the rose walk and the arboretum were in their winter slumber, but the box hedging and the miniature pines gave a splash of colour. The large stone planters either side of the turning circle were filled with heathers and Nick knew his grandmother had ordered them. She had colour in the Brocklewood gardens all year round. Out in the upper paddock, stable boys were exercising two of his favourite horses, Madge and Patcher.

As Millie spun around the huge stone fountain and drew up at the front steps, he was pleased that all was quiet. He was calm and not terrified, as he thought he might be. This was his home, he had a right to be here, and one day he would own it all. Perhaps he should have checked ahead with Floss, but he hadn't, and so he just had to hope there were no visitors in the house. His mother when she was home seemed incapable of existing without an entourage of people, always glamorous, who came for hunting or shooting or fishing or just to demand gin and tonics at odd times of the day. They would all dress for dinner, and he remembered watching from the top-floor balcony as they descended in a wave of feathers and jewels to the dining room at the gong, or for cocktails in the library in the winter or on the terrace in summer.

He wondered where Harriet Shaw was now. Edinburgh, probably, still refusing to come home after Wally's death. He wasn't sure he cared whether she was here, because he didn't really know her. He'd been shipped off to boarding school aged seven, a series of nannies before that, and even when he came home for the holidays, she was rarely there. His mother was a shadow in his childhood, if even that.

Millie and he climbed out of the little two-seater car, and together they helped Celine out of the cramped luggage space. While the girls stood together on the gravel, Millie with her arm linked with Celine's, Nick climbed the ten steps to the double-wide oak front door, newly varnished.

The stained-glass panelling on either side and above the door depicted elements of the Simpré heraldry, and the ivy that clad the façade had dropped its leaves, so the stems, as thick as his finger, visibly ran riot over the old stone.

He pulled the chain and heard a faint clanging through the thick oak. Then footsteps, and finally locks being unbolted on the inside, and the heavy door creaked open. The Troubles had made everyone very security conscious, he realised. That door had never been locked like that before.

'Hello, Armitage,' Nick said with a smile.

The old butler hadn't changed at all. Immaculately presented and in his sixties, he was tall and straight, and his white hair with a pronounced widow's peak still grew in thick profusion and was combed back from his prominent forehead.

'Master Nicholas!' The poor man, always quiet and proper, stared at him as if he'd seen a ghost. 'I...I mean...welcome home, sir, welcome home...' It was all he could manage for a few seconds. Then he rallied. 'Please, come in, come in. His Lordship is in the trophy room, and the Dowager Lady Shaw is resting in her rooms. Your mother is still visiting her relations in Scotland, I'm afraid. She will be most sorry to have missed you.' His eyes drifted past Nick to the two young women, who had followed him up the steps, both wearing their best woollen coats with fur collars, Millie in a trilby and Celine with a little felt hat pinned to her tawny hair.

Nick stood aside to introduce them. He had to hope his father didn't throw him out; the shame of it in front of the girls would be too much. Best behave as if they were staying.

'Armitage, this is Celine Ducat and her friend Amelia Leybourne. They will be taking the rose room and the bluebell room in the west wing. Can you arrange Alistair to bring up the bags from the car, and send D-D-Dorothy up with fresh sheets and fl-fl-flowers and to light the fires? And call Agnes to sh-sh-show the ladies to their rooms. She can act as ladies' maid to the both of them, I suppose, as my mother isn't here?'

'Certainly, sir, of course, sir...' The flustered old man rushed to pull several bells on the wall, summoning the various servants from the depths of the house.

'And k-k-kindly inform Mrs Mulcair that there will be three more to l-l-l-lunch.'

Nick glanced at the huge grandfather clock with the round brass pendulum glittering in the flames of the gigantic fireplace, which sent out a blaze of heat. The stone fireplaces in Brockleton were built to take huge baulks of timber, cut from their own woods and dried for several years. 'I take it we eat at one o'clock, as usual?'

'Of course, sir, and then shall I tell your father...'

'No thank you, Armitage. Once the ladies are seen to, I'll announce myself.'

A cluster of servants had arrived, fussing over bags and running for flowers from the year-round hothouse. Liza, the ladies' maid, arrived to show the girls to their rooms, and Millie followed her up the curving staircase, her nose in the air, playing the part of a gracious aristocratic lady just as well as she acted her dandy gentleman character on stage. Celine, following Millie, kept glancing back at Nick with her hand to her mouth and eyes sparkling, like she might burst out into giggles at any moment.

'Would there be anything more, sir?'

'No. Thank you, A-A-Armitage, that will be all.' He nodded at Armitage and strode by him, across the entrance hall, down the corridor that ran along the front of the house, passing the ladies' drawing room, the billiards room and the green door that led downstairs to the kitchens and the butler's pantry and the housekeeper's sitting rooms.

The trophy room, where he was headed, was a place he'd never liked. His father often used it as a living room, but the stuffed and mounted heads of deer, bison and even bears gave Nick the creeps. On the floor were two Bengal tiger skins with heads, which he could hardly bear to look at as a child.

He braced himself outside the door. He'd not seen his father in over two years. When he left that day, he'd been sure he would never return. Was this a terrible mistake? He really was beginning to doubt his decision...though it was much too late now.

He rapped on the door and awaited a reply.

'Come?' His father sounded surprised. Nobody knocked in Brockleton. The servants would never disturb the master in the trophy room, except possibly Armitage, and he would simply open the door.

Nick turned the porcelain handle and entered.

The curtains were half closed against the sunlight outside, and the gloom meant his eyes had to adjust before he could see properly. The sofa was pulled closer to the huge fireplace than he remembered it being before, and his father was lying on it. It looked as though he'd been sleeping.

Nick had never seen Walter Shaw lying down during the day before; usually he was up and striding around, barking orders at random servants, demanding his horse be saddled or fishing rods brought to him. Maybe he had changed in the last two years, as Nick had changed.

'Who is it?' his father asked, his hand flailing at the card table beside his head for his spectacles, and then he sat up with his feet on the floor, holding the glasses in his hands before putting them on, blinking feebly at Nick. Nick couldn't remember ever seeing his father without his glasses. His face looked weaker without them on, but that wasn't the biggest change. Walter Shaw looked so much older. He stood now, fumbling to hook the spectacles over his ears.

'Father, it's me, Nicholas.'

'Nicholas?' The incredulity in his father's voice was something new. Walter Shaw normally knew everything. 'Nicholas, is it really you?'

'Yes, Father, it's me.' He braced himself for what was coming. Cold dismissal, a derisory laugh, a tirade of fury at his sudden departure, a blow even. He knew his father would not be pleased to see him, but what form that displeasure would take was impossible to guess.

'My son, Nicholas? Is it really you?' Walter Shaw had got his spectacles in place and came slowly towards him. He was somehow smaller than Nick remembered. His father had been a wrestler at school, as he was fond of telling his sons, and had always been an intimidating physical presence, but he seemed to have lost a lot of weight, and he no longer towered over Nick; they were about the same height now. His hair too seemed thinner, not the lion's mane of old. Was it possible for someone to be so diminished in just two years?

'Yes, Father.' He'd been subjected to so many tirades from his father, with his father saying that he was disgusted by him, that his stammer was shameful, that he was a defective human being, someone to be embarrassed by. But he was no longer a scared child. He would remain calm and reasonable, whatever his father might say or do. He needed to claim his inheritance, for Peter's sake if not his own, so he would endure whatever Walter Shaw was going to say.

His father kept coming towards him, his eyes drinking him in. Then he stopped, a foot away, and to Nick's astonishment, he saw tears form on his father's lower lids.

'You're alive,' whispered Walter Shaw. 'But you *were* in the war?'

'I served with the Royal Irish Rifles, Passchendaele, Ypres.' He didn't bother to add 'as a private soldier'. His father knew well he was not officer material.

'You made it through. I…I…assumed you… When I never heard…' The aged man wiped his eyes with the back of his hand and cleared his throat.

'I'm so sorry about Roger. And about Wally,' Nick said truthfully.

His father nodded sadly. 'Your mother lost her mind about Roger. And then you went to war so I could keep poor Wally at home, but God took him just the same.'

'It was awful,' Nick heard himself say. He flinched then, fearing his father's rebuke, being told to pull himself together, keep a stiff upper lip, don't behave like a snivelling girl. But he was once again surprised.

'Yes, it is all awful. So many of our young men, fine, strong young men, and they're gone, or worse. Roger among all the others. When I see how some of them have returned, I thank God that Roger is dead. There are worse things than dying. But now' – he shook his head sadly – 'the big houses decimated. And then Wally in a stupid accident...' His grief was palpable. 'But you... Let me look at you.'

Nick tensed but stood his ground. And his father held out his arms, and a smile came to his face, and Nick realised it was the first time in his life his father had ever smiled at him.

'A real live son, my boy, home in one piece. Nicholas, my dear boy...'

Then before Nick knew what was happening, Walter Shaw drew him into a tight embrace, his arms around him. And it wasn't until he felt the moisture on his neck that he realised his father was sobbing. 'Oh God, I've been a fool,' wept Walter Shaw, the fifth baron de Simpré. 'An arrogant fool who didn't deserve a boy like you. I'm so sorry, Nicholas, so very, very sorry. But now you're home.'

# CHAPTER 17

 *ETER*

PETER WATCHED MAY SLEEPING, her hands under her cheek, her long blond hair fanned out over her bare shoulders and down her back. He eased himself quietly out of bed, and she stirred but didn't wake. He decided to leave her to rest; she'd looked tired and pale the last few days. She could follow him to the tent site when she woke up naturally.

He crept downstairs and got himself a cup of tea in the kitchen. They were staying in a private house this time, just him and May, and the owners had told them to help themselves within reason but not to expect to be waited on. The other performers were scattered in similar digs all over the little town of Rush, County Dublin, which was too small to have proper guest houses.

He ate a slice of stale soda bread he took from a tin and planned his morning. Today was a moving day, so there was much to be done. The men would meet in the field where the tent was erected in the next hour or so and begin the dismantling. The women would arrive an hour later and start packing up the props and costumes. Each person was responsible for their own belongings, but there was a collective sense of responsibility to ensure nothing was left behind. It was the thing he was most proud of, everyone pitching in, no prima donnas, nobody saying 'it's not my job'.

Then the landowner's labourers would arrive – which the farmer would charge Peter a fortune for while only paying the poor men a pittance – and the men would help manhandle the equipment across muddy fields into the lorries waiting on the road, unable to drive across the rain-soaked fields.

It was going to be tougher when all this had to be done with rain and sleet and even snow driving into their faces. He and May had considered going into a theatre for the worst of the bad weather, but in the end, they'd decided to stick it out because they needed every penny they earned to keep afloat. Paying a theatre owner the lion's share of the door wasn't an option.

Money was so tight, he'd been pleasantly surprised when May had agreed to employ Clive Stephens without even putting up an argument. Her time in Dublin with her mother seemed to have softened her for some reason. In the weeks since she'd come back, she'd been much more amenable and loving, and more willing to do things his way. She'd even stopped worrying him about starting a family. She had an idea to have Nick dress up as Father Christmas as part of the finale, and on the last night gave out sweets to the children. The tent was decorated for the season with a large tree, covered in lights.

He hadn't meant to hurt her the last time they'd talked about it, and maybe he shouldn't have been so honest about his relief that they weren't stuck with a child at this stage. He didn't mean never, obviously, but now would not be a good time to have more people depending on him than he already had. And thankfully May seemed to accept that. Last night they had made love for the first time in a while, and he was fairly sure she'd used that rubber thing she got in England to stop her getting pregnant but didn't want to ask. Things were better between them, and he wasn't going to rock the boat.

After leaving the house, he strolled down the dark town towards the field. It was a beautiful location overlooking the coast, and the first pale-yellow dawn light was just appearing over the sea. He stuck his hands in his pockets and whistled as he tramped down the road.

Before Nick had set off for Cork yesterday to see his father and grandmother with Celine and Millie, he'd told Peter that his father owed him five hundred pounds and he would lend it to Peter as soon as he got back. What a weight off his shoulders. As much as he hated the idea of borrowing money off his old friend, a few hundred pounds would get them out of the sticky patch they were still in after taking on Clive, and maybe it would get them another couple of acts as well. He'd been so right about expanding. His show was much sought after all over the country, and he had invitations to various places right up to the middle of next year. If he could just be single-minded now, no distractions, he could really take them to the next level. Touring, not just Ireland but England, and then – the dream – to America.

He crossed the field towards the tent as the first rays of winter sun crept across the field. And then he stopped at the entrance, frowning. He was sure he'd heard a cough, a rattling raspy cough, coming from inside. Squaring his shoulders, he threw back the flap and marched in, fully expecting to find some young lad who thought he could get away with a bit of romancing with one of the chorus girls while nobody was about, but what greeted him was not that.

The stage was still up, and on it lay two wounded men. Three other men, including one who had a doctor's bag with him, were seeing to them, washing and bandaging one man's shoulder and cutting a broomstick to bind a splint to the other man's left leg.

As he stared at the scene in bewilderment, Eamonn walked towards him, smiling, his hands up in a gesture of calm. 'Peter...'

Peter exploded. 'What the hell is this?'

'It's nothin'... Calm yourself, will ya?' Eamonn's smile dropped as he grabbed Peter by the arm and pulled him none too gently back outside.

'Calm myself? Calm? Are you out of your mind?' Peter, enraged, shook him off. 'What do you think you're doing? What are they doing in there?' Though he knew without being told. Since the 1916 Rising, he'd known his brother was involved in the Volunteers, and later the IRA, and though he'd never asked, he suspected Eamonn was fairly high up.

'I had to take them somewhere, and I knew you were in the area, and it gave our doctor somewhere to treat the men. We got into a bit of a set-to with the Tans. We left them worse than us, though.'

'A bit of a set-to? Are you mad?' He could barely speak, he was so angry. 'Because the Tans *are* mad, stark-staring bonkers. We had to turn some of them away a few nights ago in Drogheda because they were so drunk and disorderly.'

In response to the relentless campaigns of assassination of policemen and Crown forces, the English had sent over the Black and Tans, a motley crew of dangerous thugs from what Peter had seen of them. He'd warned every one of the company to steer clear. He wanted no trouble; he'd seen enough blood and guts in France to last a lifetime.

'Eamonn, I'm trying to run a show here, and I want nothing what-soever to do with this – nothing, d'ya hear me? I won't put my people at risk, so you can get them fellas off my stage and away from my theatre. And I'm sorry if that's disappointin' to you, but it's how it is.' In his anger, he could hear himself revert to the working-class Dublin accent of his youth, sounding more and more like his brother.

But instead of apologising and going to do as he was bid, Eamonn stood his ground, looking disgusted.

'Well, isn't that nice for ya? The rest of us are risking life and limb every day to rid our country of that shower of murderers and their English paymasters, but you've a business to run, have ya? No interest in this stuff? Want nothing to do with it?'

Peter was incensed. How dare his brother come in here spouting this at him?

'It's not about want – it's about can't,' he hissed. 'We can't do anythin'. We're actors, singers, dancers, and we're not doin' nothin' to help. We're brightening people's lives when they're scared to death of the Tans, and of you and your gang, doing terrible things to the Crown forces, drawing their anger down even more on ordinary people. No, Eamonn, no way. I swore the day I was sent home from France, I'd never be dragged into a war again. I've seen too much slaughter in my life. I can't go back to it – I just can't. And what's more, I won't.'

Eamonn's eyes flashed hotly. '"Won't" is not a luxury any Irishman can afford any more, little brother. It's the English who won't stop till they destroy us, every last man, woman and child in this country, crushed under their boots. Did you hear what they did two nights ago? One of our lads was involved in an attack on the police barracks, so the Tans went to his house, where his mother, his grandmother and his two young sisters were, on their own, no man around the place. They tied his little sister down – she was only eleven, Connie's age – and cut her hair off, and then they dragged her inside the house and assaulted her. Another of them got the other girl, but she managed to bite him on the neck to stop him raping her. But then the grandmother was trying to pull him off her, and another one of them hit her in the head with the butt of a rifle. The old woman is dead, killed outright. And his mother was held down while she watched this, her daughters being violated, her mother killed and they roaring at her to tell them where her boy was.'

Peter shivered but stood his ground. 'I'm sorry for their troubles, but you know well her son attacked the barracks and brought it down on them.'

Eamonn stepped closer, his voice low and throbbing with rage. 'Don't you dare blame the boy. He was doing the right thing, protecting his people. Every day, every single bloody day, we are hearing stories, down in Cork and Kerry and Tipperary especially, torturing people for information, shooting on sight, women, girls – they don't care.' He was ranting now. The veins stood out in his neck, and his breath was heavy on Peter's face. 'The time for trying to get along and stay out of their way is over, Peter. We need to fight back with every shred of strength we have, every one of us.'

'And if they come and find IRA men bleedin' all over me stage? What then, eh? I'm supposed to clatter 'em or shoot 'em, am I? Or send the girls off to gouge their eyes out with their high heels? Talk sense, will you, Eamonn? I have people to protect, especially my wife.'

'Your wife?' Eamonn's eyes glittered with rage. 'May knows better than you what needs to be done for this country.'

'What's that supposed to mean?' demanded Peter in fury. 'May thinks the same as I do. How would you know what May feels about this or anything else?' Though it was true May had surprised him with how in favour of the rebels she'd become of late. And he was inclined to agree with her in private, though at the same time, he was very sure her sympathies did not stretch to letting Eamonn land a bunch of wounded rebels on their doorstep, and on moving day as well, when people would be swarming over the place within the next hour.

His older brother held up his hands in resignation and took a step back. There was something else in his eyes now – as if he knew he'd gone too far, dragging May into the argument. 'Nothin'. Look, I don't mean anythin'. Just she's a good person with her head screwed on and she knows what's at stake here, but I'm not asking you to get her involved. I'm sorry. It was a spur-of-the-moment thing. I was desperate. I needed some place to bring the lads to be doctored. Their homes aren't safe – too many paid spies and informers – and they won't go there anyway because it's putting their families at risk –'

'But you didn't mind putting me and mine at risk?' snarled Peter. 'Look, Eamonn, I have Nick and Enzo and all the lads turning up in half an hour to strike the tent, and then the girls will be here and then the local labourers – you couldn't have picked a worse time. You can't be here when they get here.'

'All right, all right. Give me a few minutes.' Eamonn went into the tent, then reappeared. 'Ten minutes, tops, and we'll be gone. The doctor has told me he knows a safe house not too far away. Look, Peter, I'm sorry.'

Something about Eamonn's demeanour unsettled him. His brother never apologised to anyone, and it wasn't like him to back down.

He watched his brother turn to go, but then Eamonn came back, lit a cigarette and offered him one. After a moment's hesitation, Peter took it. Eamonn struck and held the match for him, one hand cupping

Peter's chin, and that intimate gesture, along with Eamonn's brief apology, dissolved Peter's animosity.

Since he could walk, he'd looked up to Eamonn, always wanted to be with him, to be him. He was his big strong brother, his protector. He had saved Peter's life that night when their father tried to kill him; his brother was his hero. And maybe Eamonn was right about the need to fight. Peter didn't like to admit it, but things were getting worse and worse. People were scared. 'Can we win, do you think?' And he realised he'd said 'we' instead of 'you'.

Eamonn nodded. 'I think so, but it might kill us all in the doing of it. Our plan was to drive the police out of the small rural barracks, keep attacking them, so the top brass would move them into the towns where they're safer, but it means leaving the country unpoliced. That was working fine till they sent the Black and Tans over. That's changed everything.'

'They're everywhere,' Peter said.

'I know.' Eamonn picked a leaf of tobacco off his lip and spat it to the ground.

He'd aged, Peter realised, in the last year or so. He looked badly in need of a scrub, a haircut and a shave.

'But they wouldn't have sent them if they weren't scared. Every official they send to Dublin Castle, we put a bullet in him. The police have all been warned to resign or face the consequences.'

'But, Eamonn, they're Irishmen, just doin' their jobs.' Peter had heard of a man in Ballina, a rural policeman, a member of the Royal Irish Constabulary for the last twenty years. He'd a houseful of children and his wife was dead, and he was told either give up the job or be shot as a traitor to the Irish Republic. He'd refused, asking if the IRA would feed his kids, but they weren't making idle threats. He was shot dead walking out of the barracks the following week. Everyone had been horrified, but more and more people were coming around to the IRA's way of thinking. You're either 'with us or agin' us', as the old saying went, and it was time to make up your mind. Sending the brutalising Black and Tans had done wonders for recruitment to the IRA.

173

'They have a chance. We give everyone a choice, but we can't be soft. If they choose to take the king's wages, then they're an enemy and will be treated as such. It's hard, I know, but it's how it has to be. No special cases, no "what abouts". Eamonn ran his hand through his hair, and Peter saw the blood on his knuckles and a vivid bruise on his neck.

'What happened to you?' he asked quietly.

Eamonn examined his hand. 'Ara, nothing much. I'm grand.' He turned to face Peter then, his eyes boring into Peter's. 'Will you help us with one thing, Peter? Something I was going to ask anyway. If I've healthy men I need out of the way for a while, could you take them on as your labourers and have them travel with you? You wouldn't have to pay them, so that would save you a load of money.'

Peter stared at him, astounded. 'Ye're askin' me to put IRA men on my payroll?'

'Only on paper,' said Eamonn quickly. ''Twill cost you nothin' and save ye a lot. The organisation will pay for their food and everythin'. Peter, the English know who lives where – they're keeping records on everyone. But ye travel around, there's loads of ye, nobody counts ye – it's a perfect cover.'

'I… What… But where would they sleep? I can't be putting them up all over town?' Peter couldn't believe he was even considering this madness.

'In the tent. Like, you leave it up, don't ye, when ye travel? Just let them kip in the back there with the stuff, and they'll pitch in and take it down and put it up again when you need them to. They won't always be the same lads, but there'll be three or four of them at any time.'

Peter hated to refuse him, but there was no way he could take such a huge risk. 'And what am I supposed to tell May? She'll go mad if I tell her we're getting stuck in this… And I'll have to tell her – she'll see we're saving on the labour.'

Eamonn gave him a funny look then, just for a second, one Peter didn't understand. 'I know you'll have to tell her the truth, but I'm sure she'll be fine with it. Tell the others nothin', though, just that you think it's cheaper to have your own labourers. Or however ya want to tell it. You're the boss.' Eamonn pucked him gently on the shoulder and crushed the cigarette with the heel of his boot. 'Now I better help move on the wounded men – we've fence pallets for stretchers. I'll send the other three back in a while. Diarmuid Sweeney, Pat Murphy, Tom Collins. They're not their real names, but they'll know to answer to them. Any men I send to you, use those names.'

Eamonn just assumed he'd do it.

Eamonn started towards the tent, but Peter caught his arm and pulled him back again.

'Eamonn, are Ma and the girls in danger from what you're doing?' He needed to know.

His brother shook his head. 'Well, I'm not in Dublin much these days, so no. The English know I'm gone. Sightings of me in America have been fed back, so they think I'm over there, and Ma or the girls wouldn't have a clue how to find me, so I think they're OK. I've people watchin' out for them anyway – don't worry.'

'But I heard the boy Maggie was seeing was put on the boat?'

With a grimace Eamonn stretched up his arms, closed his eyes and allowed his head to roll right back. 'Sleepin' in ditches is no good for the spine...'

'Eamonn, answer me.'

'Ah sure, a blabbermouth he was, too much to say for himself.' He still didn't meet Peter's eyes.

Peter knew that was as close to a confession as his brother was likely to give him. The rebellion was serious stuff. Spies and informers got no quarter and no second chances. By the sounds of it, the boy was lucky to get away with his life.

He made up his mind. 'Look, if May agrees, and that's by no means a guarantee, then I'll do it, but only if no one comes sniffing around, all right? Nothing more. I've too many people to protect here.'

'May'll be grand, good man.' Eamonn grinned and gave him a quick one-armed hug. 'Now I'd better go help shift the fellas bleedin' all over your stage. Stay away. We'll take them out the back, and that'll be the last you see of them.'

'Eamonn.' Peter called after his older brother as he stepped into the tent. 'Watch yourself, will ya, for God's sake. The English aren't messin'.'

'Neither are we, Peter,' Eamonn said, looking back with a wry smile. 'Neither are we.'

The morning passed quickly, and Peter was anxious. Eamonn and his wounded men were long gone, but he wanted to get out of the area as fast as he could, and he wasn't looking forward to the arrival of the so-called Diarmuid Sweeney, Pat Murphy and Tom Collins. He was so jittery that when someone came up behind him and covered his eyes with their hands, he nearly jumped out of his skin.

'It's only me.' May laughed as she turned him around to see her.

'I'm an eejit,' he said, embarrassed by his cowardice. 'How are you feeling?' She looked a bit less pale and tired, a touch of rose in her cheeks.

'Much better for you letting me sleep in. Thank you, Mr Cullen. Now what has you so nervous?'

'Nothing, I'm fine...' He knew he should tell her about Eamonn and everything before the three men appeared. He turned from her and called, 'Two-Soups, can you supervise the loading of that trapeze? The girls are buckling under it over there.'

Two-Soups nodded quietly and went off to help the chorus girls.

Poor Two-Soups wasn't even close to coming to terms with the loss of Betty. On stage, he was still hilarious, and not just in the way he told jokes; he had a way of observing life that was really very funny. He had a new routine with Millie, a conversation between an Irishwoman and a Scotsman in a shop, both accents only intelligible to natives, and the ensuing confusion had the audiences in stitches. His act was perfect every single night.

Off stage, he was equally hard-working, putting up and striking the set like a man possessed. But it was clear he was hollow with grief inside. It was hard to watch. One of the chorus girls, Delilah – probably she was called Mary, but they'd all adopted fancy stage names – had tried to befriend him, even flirt a bit to cheer him up, but he just looked at her blankly, gave her a sad little smile and shook his head.

A BEAUTIFUL FEROCITY

There was one woman for him, only one, and she had been knocked down and killed in the street in London. There would never be another. Everyone's heart went out to the big man, but he was hard to reach.

Once the trapeze was being sorted, Peter drew his wife to a corner of the tent, out of earshot of everyone else, and told her of his encounter with his brother.

'And you said we'd help?' she asked, her cheeks flushing a deeper rose.

'May, I said I'd ask you. And if you say no, then it's a no. I know it's probably crazy, and I told him if there was a single hint of the Tans sniffing around...'

'No, it's right for us to do it. Is Eamonn hurt?'

'You don't mind about the men?' Again she'd surprised him. He'd been afraid she'd go mad.

'No. We all have to do our bit. And he's right – there are so many people coming and going here, three more won't make any difference. Is he hurt, though?' she asked again, her eyes on his face.

'No. A bit bruised and stiff, but he's fine. He's on the run, I'd say, so living out in the wild. Ma would have a stroke if she saw the cut of him.'

'At least that, he's still all right.' She gave a firm little nod. 'You did the right thing.'

'I suppose so...' Something really had changed in her of late. So much softer, yet somehow stronger too.

'We have to do this, Peter. Otherwise we're under the yoke of British imperialism forever, and it will only get worse.'

'Well, exactly, or so Eamonn says anyway.' He smiled, trying to lighten things.

'He's right.' She seemed certain of that. 'Now I'll get the accounting books, and I'll put these three names on the payroll, and everything will look official and above board when they get here. And then I'll get on with helping the girls pack up the costumes properly.'

# CHAPTER 18

ICK

CELINE WAS ENCHANTED by the scenery of Cork, and in love with Brockleton.

As they strolled over the ancient stone bridge decorated with gargoyles that traversed a lily pond, she could hardly stop gushing. Alternate stone tubs of purple primula and white snowdrops were dotted along the gravel walkway and winter honeysuckles grew in the hedges.

Hares and eagles and wild Irish red deer still roamed the grounds, and in the distance, sheep moved gently on the hills.

For once it was just the two of them. It wasn't that he didn't like Millie – he did, very much – but having Celine all to himself was bliss.

There was a stone seat set into the wall around the pond, and Celine sat down, smiling up at him and shielding her eyes from the low bright sun with her hand. It was cold but bright and hard, typical Christmas weather. She had on a simple dark wool dress under her coat, and her hair was pinned up loosely under her hat. She wore beautiful lace dresses and lots of make-up on stage, and though she always looked lovely, this was how he preferred her, just ordinary, normal-looking, naturally beautiful.

She patted the seat. 'Sit with me, Nick?'

He sat down and felt huge beside her. She was slim and petite, a mere five foot to his 'six four, built like a door', to quote Enzo. It was part of the reason he was afraid to ask her out properly. She was so beautiful, ethereal like a butterfly or a delicate flower, and he was twice the size of her.

She touched the ring on her little hand. 'You know how we told my papa we were engaged? And now you've told your father and grandmother the same thing?'

Nick's heart sank. Now it was coming, the moment when Celine would give him back her ring. It must have been the way his father and his grandmother fussed over her yesterday when Nick introduced her as his fiancé.

He'd been worried about his father's reaction, because he knew his father would have preferred some titled girl, someone of their class, but it was a testament to how much Walter Shaw had changed that he had marched across the room and planted a kiss firmly on Celine's cheek. 'Welcome to the family, m'dear.'

The downside was that Walter and Floss had immediately begun planning a huge Brockleton wedding, and much, much worse, his father had started talking about future heirs. 'Plenty of sons, Nicholas, five or ten, so that cousin of yours, Harvey, can't get within a lion's roar of the place.'

Nick hadn't known where to put himself; he must have been the colour of beetroot. Millie smirked, and Celine had looked quite faint. He'd had to put his foot down very firmly, stammering that marriage wasn't on the cards any time soon, that they were both very young and there was plenty of time for all that.

'Are you all right, Nick?'

He wished he was the kind of man to charm her, to woo her, but not a single word came to mind. His palms were sweating, and the familiar restriction in his throat that came on when he was nervous, which led to his stammer making him unintelligible, was increasing by the second. He would just have to nod or something. *Oh God.*

'Hmm.' It was the closest to a word he could make.

'Well, I was thinking...'

This was excruciating. He opened his mouth, but no sound came. If he could only get the words out, he could save himself from the coming rejection. He would tell her that she was off the hook, that he never thought it was serious anyway, that of course she wasn't beholden. He wished he could laugh. What an idea, Nick and Celine – who would have imagined such a ridiculous pairing?

'Perhaps...' She got up then and, to his utter confusion, knelt before him and took his right hand in hers. She took a breath, smiled shyly and said, her voice steady and composed, as if she'd rehearsed it many times, 'Nick Gerrity – I know you are Nicholas Shaw, but to me you will always be Nick Gerrity – I was hoping that maybe you could do me the honour of becoming my husband very soon?'

'Wha...?' The sound came out choked, barely recognisable as a word.

'If you don't want, of course, I won't hold you to our engagement, and I know it was just for my papa, and then so I could travel with you without scandal. But, Nick, you are the man in the world that makes me feel safe. Nothing bad will happen when you are by my side, and I love you. And not because of all of this.' She waved her hand around. 'It is beautiful, but please believe I would not care if you had nothing.'

'I...I...I...' He stopped and took several deep breaths, trying to loosen his tongue.

'I'll make this easy.' She smiled, still holding his hand. 'Yes or no?'

His head felt like it was going to explode. She'd said she loved him. Celine *loved* him. It was incredible. He would have settled for 'I'm fond of you', even 'I quite like you', but she'd said she loved him. Maybe Brockleton had done it, maybe it hadn't, but did it matter? She would never ever be able to love him as much as he loved her, that much was certain, but the fact was, she was asking him to marry her...offering to

actually marry him for real, to have his heirs if they were so blessed...
Was this really happening?

'Nick? Yes or no.'

'Yes...p-p-please.' Finally he'd found his voice.

She squeaked with joy and threw her arms around him then,
hugging him tightly. Gently, fearfully, afraid this was a dream, he
allowed his arms to go around her, and then he buried his nose in her
hair, inhaling deeply. From that first night in the Aigle d'Or a lifetime
ago, there had never been anyone but her. Yet despite his friends
telling him to declare himself, he never could, and now, here she was,
proposing to him. Was he dreaming? He must surely be. But no, it was
real.

It was time for afternoon tea, and Floss would be expecting them,
so they walked hand in hand back to the house. 'So we marry very
soon?' asked Celine, skipping along like a child at his side to match his
long strides.

He felt weak with joy at her eagerness. 'Of course. What k-k-kind
of wedding would you like? It doesn't have to be the b-b-big intimidating celebration my father was talking about – that would t-t-take
months in the planning. We c-c-could have a small wedding in France
if you want? So your papa c-c-can be there.'

He personally would have liked nothing better than to marry her
in that little church down the street from her father's establishment
and have the reception at the Aigle d'Or, where they'd sung their first
love duet.

'You see?' She reached up to caress his cheek. 'This is why
everyone loves you, Nick, always you think of others. But *non*, we
should marry here, should we not? And perhaps my papa could
come?'

'If it's what you want. We will d-d-do whatever you want.' He
smiled down at her, raised her hand to his lips and kissed it.

'Oh, it is what I want, a wedding here, with our friends, your
family, my papa – it would be perfect. And your own mama perhaps?'

Nick shook his head. 'I doubt she'll come.'

The baron had telegrammed Nick's mother at once to let her

know about her third son's return but had received only the briefest of replies. Harriet Shaw, the second cousin of the Earl of Perthshire, had returned to her own family after Roger's death, and a divorce was in the pipeline. His wife leaving hadn't turned a hair of the baron de Simpré's head. It had been a marriage of convenience that no longer served anyone, so it was gone, and good riddance to her and his marriage as far as the baron was concerned.

Nick had rather hoped his mother would at least be pleased at his having survived the war, or better still realise she loved him after all, as his father had done. But her telegram, which had arrived at breakfast that morning, presented by the footman on a silver platter, read only: *Give Nicholas regards STOP Poor Harvey STOP*

The baron growled and grumbled. 'Your foolish mother was always too fond of that slimy Harvey. She wanted him to be Roger's godfather, you know, but I put a stop to it. Can't stand the man. Suppose we'll have to tell him you're back, though, and he can give up dreaming about getting his hands on Brockleton and all the rest.'

Celine, sitting beside Nick at the breakfast table, had taken his hand and squeezed it, with a smiling look.

She did the same now, stopping and turning to face him, taking his other hand as well. 'You believe that I do not do this now, because I find you will own Brockleton?'

He shook his head seriously. 'I b-b-believe you b-b-because I trust you. B-b-but the thing is, Celine, I d-d-don't care even if it's not true. Whatever your reasons, I'm so happy. I never thought, never, that you felt anything for me b-b-but friendship, and I've always loved you, you know that. Everyone knows that.' He laughed ruefully. His infatuation with her was Cullen's Celtic Cabaret's worst-kept secret. 'So if you'll marry me, then I'll just b-b-be so very happy...' To his horror he felt tears on his face.

She brushed them away with her fingertips. 'I want to make you happy, Nick. I need you by my side. I want to be a good wife to you, and I'm so happy too.' She stood on her toes, kissing him gently on the lips. The ducks and drakes on the pond seemed to start quacking in concert at that moment, and it made them both laugh.

He kissed her then, gently, their lips just barely touching, but he felt as if explosions were going off in his head. He'd never kissed any woman before. His lack of experience was terrifying; what if he messed it up on their wedding night? Obviously he'd seen the post-cards and magazines at the front and listened to Enzo wittering on – his education was complete in that regard. But did one really do that with the woman you loved? A beautiful, innocent girl like Celine? It all felt a bit boorish and uncouth.

Floss, Walter and Millie were in the west wing drawing room when they got back to the house. Walter was showing Millie his latest hunting rifle; he'd gone straight back to his old interests now that he had his son back. Floss was perched on the couch, already enjoying her afternoon tea. The dowager had coffee at every other meal, though her son and daughter-in-law had tried their best to eradicate what they saw as an American habit, but she did accept tea in the afternoons, along with cucumber sandwiches and sometimes a scone with jam and whipped cream.

Celine dropped her gaze and hung back demurely as they entered the drawing room, but Nick noticed that she and Millie exchanged a look. Had Millie known about this proposal? Was it even her idea? Nick thought it might have been, and he was filled with gratitude for their slightly peculiar friend, who had always supported him and encouraged Celine to see his good points.

'We have an announcement,' he said, beaming with pride. Walter looked up from his Winchester, and Floss paused with her scone on the way to her mouth.

'What is it, Nicholas?' asked his father.

'Celine...and I...we've d-d-decided not to wait any longer. We will be married as soon as we can, here in B-B-Brockleton.'

'Well, well, well...' Walter was clearly delighted, rubbing his hands together. 'Wonderful news. Why wait, indeed? Times have changed since your grandmother married my father, and I married your mother. It was all cold-blooded stuff then, money and land. These days nothing should be allowed to stand in the way of true love, and the earlier you get going, the more babies you'll have. That's what we need, protect the old place from the likes of Harvey.' He pulled the velvet rope beside the fireplace, summoning Armitage. 'Champagne, Armitage, please. My son is to be married.'

Millie hugged Celine, who was blushing, and then Walter hugged her, and then Floss, and finally Nick got to hug her again.

It wasn't till the hubbub died down and everyone had a flute of Taittinger that Floss sidled up beside him, tall and elegant as ever. 'So I was right. This old place did the trick then?' she murmured in his ear.

'She says she d-d-doesn't care that I'm rich, but I t-t-told her I d-d-don't care why she's marrying me, so long as she is.' He grinned back.

'That's my boy.' She winked as she squeezed his arm fondly.

* * *

WALTER SHAW WAS NOT best pleased when Nick confessed to him over a game of billiards that he and Celine intended to keep working for the foreseeable future with what the baron insisted on calling the 'travelling circus'.

'Good lord, man,' he boomed, banging his cue on the floor. 'The house of de Simpré will be the laughingstock of the country.'

'Nonsense, Father. Look at all the things the other children of your Anglo-Irish p-p-peers get up to. Take Florence P-P-Postlethwaite – I mean Lady Gamminston. She and Lady Lavery, and the Honourable Sarah Bottomley, they spend their time arranging themselves in the shape of famous p-p-paintings, and lots of p-p-people come to see them.' His stammer, which had been improving around his father, had worsened again with the stress of standing his ground, but he was pleased to note his father didn't wince and sneer as he would have done in the old days.

'Ugh, don't quote Florence Postlethwaite at me, or her sisters. Ernest Gamminston has decided his wife is far too…hmm…sociable to be left in London alone while he goes on business to India, not a good idea at all. He's insisting she stay home in Cork under the watchful eye of her parents. On and on he went about the dratted woman when I met him at the races recently, and I was only there to see a new two-year-old gelding Larry Ellisson had brought over from Kentucky.'

'Florence is here in C-C-Cork?' Nick chuckled to himself as he potted a ball. If Lord Gamminston knew Enzo was around, he might not think his sociable young wife was that safe in Ireland after all. 'Well, she's a great fan of the c-c-cabaret. If she had her way, she'd be high k-k-kicking with the chorus girls.'

'Very funny, young man.' Walter raised a hairy eyebrow. 'I hardly think that's what her long-suffering husband has in mind. Which is why he's not just relying on her mother to watch over her – he has a private detective on her tail as well, would you believe? Women are more trouble than they're worth, son, but you need to figure that out for yourself, I suppose, and your little slip of a thing will hardly get up to much.'

'Celine is wonderful, Father. I'm so lucky that she agreed.'

'You're the lucky one, eh?' His father chuckled. 'If she's convinced you of that already, then maybe she's not as gullible as she looks.'

'She hasn't convinced me at all. I just know it.' Nick was quick to defend her. 'And you should see her on stage. She's mesmerising...'

'The baron and baroness de Simpré simply cannot be cavorting around the stage, all this flamboyant nonsense.'

Nick realised his father was trying to railroad him, gentler than before undoubtedly, but he was bossy and used to having his own way.

'The cabaret is everything to both of us. I'm serious, Father. These are my friends. I can't let them d-d-down. Even if things change later, I can't just abandon them.'

The baron huffed and puffed, but he was having to come to terms with the new Nicholas, a grown man with his own thoughts and ideas who would not be bullied. Walter was softer than Nick ever remembered him. He'd aged, and the loss of his sons had taken a heavy toll, though Nick's return, safe and sound, had lifted him up a great deal. And Nick understood why his father wanted him at his side. Partly it was paternal love, but also it was because no peer wanted to be the one that lost the assets or ended the line. It was shameful to break the chain of generations.

'Well, perhaps once you're married,' said Walter hopefully.

'We'll t-t-talk about it then, Father.'

'Anyway, once your filly is in the family way, well then, of course she will have to stay here at Brockleton, even if you insist on these ridiculous goings-on, and that will be company for me in my old age and your dear grandmother as well.'

'Father, we're not even married yet. Do stop t-t-talking about Celine like she's a b-b-brood mare.' Nick felt a wave of heat wash up his neck. His father discussing his and Celine's ability to procreate like they were race horses felt deeply awkward.

'Pshaw – why not talk about it? It's what the whole thing is about. How else can we retain the lands and titles for the de Simpré blood-line? By the way, talking of the loathsome Harvey, the man has invited us to Cushing Hall on Saturday.'

Nick winced as he potted another ball. 'Ugh. Is that really neces-sary? I c-c-can't stand the man any more than you can, and I d-d-don't know if I'd want Celine anywhere near him.'

'Normally, Nicholas, I'd agree with you. The man is a cretin and a cad, but he's being surprisingly civil about the whole inheritance thing, so I feel we should fly the flag. He's holding some sort of gymkhana and a champagne lunch in a marquee to celebrate your return, and I said we'd be there.'

The door to the games room opened before Nick could reply, and Armitage appeared. 'Apologies for interrupting, my lord, but Mr Pat Twomey is here. He wishes to discuss the pigs with you, sir?'

Walter slotted his cue back into the rack, happy to abandon a game he was losing. 'Ah yes. Nicholas, we're experimenting with a breeding programme for the saddlebacks. Excuse me. It's nearly dinner time anyway – will you gather the troops? And that friend of your fiancé's, for God's sake get her out of trousers and into a frock. Call me old-fashioned, but it makes me feel quite uncomfortable to see her looking like a footman. I've told her she can help herself to Harriet's old things. If nothing else your mother did know how to dress.'

Nick potted the remaining balls and went in search of the women.

As it happened, Millie seemed to have taken his father's advice; when he came on her, she was already dressed for dinner, in a rather elegant red silk dress that Nick recognised from his mother's wardrobe, and with a slash of red lipstick to match. She, Celine and Floss were in the small sitting room, discussing the latest rebel attack; a bridge had been blown up between Brockleton and Cushing Hall.

The three women were sitting on the striped couch with their backs to the door where he was standing, and Nick stood and listened, happy to admire Celine without her noticing his presence.

'Well, the Anglo-Irish aristocracy are usurpers here. I've always thought that,' Floss was saying to his fiancé. 'Your country and mine, France and America, we have both had our revolutions to get rid of the monarchy, but Ireland has yet to throw off the yoke of English rule.'

'Mm…' Celine, who was wearing a delicious pink silk dress, had become distracted by a robin that had landed on the windowsill, but Millie answered for her.

'Surely the de Simprés have been here long enough to count as Irish?'

'Oh, they've been here a very long time,' agreed Floss. 'My husband's family was given this land by Queen Elizabeth the First in the late 1500s. The problem was, it wasn't hers to give. The tenant farmers who lease it now are the descendants of those who owned the land in the past. Now they pay us rent for the use of their ancestral lands.'

'But the tenants seem happy? Walter was showing me around the estate this morning.'

'My son is a decent landlord – I made sure to raise him to be. But his father wasn't, and before him were more than enough Shaw tyrants, and people have long memories. But times are changing, my dear, and who knows what the future may bring? However good a landlord my son may be, we are still seen as symbols of all that is wrong.'

'Well, I think Brockleton should remain in the de Simpré family,' said Millie firmly. 'The family can hardly be blamed for what was done centuries ago. Oh, Nick, here you are – what do you think? Your grandmother seems to think you should hand over all your land to the rebels. She's quite the Bolshevik.'

'I am certainly not that, my dear,' his grandmother cut across her coldly. 'And I said no such thing.'

Nick laughed as he came into the room.

Nothing could be further from the truth than calling Alicia Shaw a Bolshevik. She treasured a brocade bag that her mother-in-law had got as a gift from the tsarina of Russia when she and her husband, two barons ago, had visited the Winter Palace in St Petersburg. When Nick had once referred to the former capital city as Petrograd, which is what the Bolsheviks had renamed it after their revolution, she'd got quite cross. Though an ardent supporter of Irish independence, she abhorred the behaviour of the Bolsheviks and what they'd done to the Russian aristocracy. 'Your grandmother would have Lenin's head on a spike if she could, yet she has nothing but sympathy for the rabble who seek to throw us out of our home,' his father had grumbled over dinner the night before.

Nick could see both sides. Of course this land of Ireland should be owned by the Irish, but how long did one have to live here to be considered Irish? His family had been born and raised here since the sixteenth century – wasn't that long enough?

Though the problem wasn't longevity, he knew. As far as the rebels who were wreaking havoc all over the country were concerned, he was British. His family was Protestant, they were loyal to the Crown and represented British rule in Ireland, and for that Brockleton was a possible target; there was no getting away from it. Meanwhile he knew most of his friends in the cabaret had rebel sympathies. He'd always found it better not to talk about it.

'Go on, Nick, what do you think?' repeated Millie, but before he could reply, the dinner gong sounded and he was off the hook.

They'd hardly sat down for the soup when Walter returned, red-faced and flustered. 'Bloody Auxiliary captain shot one of our sows last evening,' he snarled, throwing himself into the big wooden chair at the head of the table.

'What, why?' Nick was aghast.

'No reason apparently. He arrived looking for information about young Walsh, and when nobody knew what he was talking about, he just shot the sow.' He slammed his meaty fist on the table, furious. 'And they wonder why they're hated? Bloody IRA. But that Penny-weather, damn his eyes, antagonising them…'

Walter had refused to allow Brockleton to be a place of refuge or entertainment for the officers stationed in Bandon or Cork, though many of the big houses had done so, including Cushing Hall. But Walter had taken his mother's advice not to antagonise the tenants yet further. Her idea was to be the best possible landlord, treat everyone fairly and try to stay out of everything else, but the behaviour of the Crown forces was becoming more and more difficult to defend.

'What did Pennyweather do now?' Floss asked wearily.

'According to Pat Twomey, he's ordered that all men over the age of sixteen in the county must not have their hands in their pockets – if they do so, they'll be shot on sight. This is ridiculous. The Black and Tans went on a rampage last night out near Macroom, set fire to cottages, terrorising innocent people. And Pennyweather, who is supposed to be an Auxiliary officer, is only fanning the flames.'

'It was Harvey Bathhurst that suggested the whole thing to Churchill,' Floss pointed out. 'Thank goodness he's no longer your heir, Walter. Brockleton would be up in flames.'

'You're right, Mama. Nicholas's return has saved the old place from being blown up, that's for sure.'

The story went that Harvey Bathhurst had met Winston Churchill in a club in London and had made the suggestion that the police in Ireland be expanded to form some sort of special force, dedicated to the routing out and destruction of the IRA. Apparently Harvey had been taking the credit, however true or not it was, for the British deci-sion, which was the arrival in Ireland of the Auxiliaries and the Black and Tans. The Auxiliaries, or Auxies, as they were known, were from the officer class mainly, whereas the Tans were just ordinary Tommies of the sort Nick, Peter, Enzo, Two-Soups and Ramon had fought alongside in the trenches. But many of them were so traumatised by the war that they were violent, alcoholic and so destructive. Whatever their motivation, they certainly were not helping the situation at all.

'Yes, but he clearly didn't know what he was raining down on all of our heads, did he?' Walter poured himself a large glass of claret as the second course arrived, a brace of pheasants. 'The attacks are becoming more frequent and more bloody. Castleshane, Runnamoat House, the Balfe's place, in Roscommon...' He paused to think.

'South P-P-Park House? I heard it was burnt down,' Nick interjected. He remembered South Park as a child, a handsome little manor house belonging to a cousin of Florence.

'Yes, that place, and did you hear about John Browne?'

Nick knew he was referring to Baron Kilmaine of Gauleston House in County Westmeath. 'That too?'

'Oh, up in flames, almost nothing to salvage.'

'Are we at risk here?' asked Millie, with a look of concern.

'I don't know, Miss Leybourne.' The baron tackled his pheasant with knife and fork. 'Our tenants are happy enough, I think, but with the Irish, one never really knows. They could be plotting our demise while shaking my hand – it's impossible to tell.'

Nick winced. In the old days, he wouldn't have noticed the inherent mistrust and superior attitude his father had towards the Irish, but now it rankled. Peter, May, some of the chorus girls, the many people who came to the shows, sometimes over and over, were Irish and more or less sympathised with the rebels, even if they weren't actively involved. They'd lived under British rule for centuries, rebelling frequently but to no avail. But since the Rising of 1916, they felt entirely justified at reacting to the brutality the British meted out, and Nick couldn't bring himself to condemn them.

His father was helping himself to mashed potatoes. 'Harvey now, he's very connected to the top brass in Dublin, spends a lot of time there at the Castle these days. But I tend to steer clear of politics myself. Doesn't do to be seen to be too cosy with the forces of His Majesty.'

Nick frowned, remembering Harvey's invitation to his house. 'Perhaps it would be best to steer clear of Cushing Hall as well then, Father?'

'Ah, it's only a bit of a get-together nothing political, can't do any harm. Life must go on.' And then Walter started telling them all what he considered a side-splittingly funny story about one of the tenants who bought a greyhound without seeing the animal, and how when it arrived, it was some kind of a mongrel and bore only the slightest resemblance to a greyhound. The tenant was furious with the seller, until the dog won at the race track. And then he changed his tune, calling the animal the finest greyhound ever seen. 'That's the Irish for you,' said Walter Shaw pompously, making Nick cringe again. 'Fickle as the wind.'

# CHAPTER 19

ICK

It was another bright but cold day and Walter insisted on driving to Cushing Hall himself, leaving the chauffeur behind. He had a magnificent open-topped Bentley, and he'd swathed himself in a woollen scarf, hat, goggles and gloves, while the rest of them covered themselves with tartan blankets against the cold. Floss waved them off from the steps. She was staying at home; she couldn't stand Harvey and was too old, she said, to pretend any more.

Despite Walter's dangerously fast driving, the journey took much longer than it normally would have because so much destruction had taken place in this part of Cork. Not just the bridge but roads and railway lines were bombed or blocked, and the Bentley leapt and bucked as Walter Shaw, never the most careful of drivers, hit one pothole after another.

When they eventually arrived, Nick was surprised at how small the house was compared to Brockleton; he remembered it as larger from visiting it in his childhood. Not only that, but it was in need of some repair, the drive needed surfacing, the grounds looked shabby and uncared for, and there were only two maids and a footman to serve the picnic in the canvas marquee. Still, the booze flowed and food was plentiful, and it seemed everyone who was anyone in the Anglo-Irish social set was there, entitled wealthy people simply carrying on as if nothing was happening. It felt ridiculous to Nick to be doing something as frivolous as going to a party in the middle of such a war, but 'life went on', it would seem.

Florence Gamminston came bounding towards him, throwing her arms around him. 'Nicholas, darling, Harvey tells me you're engaged. Congratulations, darling.'

'Florence, this is my fiancé, Celine,' said Nick, with an apologetic glance at Celine. 'I believe you've met before.'

'Oh, we have. I remember now – Enzo introduced us.' Not one whit embarrassed, Florence released Nick and hugged Celine. 'Your voice had every soldier in the place eating out of your hand. And you're so pretty. Well done, Nicholas. Your babies will be beautiful.' She glanced around furtively and dropped her voice to a whisper. 'Is Enzo here with you as well?'

Remembering what his father had told him, Nick took Florence's arm and drew her away. 'Millie, would you find Celine a glass of champagne and a seat?' he said over his shoulder. 'I want to talk to Florence in private for a moment.'

'Ooh, so he is here?' gasped Florence excitedly.

'He's not, but he is in Ireland…'

'Oh my God, where?' Her eyes lit up.

'Lots of different places. We're touring with Cullen's Celtic Cabaret – we're a fit-up now. But listen, Florence…' He drew her into a quiet space between the marquee and a high red stone wall, between two guy ropes. 'I have to tell you, your husband is having you followed by a p-p-private d-d-detective.'

Florence's eyes widened, and then she trilled with laughter. 'Oh my goodness,' she chortled. 'So that explains the chap in the bowler hat who keeps bobbing up and down behind the hedges. Aren't men stupid sometimes? He's getting as bad as Blimpy.' She paused and then spoke quietly. 'Nicholas, since we're being honest allies, you should know this. Blimpy was so furious with your brother for getting up to all sorts with Maud, he shot him. Claimed it was an accident, of course, but Maud told me he goaded her, saying he'd shot her lover. She claims they were never together, that Blimpy just got it into his fat head and there was no talking to him.'

Nick felt a pang of sadness. He hadn't been close to his boorish brother, hadn't even liked him, but poor Wally didn't deserve to die, even if he had been romancing Maud Banting-White. Though Nick had to admit, he might feel pretty murderous himself if some other man came chasing after Celine.

'Was it that obvious Wally was seeing Maud? I suppose it was,' he added, without waiting for her reply. 'I mean, you knew all about it when I met you in London.'

'Oh, don't worry, there was no big scandal. It wasn't common knowledge – that's why no one suspected Blimpy. Maud confided in me recently, but I knew it before because Harvey whispered it to me himself at Pippa Hillsdan's twenty-first birthday party when we all ended up in some terrible club in Soho.' She shrugged and smiled. 'He wanted me to tell Blimpy about the affair, seeing I was so fond of him, but of course I wouldn't. Like I told Harvey, Blimpy Banting-White was such a jealous man, I knew what would happen if he found out. Which he obviously did,' she finished regretfully.

'Do you think Harvey told B-B-Blimpy about Wally and Maud, knowing what he'd do?' Nick was stunned; it was the first he'd heard of any of this. 'He assumed me dead, and Wally was in the way of him being my father's heir.'

'Goodness, I really don't know. Would he really do that, do you think? I did say to him I didn't think it was true. Maud was always batting those long eyelashes of hers at Wally, even when he was going out with my sister, and he never seemed interested, although I suppose that could have changed.'

'So do you think it wasn't t-t-true?' There was an awful sinking feeling in his gut as he took in what she was telling him. 'You think

Harvey could have lied about Wally to B-B-Blimpy, after you'd told him the way B-B-Blimpy was?'

Florence looked thoughtful. 'I suppose Harvey was always one for dripping poison in the ears. He enjoys pushing people around like pawns on a chessboard. But surely even he...after what I said to him...'

A terrible rage rose in Nick's chest. He marched out from behind the marquee, nearly tripping over the guy ropes. 'Where is he?'

'No, wait, stop.' Florence cried, hurrying after him in alarm. 'You can't go bandying accusations around with no proof. And anyway, it probably was an accident, Nicholas. Everyone says so. You can't go dragging it all up again – it won't bring poor Wally back. Oh, hello there.' She waved vigorously to a man in a bowler hat, who looked embarrassed and disappeared behind a rhododendron.

'Right, everyone,' commanded a smooth baritone voice from inside the marquee. 'We've set up a little course in the water meadow for the ladies, and for the gentlemen, there's a set of jumps in the long meadow. Just filter down to the stables – there's a horse for everyone that wants it. Let's have some fun, shall we?' The next moment Nick's nemesis came strolling out of the marquee, with his hands resting on the waists of both Celine and Millie.

Florence placed her hand on his arm as he watched, fury burning inside him. 'I'm not saying do nothing, Nicholas. I'm just saying you need to bide your time, do some digging if you have to, find out more. Harvey's slippery as an eel. You need to be clever.'

He nodded his agreement, knowing she was right.

Hurrying across the grass, Nick seized Celine's hand and pulled her away from Harvey. 'Are you all right, darling?'

'Oh, don't worry, I've been taking good care of her.' The other man smirked. Nick's distant cousin by marriage was a pale, slender man with brown hair and grey eyes, not at all ugly, though Nick had always found him repulsive, especially after the strange incident at the Christmas ball when he was fifteen and Harvey seemed to mistake him for a girl.

'Of course I'm all right, Nick. This is great fun.' Celine dimpled up at him, hugging his arm.

'We should go home.' He had to get her away from his poisonous cousin. 'I know you don't ride, so we can just go back to Brockleton and have afternoon tea with Floss. I'll get one of Harvey's grooms to bring us in the trap if Father wants to stay.'

Celine's little face filled with disappointment. 'Oh, but I want to stay too, Nick. I had a pony in France on my grandmother's farm, and Harvey has said he'll put me and Millie up on the gentlest of horses. Please don't make me go home, Nick. Come on, I'd love to ride. Can we?' She looked so hopeful, he relented, and let her tug him along after Harvey and Millie, who were walking ahead, chatting very civilly together.

Florence caught them up and took his other arm. 'Now don't we make a happy little group? We'll have a wonderful time,' she trilled.

The stable yard was a hive of activity, and a young groom led all the women to a line of ponies, tacked up for riding side-saddle, though Millie said she would prefer to ride astride; she had jodhpurs on under her calf-length skirt. It caused a few raised eyebrows, but the groom acquiesced. She casually slipped her skirt off to reveal men's breeches and easily mounted a grey mare.

Nick lifted Celine up onto a gentle dappled pony, and Florence, an experienced horsewoman, chose a handsome roan, and she led all the ladies out along the riverside track to the water meadow.

Nick's father was already mounted on a mighty cob, who was bucking and dancing and looked none too pleased to have heavy Walter on his back. Harvey brought out two Arabs from the stables for two other gentlemen. Another young groom appeared beside Nick, leading a chestnut stallion with a white star on his forehead, who whickered as Nick stroked his neck. 'M'lord says you're to have Star, sir...' The groom lowered his voice. 'But keep him out of the water, sir – he don't like it.'

'Thanks for the tip. I will.' Nick swung into the saddle, and the beast stood docile as he found his stirrups and gathered up the reins.

He was surprised at how easily becoming a member of the aristocracy again was for him.

All the other men were mounted and headed for the long meadow. Star was a good jumper and a powerful horse, and Nick began to enjoy the feel of the wind in his face and the rhythmic vibration of the horse's hooves on the hard ground as he jumped fence after fence. It had been a while since he'd ridden, but his father's barked instructions from his boyhood were impressed on his memory: left leg behind the girth, right in front, sit in deep and squeeze with the knees, hands on the withers.

After maybe twenty minutes, Harvey stood up in his stirrups and waved his hat, shouting, 'Let's join the ladies.' Then he galloped at speed towards a high ditch, eight or nine feet at least, at the end of the field, with Walter Shaw and the other gentlemen in eager pursuit.

Nick remembered the groom's warning, but it had not rained properly for weeks, they'd enjoyed an unusually dry November and December, so even the water meadow, which would flood when the river was high, was firm and dry. He headed for the ditch with the wind in his hair, and Star leapt powerfully as he leant forwards in the saddle.

It was only as they crested the jump that he realised there was a shallow tributary running down the other side of the ditch. His father's horse had just landed in it with a mighty splash, Walter roaring in amused indignation as his legs got soaked – but Nick had way worse problems. As Star plunged down towards the water, the animal's nostrils flared and his eyes rolled; he neighed and writhed, then crashed, flailing, into the stream, landing awkwardly on his side, pinning Nick beneath his bulk, the muddy water closing over Nick's head...

'Nick!' Millie was there, grabbing the reins and urging the terrified stallion to his feet. The poor horse made an effort to roll away from Nick before it fell to its knees; it had broken its right foreleg.

'Thank you...' Nick gasped for breath as he got to his knees in the stream, spitting out muddy water.

'Good lord, Nicholas, what happened?' His father was there, and for a moment, Nick thought Walter was going to berate him for being a terrible rider. But instead his father leant over him tenderly. 'Are you all right, son? I looked back when I heard the scream, and I thought you were a goner there...'

'Nick!' Celine had managed to get down off her pony and came running up, equally distraught. 'Nick, are you hurt?'

'Just my shoulder. I think it's d-d-dislocated. But the poor horse...' His heart was breaking for Star, even though the stallion had nearly killed him. 'His leg is broken...'

'About bloody time he was shot.' Florence had arrived on foot, leading her roan, looking furious. 'That's Star, isn't it? Why were you on him? He nearly killed Oliver Wellington last winter. He almost drowned as a foal and is terrified of water.'

Nick couldn't focus on what she was saying; the pain in his shoulder was threatening to make him vomit. His father tried to help him to his feet, but Nick shook his head. 'Wait a moment...' The world was turning grey.

He could hear Celine sobbing in panic. 'He needs a doctor, Lord Shaw.'

'You're right, my dear. You there, stable boy, whatever your name is, take my horse and head back to the house and call Dr Ashley.'

'My poor dear cousin.' Nick heard Harvey's silky tones as he arrived on the scene. 'I didn't realise you were so inexperienced...'

'He shouldn't have been riding Star, Harvey, and you know that.' Florence was furious. 'You said you'd get rid of him after he nearly killed Oliver. A horse that's afraid of water is dangerous!'

'I completely forgot about the water thing. I'm quite sure riders have ridden him since without incident – I know I have. But yes, in this case I should have recalled.' He sounded not even slightly contrite. 'Here, cousin, let me help you up...'

'Don't touch me,' Nick mumbled, then tried to get up by himself. And passed out.

* * *

WHEN HE CAME TO, he was in the living room of Cushing Hall. His old childhood doctor, Dr Ashley, was standing over him administering an injection, and his arm was bandaged to his chest.

He made an effort to rise from the sofa, but the doctor pushed him down again. 'You shouldn't get up – you need to rest,' he said disapprovingly. 'I've set your shoulder and strapped it up, so you'll be fine, but you need to rest now.'

'I'll rest at my own house.' He would not spend one more minute under this man's roof.

'I really must insist –' the doctor began.

'Celine? Millie?' Nick called hoarsely.

The two women appeared instantly; they must have been listening just outside the door.

'We'll take care of him from now. Don't worry, Doctor,' said Millie firmly. 'And if he wants to go home, he shall.'

\* \* \*

WRAPPED up in tartan blankets in the back of the car, Nick winced and groaned under his breath as Walter Shaw navigated the badly surfaced sweep of gravel outside the steps of Cushing Hall. Millie, sitting up front, had offered to drive home – 'to give you a rest, Lord Shaw' – but Walter had spluttered with astonished laughter at her suggestion and was now reversing the Bentley to and fro in the turning circle over a series of deep potholes.

'Oh, Nick, my love...' murmured Celine, holding his hand under the blankets, tears in her eyes every time he groaned. 'I wish I'd let you leave when you wanted to leave.'

'Not your fault.' He squeezed her hand feebly. As Walter finally got the car lined up with the avenue, Nick glanced back at Cushing Hall and saw Harvey in the window, a cup and saucer in his hand, watching. A slight smile played around his thin lips as he raised his cup in salute.

\* \* \*

THE FOLLOWING week was pure heaven despite the pain. His shoulder was healing well, and he had full use of it once more, though there was an ugly yellowing bruise where the doctor had had to apply pressure to relocate it.

Millie had returned to the cabaret, leaving him and Celine to enjoy Christmas at Brockleton, and it was wonderful how much more time that gave them together. Celine was so sweet and loving and kind, waiting on him with cups of tea and a glass of wine in the evenings, and one lunchtime she even made him a thick onion soup with a slice of cheese and toast floating on it. It was a French recipe and Mrs Mulcair was not impressed, but it was delicious.

The Christmas tree twinkled in the entrance hall and Floss and Celine gave all of the staff beautifully wrapped gifts. Celine showed the same kindness and generosity of spirit to the people who worked at Brockleton as she did to the soldiers and Nick watched with pride how everyone loved her.

And his father was being so good to him as well. He had been shaken to the core by the idea he might have lost Nick the way he'd lost his other sons. He'd given him an exquisite pocket watch, engraved with his initials and the coat of arms of their family as well as a sizable cheque over and above his generous allowance.

Celine bought thoughtful gifts for Walter and Floss and they'd enjoyed a lovely few days together.

Never had Nick felt so loved.

A beautiful vision was opening up to him, of this being the way his life was going to be from now on. After all the misery of his childhood, and then the war, where until Peter rescued him, he hadn't much cared whether he lived or died. Imagine if he *had* died at the front, blown to bits like May's brother must have been, and he'd missed all this. It didn't bear thinking about.

The icing on the cake was a letter from Florence, which the butler brought to him as he was reclining on the stripy couch in the small sitting room, in late December, waiting for Celine to come back from Cork City, where she had gone with his grandmother to get measured for her wedding dress.

*Dear Nicholas,*

*I have interesting news. That day at Cushing Hall, I was so cross with Harvey, I decided to ask the man in the bowler hat what he thought about things, him being a detective and everything. He was a bit startled when I came on him behind the rhododendron, denying everything, but soon he realised that was silly. I told him all about Wally and you and Harvey and the inheritance and everything, and how if Wally died, and now you, that would have put Harvey next in line, and he thinks it's all very suspicious, though of course he IS a detective, so it's in his nature to be suspicious. He's seen the dark side of human nature, so to speak.*

*Anyway, John Smith as he calls himself, definitely not his real name, he has this camera, a box Brownie, and in return for me promising to pay more than my husband for the use of his skills, he agreed to follow Harvey around for a couple of days. He ended up in some dreadful opium club in Cork, stank to high heaven apparently, and there was an English general in it, would you believe. Anyway, he came back with all these photos of your awful cousin with a boy in that place – he couldn't have been older than ten or twelve, and Harvey was, well, you know, fondling him. Anyway, I've sent them to you, so you can see for yourself...*

Feeling slightly sick, Nick dug into the envelope, and sure enough there were four small black and white photos, a couple of inches square, all showing Harvey with a miserable-looking boy on his knee. In one he was kissing the boy's neck and the child looked terrified. In another, his hand was wandering in the boy's lap.

*So I was thinking, and John thinks so too, it might be a good idea to let your cousin know you have these in your possession, and that if anything happens to you, they will come to light.*

*Darling Nicholas, I think Celine is absolutely lovely. Please remember me to our mutual friend when you see him. I'm hoping I can persuade John to let me out of my cage for a few hours of freedom one of these days. He is a very sweet and helpful man when you get to know him.*

*Yours lovingly,*

*Your childhood friend,*

*Florence*

Nick folded the letter away thoughtfully, along with the photos. It was tempting to do as Florence and the detective had suggested, but Harvey had friends in Dublin Castle, no doubt including the English general who had been with him at the opium den. And there was no real proof Harvey had schemed to have Wally murdered, or intended to have Nick break his neck. The more he thought about it, the more far-fetched it seemed. Harvey would just laugh at him if he confronted him.

Still, he would keep this letter and these photos with him, just in case they ever came in handy.

# CHAPTER 20

AY

A WEEK LATER, May stepped out of a small caravan, carrying a load of clothes she'd just begged from Two-Soups: a striped grandfather shirt, a jacket with patched elbows, a pair of worn black trousers and an old cloth cap. The outfit had belonged to the Scotsman when he worked on his fiancé's farm in Scotland, but they no longer fitted him because he'd lost so much weight since Betty's death.

A few snowflakes drifted down as she walked across the muddy ground towards another caravan in the neighbouring field; this one belonged to her and Peter.

Nick had returned from Brockleton a few weeks ago with one thousand pounds for the cabaret, as well as a wedding date, and it was hard to know which of these facts was more astonishing or more welcome.

Celine seemed very happy – she'd already been measured for her wedding dress – and everyone was delighted for Nick, who was walking on air. And Peter was thrilled with the money, which was twice what Nick had promised him, and was already scouring the papers looking for acts he could poach from other companies.

May had insisted, though, that they spend part of Nick's money on eight caravans.

She was determined that they would pay Nick back, even though he insisted the money was a gift, not a loan, and not having to pay for accommodation meant they could save so much money in the long run. And the caravans were lovely. Each had a door in the middle and three oval porthole windows, and she'd made sure they were painted bright colours to add an air of gaiety to the entire camp. Everyone had to admit they were very comfortable, and it certainly beat damp beds and cranky landladies. May had employed a cook as well and provided her with a fit-up kitchen, so meals were available to anyone who wanted one. People were now happily going to the grub tent and helping themselves. It emerged that the cook, Mrs Toohey, was a widow whose house had been burnt by the Tans, and Eamonn had suggested her to Peter for the position. Her son was one of his men, on the run out in the wilds.

The growing unrest all around the country was making them all jumpy. Of late the troupe was staying close together and keeping their heads down, so it was good not to have to go into the towns for anything but supplies. The Black and Tans, British Army, RIC and Auxiliaries were crawling all over the place, and the IRA were effective and swift in their attacks, so almost everyone had had a close call at this stage. The Crown forces were trigger-happy at the best of times, but now they were like caged rats – terrifying.

For the last while, May and Peter had been hiding IRA men, letting them sleep behind the stage in the tent, passing them off as odd-job men they hired from time to time as they went around the country.

And last night Eamonn had turned up as well, looking bloodied and battered and wanting a bed and a much-needed wash and shave.

It had given her a terrible turn, seeing him for the first time since that night in Doyle's, which she'd tried so hard to forget about, but apart from meeting her eyes for the briefest of moments, he'd focused all his attention on Peter, giving her time and space to recover. And all his conversation was about politics.

The war was going well, he'd said. Michael Collins had the enemy on the back foot. The savagery of the Black and Tans and the Auxiliaries was being met, blow for blow, with a cold-hearted violence never before seen in Ireland. Michael Collins seemed to be the orchestrator of the whole thing, and his decisive and often brutal attacks on Crown forces and those in their employ were staggeringly effective.

Any efforts at negotiation or peace talks were out the window, as every day, assassinations of British intelligence, police and soldiers were conducted and barracks burnt out. The IRA were ruthless and relentless, and they were winning.

The Dublin dock workers, as well as the train drivers and all members of the General Workers' Union, refused to handle or transport British weapons or troops, and despite the economic hardship brought down on them with no wages, they were holding tough. It felt like every man, woman and child in the country was in concert in making life extremely difficult for the British authorities, which was precisely Collins's objective.

Eamonn explained how Dublin Castle, the administrative centre of British rule in Ireland, was in a spin and panicking. Many of the aristocratic families had shut up their Irish residences and retreated back to England, fearing being burnt in their beds or shot by a sniper's bullet. Eamonn told them of men secreted away to America to keep them out of British hands, the most recent being the man who shot and killed a member of Parliament.

Meanwhile, it was January of 1920, and the weather was freezing cold and relentlessly wet. May could only imagine how hard it was camping out in the ditches or, if they were lucky, in a farmer's barn.

Peter offered his brother to sleep on seat cushions on the floor, but May said he could take her half of the bed. She had no intention of staying in the same space as Eamonn. She'd worked so hard to put his physical presence out of her head, and now he was here, occupying all the space in their tiny home. She went off to share with Millie and Celine.

Then this morning Peter had popped his head into the girls' caravan while Aida and Celine were rehearsing and asked her to find Eamonn something to wear that was less conspicuous than a blood-covered uniform, things that no one wanted any more, farm labourer's clothes if she could find something like that. And he told her to bring scissors – he was going to give his brother a haircut.

As she walked across the muddy grass between the caravans with her bag of old clothes and a pair of scissors, as well as the cloth cap, which had been left behind one night by a member of the audience and not reclaimed, three men she'd never seen before passed her. They were Eamonn's latest lads, no doubt, following their noses to a huge cauldron of something that Mrs Toohey had made.

She reached the door of her and Peter's caravan and opened it a crack.

'It's only me, Peter,' she called in. The door opened wider, and she saw Eamonn, clean-shaven now and with his black hair washed.

'Oh, I thought Peter would be here...' She backed away, her heart beating hard.

'Some emergency with the piano. He's gone into town to find a tuner.' He stood just to the side of the door, in the shadows, his chest bare, his braces hanging by his sides.

'Right, I'll let you dress so. These were lying around, so you're welcome to them, and here's the scissors.' She shoved the bundle of clothes in the door, her cheeks burning.

He took the clothes from her, his face impassive, and closed the door.

May's heart was pounding. Sweat trickled down her back, and without warning her stomach rose. She ran into the patch of grass behind the van and was sick. It wasn't just the shock of seeing him. This was the fourth time this week she'd thrown up, and a terrible realisation had been dawning on her for a while now, but one she hadn't come to terms with yet. Sinking into the grass, out of sight behind the van, she sobbed quietly.

A movement behind her startled her. She wiped her mouth and jumped to her feet.

It was him.

'So.' He stood looking down at her with his hands in the pockets of the trousers she'd given him and his grandfather shirt half buttoned. 'What will we do now?' His voice was deep, gentle and concerned.

'I… Eamonn, I just felt a bit… I ate something…' She was mortified, being found like this.

'Come inside. We can talk there.' He turned away. The biting wind had sleet on it, and she felt so thoroughly miserable, she did as he asked.

She crept back around the corner and entered the little van, a bed made up at one end and a U-shaped seat around a table at the other. Eamonn indicated to her to sit down and brought her a glass of water.

'Is it mine?' he asked bluntly as he handed it to her, direct as ever.

'Is what yours?' This was awful. She'd not even accepted in her own mind what was happening to her, let alone discussed it with Peter, and now Eamonn was here asking questions. *How could he know?*

'The child you're carryin', May, is it mine?' He sat down on the other side of the U-shaped bench, his hands resting on the small table, bolted to the floor, on which she and Peter took their meals. 'Tell me.' His voice was rough with emotion.

May studied him from under her eyelashes for a moment. There was something vulnerable about Eamonn, she realised, despite his physical toughness. Peter was cool and self-sufficient; he was a born survivor who relied on no one, not even her. His older brother was different. Passionate, impulsive. She felt hot, as if heat was radiating from him on this cold morning in this confined space. This was wrong; he was her brother-in-law. She should be hanging her head in shame at how they'd behaved. It was a moment of insanity, she'd convinced herself in the weeks since she'd seen him, but now that he was here, in front of her, it was oppressive, the weight of her feelings.

'Eamonn, I'm not sure I even am…'

'You are. I've seen it in women before, wives of my friends. You've got bigger up here' – he pressed his hand to his own chest, covering his heart – 'and you're pale and sick. And maybe you're not showin' 'cos you're young, but you soon will be. So I have to ask you again, after what you were telling me about worrying you'd never have a baby with my brother... Is this child mine?'

So little time to think of the right answer. She clenched her hands under the table and made her decision. 'No. If I'm expecting, then it's Peter's.'

Relief? Pain? Regret? What was that split second of emotion on his dark, handsome face?

'How do you know?' he asked thickly.

She thought desperately back to the physiology lesson Dr de Vries had given her. 'Because I had my...my monthly...after we...well, afterwards...and then...well, ten days later...with Peter. So...'

Even as she spoke, she could feel the hot, ugly splodge of shame spread from her cheeks to her chest. This was excruciating; she was telling this man a barefaced lie. There had been no period. She longed to scratch and itch her burning neck. Instead, she put her hand to her throat.

'I'm glad,' he said very softly, looking away. 'Congratulations.'

She swallowed. 'Thank you. I haven't mentioned anything to Peter yet.'

'Why not?' His blue eyes came straight back to hers, searching them for answers.

'Because I wasn't sure until now, and we've just been so busy and...' She bit her bottom lip.

'And you're afraid it's not what he'll want?' He leant forwards, his gaze still fixed on her face.

She sat, saying nothing. What did she feel?

'You do want him to be glad of it, May?' he probed more gently.

'Yes, of course I do.' She lifted her chin and looked straight at him. 'I love Peter so much, and I want him to be happy for us.' It was true; she loved her husband. She wanted this baby to be his.

He stood then, pulled her to her feet and placed his big hands on her shoulders, towering over her in the small space.

'Well, if that's what you want, I'm happy for both of you. And he'll be glad about this child, May, of course he will. It's just a bit different for us, like. We grew up with nothin', and fear of poverty, the kind we knew, empty bellies, no heat, fear of gettin' thrown out on the street for the want of the rent – it makes a person different. You can't understand it, bein' brought up the way you were. Peter is a self-made man, and he can't ever go back to that. He just wants to provide for his family, make sure ye don't ever have to live like that. It's not that he doesn't want a baby – I know that much. Peter wants you, and this life.' He waved his hand around. 'And he'll love his son or daughter when the time comes too.'

*Peter wants you.* That sentence hung between them.

That thing, that knowledge that she'd avoided addressing since the day she met him, was there now, writ large, unavoidable. The dark truth was that she had contrived the relationship between Peter and her. She wanted him, and she was going to have him, and nothing was allowed to get in her way, even the fact that he had never loved her with the intensity that she wanted him.

She'd achieved what she set out to, believing that she loved him enough for the two of them. But the truth was that he had married her to get the money she offered, and because she was so insistent.

And now she was having a child that may or may not be his.

What on earth had she done?

May couldn't speak, so she just nodded, keeping her eyes lowered. She longed, in that moment, for Eamonn to wrap her in his arms again, as he had that night in Doyle's, but she knew for him to do so would be madness.

His hands stayed where they were, on her shoulders, his thumbs on her collarbone. He cleared his throat roughly. 'May, I want to thank you, for...' He stopped.

She raised her gaze to his face, tense, waiting.

After a long pause, he dropped his hands to his sides, the contact broken.

'For keeping the gun for me. And hiding it where you did. I...the organisation...we'll be forever in your debt.'

He picked up the jacket she'd brought him from the bed where it was lying and shrugged it on. It strained a little across his wide shoulders, but at least the arms were the right length. Then he took the cap and pulled it down low over his eyes. He looked more like an agricultural labourer now, rather than an IRA soldier who had spent the last month sleeping in barns and ditches.

Except his hair was still far too long.

'I'll be off then. I promised Peter to be gone by noon.' He twitched the curtain on the window, checking out the lie of the land, then went to the door. 'Thanks for everything, May.'

'No, wait! Come back.' She seized the scissors and glanced quickly around the tiny space. There was nowhere for him to sit where she could stand behind him. 'Kneel there.' She pointed to the floor between them.

'Kneel?' He half smiled, bemused.

'Yes, kneel down with your back to me. I'm going to cut your hair. You look very conspicuous with it that long – no farmer's wife would have the farmhand looking so scruffy.'

Still smiling a little, he knelt where she had pointed, in the middle of the caravan, removing the cap and raising his head. There was a pulse beating just under his jawline, and she noticed the skin of his neck was tanned brown by the wind and sun.

Scissors flying, she gave him a quick, rough, country cut and stood back. 'There, that's much better. You look more the part now, a typical farm labourer if you remember to keep your Dub mouth shut. Just go mute if a soldier talks to you – none of the country boys say much anyway.'

He got to his feet and checked himself in the little mirror on the wall, shaking out his hair, running his fingers through it with a grin. 'Ah, that's perfect.' He pulled on the cap again, turning to her. 'So, May, in case we don't meet again…goodbye.'

She felt a stab of alarm. 'Of course we'll meet again. I want to be around to see this great republic you're promising us, and I need you to be alive to see it.'

'That's good to hear…'

Their eyes met, and though she knew she should look away, she couldn't. She felt herself flushing. 'Of course I want you to stay alive. You're my husband's brother, and this baby...well, you're this baby's uncle. And I want you to find a nice girl and start your own family when it's all over.'

He came to her then and placed his hand on her belly. 'There won't be any other girl for me, May. We both know that,' he said softly. 'But I'll do my best to stay alive so we can meet again.'

'Go,' she whispered, standing very still.

With one last long look at her, he went.

Left behind, she sank onto the bed. That second, that fleeting moment when he'd caressed her stomach, was so confusing. She loved her husband with all of her heart. He was the one for her. But...

*But nothing.*

# CHAPTER 21

 *IDA*

THE CONGREGATION STARED open-mouthed as the troupe of travelling actors swept into the ancient stone church on the banks of a river that flowed through the grounds of the magnificent Brockleton.

Peter had explained his actors should all arrive together, at the last minute, for maximum effect. It was what Celine wanted, everyone to dress up in their best finery and make a show for her, and Nick had said whatever his future wife wanted was fine by him. He was sure his grandmother would be amused and delighted, and his father never cared what anyone thought. And his wonderfully fashionable mother, the Baroness Harriet Shaw, could like it or lump it – if, that is, she even bothered to turn up.

As Aida and Ramon led the others down the aisle, the lords and ladies and various dowagers and honourables twisted in their pews to stare in amazement, whispering and fluttering and adjusting their eyeglasses.

Aida didn't care; she was used to being stared at by now. When they arrived in a town, the actors were always the most exciting thing. They looked different, they wore flamboyant clothes compared to the dowdy browns and greys of the locals, and they were a source of fascination. But today, for Nick and Celine's wedding, Aida and the others had pulled out all the stops, and she knew they were a sight to behold. Beside the overfed and unfashionably but expensively dressed aristocracy, they looked like a flock of peacocks.

Ramon had pierced his ears – or at least Enzo had done it for him – and now he had a gold hoop in each one. This look, combined with his mop of oiled dark curls and burnished skin, made him look like a pirate from a storybook. He wore a scarlet silk shirt that billowed around his dark tanned torso, tight black trousers and his shoes with the heels. He ringed his dark eyes with kohl, and a gold bangle on his wrist glinted as he walked. He looked dangerous and titillating, and the chorus girls had been tying themselves in knots all morning to have him notice them.

Aida knew the girls were jealous of her as she walked beside him in her red and black lace flamenco dress, black lace gloves and her polished vertiginous sandals, a lace fan in her hand. She'd pulled her dark hair into a bun as usual, though as it was a wedding, she'd released a few tendrils that curled around her face. There was nothing romantic between her and Ramon and never would be.

She sometimes wondered if her childhood friend would ever settle down, but she doubted it. Ramon was like her, happy to be moving, changing places all the time. He had regular encounters with women, she knew, when he went out on the town with Enzo, but she never pried; his love life was not her business.

Enzo and Millie followed behind them, both in top hats and tails. Even Enzo had drawn the line at wearing his shining skintight green silk outfit to a church wedding, but the two of them were flamboyant enough, wearing matching cerise-pink cravats and with the sleeves of their dinner jackets turned up to reveal the pink silk linings. The acrobat's hair was long and tied in a ponytail, while Millie's was as always cropped tight to her head, the only decoration being the curls waxed to her hollow cheeks.

213

The American ex-GI, Magus Magicus, wore a normal suit, but he had covered it with a midnight-blue cape, and he'd oiled his hair back to reveal his very prominent widow's peak. His craggy face looked like it was carved from granite, and his skin was like burnished gold. He looked so darkly sinister as he walked that you'd never have known what a shy man he was underneath it all.

The ventriloquist, Clive Stephens, was dressed up as an Edwardian gentleman, in plum-coloured velvet with lace cuffs, and his 'son', Timothy, was wearing a mini version of the same outfit.

Two-Soups came next, in a cream suit that Nick had found in an attic in Brockleton, a relic from his father's youth in India, and a straw boater on his red hair. He could have been Timothy's uncle, with his freckles and wild carroty hair, and indeed the dummy always acted very fond of him.

The chorus girls were in hues of pastel, pinks and yellows and pale blues, and all wore feathers and dried flowers in their hair. May, keeping an eye on the girls, brought up the rear in a burnt-orange floor-length gown, loose-fitting with a high waist, her blond hair sleek and polished.

A young aristocrat in a grey silk top hat, with no chin and weak blue eyes, who was acting as usher, came to meet the actors and showed Aida and Ramon into a pew on the bride's side of the church before seating the rest of the dazzling troupe behind them.

Aida felt Ramon squeeze her hand, that unspoken gesture from one little Spanish boy to a little Spanish girl, one that said *look how far we've come*, and she smiled at him, enjoying his pleasure at being in these surroundings.

The church was so beautiful. It had been decorated by the gardeners of Brockleton, and winter flowers from the hothouses tumbled in profusion everywhere, from sconces in the ancient stone walls and all over the white marble altar. The air was an intoxicating mixture of incense and perfume, and shafts of sunlight streamed through the stained-glass windows, many commemorating the death for his country of yet another of Nick's ancestors. He'd taken them on a tour of the house and grounds yesterday when they arrived, and it seemed to Aida that his relations, living and dead, numbered in the hundreds.

How funny life was, Aida thought. If she were ever to marry, which she certainly would not, she had nobody, not a single person to call her own blood, and Nick had so many, remembered simply because they were rich.

On the other side of the aisle sat the groom's guests, the Cork aristocracy who were beginning to quieten now, and behind them the staff of the house and grounds, and behind them again tenant farmers and their families, in their Sunday best. Nick had explained that everyone for miles around would be here. It was a big day, not just for him but for the future of Brockleton.

In the front pew was a tall, elegant elderly woman she assumed was Floss, Nick's beloved grandmother, and beside her a florid-faced man who looked so like Nick, he must be Nick's father. They'd not been around yesterday. There was no sign of his mother. Poor Nick. Her beloved Gabriella might be dead, but at least Aida never doubted her love. Nick's mother didn't care about him enough to even turn up to her only living child's wedding.

In the family pew, but sitting away from the others, was a slim man with light-brown hair and grey eyes, his arm slung along the back of his seat and his eyes roaming the church. Just as she was wondering who he was, his eyes met hers. A small smile appeared under his moustache, and he licked his upper lip, a light flick of his tongue. She scowled coldly, but instead of dropping his eyes, he continued to hold her gaze until she broke it herself.

Standing nervously at the top of the aisle, in his beautifully cut morning suit, Nick really was a fine figure of a man, she thought, although he looked like a big rabbit caught in the headlights. Peter, his best man, was whispering to him with a wide grin on his face. Aida studied him, raising her lace fan to her eyes. Peter was wearing a tailored charcoal suit, but with a tie and pocket square exactly the colour of his wife's burnt-orange dress. May always liked to put her mark on him; she wasn't as sure of him as she liked people to think.

His fair hair was longer than most men wore it, and it was brushed back from his handsome face, giving him a rakish charm.

The string quartet started up in the gallery to herald the arrival of the bride, and 'Canon in D' by Pachelbel filled the church.

Then all heads turned, and there she was, a vision in white. Her dress was made of silk and lace and hugged her figure, and her veil had been made by Aida herself, night after night, hand-stitching tiny seed pearls and embroidering flowers.

Monsieur Ducat, who'd made the journey all the way from France to give his only child away, looked exactly as someone in that position would: proud as punch of her and a little heartbroken. And as Celine walked, her arm on her father's, towards the man who would become her husband, Aida felt her own heart, which she tried to keep so cold and hard, throb a little. To have a father who loved you, bringing you up the aisle to a man who adored you, the way Nick adored Celine…

Her mind drifted. She was so lost in her thoughts that Ramon had to nudge her to bring her back.

Celine had reached the altar, and Nick looked like he might burst. As he shook hands with Monsieur Ducat and lifted the veil with trembling hands to gaze on his bride's face, it was one of the most perfect moments, and Aida's icy heart melted a little more. There was nobody in the troupe not thrilled for Nick. He was universally adored, and the fact that he was besotted with Celine was obvious to anyone with eyes. Aida wondered what that felt like, to be so in love.

The vicar was old, tiny, round and barely audible, and he muttered his way through the ceremony. Aida thought he looked comical, with soft pink cheeks and brown curls that sprung from his head no matter how he tried to keep them in check with oil. He spoke with such gravity, but he looked like a little doll. They exchanged vows. Nick placed the ring on Celine's finger. And then, miraculously, the vicar raised his voice enough for everyone to hear the words.

'Almighty God, who at the beginning did create our first parents, Adam and Eve, and did sanctify and join them together in marriage, pour upon you the riches of his grace, sanctify and bless you, that ye may please him both in body and soul, and live together in holy love unto your lives' end.'

With the blessing over, Nick turned to Celine and took her hands in his, and they stood smiling at each other.

'Give 'er a kiss then,' called Enzo, and most people laughed, though some of the more matronly on the Anglo-Irish side of the congregation looked appalled.

Nick laughed too, then leant down and kissed his bride with such tenderness and love that Aida thought her heart would break, and she held her fan higher to hide her tears.

Celine was a sweet girl, and everyone loved Nick, who had no idea how attractive he was. Some of the catty chorus girls, who had their eye on Nick for themselves, were overheard to say how it was odd how Celine only realised she loved him when she saw his mansion, but Aida really didn't think that was true. Celine was a little aloof. She kept herself private from everyone, and Aida respected that, but she and Nick had been close from the start.

The string quartet struck up 'The Arrival of the Queen of Sheba' by Handel. The aristocrats clapped decorously, and the theatrical crowd hooted and created a lot more noise as the newlyweds made their way beaming and blushing down the aisle.

The couple were followed by Nick's grandmother, in a dove-grey dress and radiant pearls. She was supported on each side by her florid, beaming son and an attentive Monsieur Ducat, who chatted away to her in French, looking delighted with himself.

Behind them, walking by himself, came that other man, slim with light-brown hair and grey eyes, followed by a collection of Shaw cousins, distant and close. As the man passed Aida, he looked her slowly up and down, his gaze running over her face and body, and she shuddered and gazed ahead, ignoring him. A memory flashed in her mind of the landlord's slimy son in Spain, who had violated her body in return for rent and food. She never wanted any man to make her feel that way again.

Outside the church, the January sky was an ethereal blue. It had snowed the night before, and now the whiteness glittered in the sun, and the church and woodlands and the big house looked like something out of a fairy tale. Servants handed out furs and wraps, and the guests swaddled themselves and walked along freshly cleared paths through the snow-covered rose gardens and in through the high French windows to the long, elegant morning room, which in turn led into an enormous ballroom with floor-length mirrors and huge crystal chandeliers. In every fireplace, logs blazed.

There seemed to be so many rooms in this extraordinary house. Nick had insisted that the troupe all stay the nights before and after the wedding, and they'd all arrived with their bags to the house, where the uniformed footmen had borne them away upstairs.

The same footmen were there to greet them as they entered the supper room, with glasses of champagne and tasty little plates of finger food: shortbread biscuits, gingersnaps, iced fruit cake, mince pies. For the hungrier guests, there was a buffet laid out along the tables of roast beef, whole salmon, jugged hare and partridge.

The actors of Cullen's Celtic Cabaret stood around a bit awkwardly at first; they had never seen such grandeur. But though they were nervous, and the toffs, as the actors called them behind their backs, were slow to thaw, the power of drink, the delicious food and the way Celine and Nick looked so happy together eventually melted the hardest of hearts, and the party began in earnest, with people drifting with their plates and glasses into the enormous ballroom, where a small jazz orchestra had set up in the corner on a triangular stage and were playing show tunes.

After a few more glasses of champagne, the actors couldn't help themselves.

Millie and Enzo ran up onto the stage together in their matching cerise-pink cravats and had the crowd in stitches as they performed the music hall hit 'It's a Great Big Shame' in exaggerated Cockney accents, and substituting the 'Jim' of the song with 'Nick', to everyone's delight.

*I've lost my pal, 'e's the best in all the town.*
*But don't you think 'im dead, because 'e ain't.*
*But since 'e's wed, 'e 'as 'ad to knuckle down –*

*it's enough to vex the temper of a saint.*
*'E's a brewer's drayman, with leg of mutton fist,*
*an' as strong as a bullock or an 'orse.*
*Yet in 'er 'ands, 'e's like a little kid.*
*Oh, I wish as I could get 'im a divorce.*
*'It's a great big shame, and if she belonged to me,*
*I'd let 'er know who's who.*
*Nagging at a fellow that is six foot three, and 'er not four feet two.*
*They hadn't been married for a month or more,*
*when underneath 'er thumb goes Nick.*
*Oh, isn't it a pity that the likes of 'er should put upon the likes of 'im.*
*'Now Nick was class, 'e could sing a decent song.*
This led to whoops and clapping,

*AND AT SCRAPPIN' 'e 'ad won some great renown.*
*It took two coppers for to make 'im move along,*
*and another six to 'old the fella down.*
*But today when I asked would he come an' 'ave some beer,*
*to the doorstep on tiptoe 'e arrives.*
*"I daren't," says 'e. "Don't shout because she'll 'ear.*
*I've got to clean the windows an' the knives."'*

After repeating the verse again, they carried on, as Celine laughed and clapped and Nick stood listening and grinning happily, his arm proudly around his wife.

*'On a Sunday morn, wiv a dozen pals or more,*
*'e'd play at pitch and toss along the Lea.*
*But now she bullies 'im a scrubbin' of the floor.*
*Such a change, well, I never did I see.*
*With an apron on 'im, I twigged 'im on 'is knees,*
*a rubbin' up the old hearthstone.*
*What with emptying the ashes and a shelling of the peas,*
*I'm blowed if 'e can call 'isself 'is own.'*

. . .

AFTER ONE MORE CHORUS, in which all the actors joined in, Millie jumped down and was hugged by both Celine and Nick, while Enzo double-somersaulted off the stage and cartwheeled all the way back to the supper room.

Lady Florence Gamminston, who had been so keen on Enzo in London, was in the crowd, and she started to go after the acrobat, but the man she was with put his hand on her arm and stopped her, much to Florence's obvious annoyance.

Next, Magus gave a hilariously serious version of 'Daisy Bell' and never cracked a smile all the way through. Then Peter sang 'Burlington Bertie from Bow', made all the funnier now because the 'toffs' mentioned in the song were all in the audience, and Nick jumped up to accompany him on the piano.

Millie made the bride and groom sing their most popular number, 'If You Were the Only Girl in the World', and as they gazed into each other's eyes as if both of them could never ever get enough of each other, the stuffiest of the aristocrats had to smile and a few even wiped an eye. And by the end of the number, every voice in the house was raised in song.

Aida suspected they'd never seen a wedding like it.

The string quartet from the church joined the jazz trio in the corner of the room. Together the musicians launched into a slow waltz, and it was time for the dancing to begin. Nick and Celine took to the floor first, and then Peter took his wife's hand. May beamed so much, Aida thought she looked even happier than Celine.

Aida danced with Ramon, and then Two-Soups, who was making an effort to be carefree, then several of Nick's very distant male relatives, all of whom she liked except for one, that slim man with light-brown hair, who greeted her with a smile that never reached his eyes. He insisted on a waltz, and he was perfectly charming, polite and engaging, but something about him made her skin crawl.

She got away from him as fast as she could, fetched one of the furs that had been left in a pile for the guests to use if they wished and wandered out into the magical snowy garden, where glowing Chinese lanterns were strung between the trees. It was snowing lightly again, but it was so beautiful, she didn't want to leave it. Sitting on a stone bench, with a woollen scarf around his neck, smoking a cigarette, was Peter. She sat beside him, pulling the mink wrap around her.

'It's beautiful, isn't it?' she said as he glanced at her, unsmiling.

'Yeah. Who would have thought Nick came from such riches? No wonder Celine changed her mind about him as soon as she saw the place.'

She nudged him, frowning. 'Don't be so...what is word? Not believing nice things can be true.' Despite her own cynicism, the wedding had made her want to believe in love for once. 'You can see how much Celine adores him. Not everything is about money.'

'I'm not saying she isn't very fond of him,' he agreed, without much enthusiasm. 'But come on, Aida. After all this time ignoring him making puppy eyes at her, day in, day out, then suddenly he takes her home for the weekend, and just like that, the date is set.'

She looked around in alarm in case they'd been overheard. 'Peter, this is their wedding day. Don't speak like this. Supposing someone had said this to you on your wedding day, that you were only marrying May for her money?'

He shot her a wry smile. 'Funnily enough, that's exactly what my brother, Eamonn, did say to me when I told him that May was giving me her inheritance to start the cabaret.'

She was shocked. 'You must have been so very angry with him. No wonder you don't see him any more.'

'Oh, it's not that – we didn't fall out over it. It's only Eamonn thinks so highly of May, and he thought I wasn't acting excited enough about marrying her. But like I said to him, me and May are a great team. She's beautiful, she makes me happy – what was the point of me holding off in case I find someone better, when the chances are I never will?' He dropped his cigarette on the ground, then kicked snow over it to hide it.

She sat looking at him for a while, wondering what was making him so dull and joyless today. 'What's the matter, Peter? We're at your best friend's wedding, and you're moping around out here in the cold.'

She couldn't help herself – he looked so sad, she put her hand on his thigh.

He smiled at her then. 'Ah, nothin'. I'm grand, all the better for you being here.'

'Good evening...' It was that cousin again, the creepy one, sauntering down the snowy path in a heavy black fur coat.

'Good evening,' said Peter automatically, as Aida shrank against him, instinctively seeking his protection. In response, Peter slid his arm around her, warming her.

'Harvey Bathhurst,' said the man, stopping in front of them.

'Peter Cullen.' Peter held out his hand, and Harvey shook it.

'And this is your charming...?'

'Peter, we should go in,' said Aida quickly. She didn't want this man knowing her name. 'I'm getting cold.'

'You're right, we should go in.' Peter sensed her discomfort and gave the man an odd look before standing and holding out his hand to help her up.

She took it and walked with him back towards the house, leaving Harvey Bathhurst staring after them.

Snowflakes whirled through the air around them. 'What is making you so sad, Peter?' she asked after a while.

'Nothing, I'm fine.'

'Peter, stop, look at me.' She turned to face him. 'There is.'

He stopped then and turned to her. There was an arbour over his head that would be flush with roses in summer but was now heavy with snow. He looked at her, clearly weighing up telling her, and then said in a flat voice, 'May is expecting a baby.'

Aida's heart contracted. It was such a surprise. She said brightly, 'Congratulations! This is wonderful, is it not?'

'I suppose, but I...I don't know, Aida. I never envisaged it, and I didn't think we'd...well...'

'Well, you do know what causes it, yes?' she asked, a little sharply.

He smiled and did that thing with his lips he often did, pursing them to the side while he was thinking. 'I know all of that. I just don't feel ready. It doesn't suit me, not with the way our lives are. I mean, adding a baby when we're only just getting going?' He pushed his hands through his long fair hair. 'I don't know – I'm just a bit shocked. I love our life as it is – this is a dream come true for me. But...'

She rested her hand lightly on the lapel of his coat. 'Peter, you are going to be a father. This is your life now, and you're going to love this baby when it comes, I know you will.'

'I know, but...' He put his hand over hers.

The cough made them both look up. May was standing on the stone veranda overlooking the path, watching the scene from above. Aida removed her hand immediately, but it was too late. She saw the hurt, the fear, the fury in the other woman's eyes.

'May, what are you doing out in the cold?' Peter ran up the five stone steps from the path to the veranda.

'Wondering the same about you,' May said coldly, her voice carrying through the clear, icy air. 'But now I know.'

'What? What do you mean? I was just telling Aida about the baby.' He followed her out of sight across the veranda, and Aida could hear them arguing in low voices but not the exact words. A door opened and closed, and all went silent.

Shivering, she turned back down the path and walked the other way around the vast house, searching for another entrance so as not to run into the two of them again.

It annoyed her that May had been angry just because she'd caught them talking. Aida and Peter were simply friends and colleagues, and it was immature of his young wife to be so suspicious of their relationship. There was nothing between them, nor would there ever be, not in a million years. Aida had no intention of ever going with a man again.

She did feel a bit sorry for May, though. The poor woman loved Peter so visibly; she was like a lovesick schoolgirl over him, even though they were married. And she wasn't surprised May had made sure to get pregnant. She obviously wanted to be a mother, but she also, Aida would bet, wanted to solidify her relationship. A baby was going to change things, that was for sure. It would make May feel more secure to make a family with Peter. And that's what most women wanted in the end.

Not her, of course. She would never be a mother or a wife – she couldn't think of anything worse. But most women did want that.

It struck Aida that while everyone said it was a man's world, women really did have an ace card in the form of procreation. Celine and Millie had told her how Nick's father had immediately started talking about the importance of Celine bearing Nick several sons, before she and Nick had even set a date for their marriage. Both of them had giggled at the memory, but Aida had thought Celine was giggling more from nervousness than anything. Sometimes she thought the French girl had the same aversion to men as she had herself. She hoped it wasn't for the same reason.

'Hello, my dear.' It was that brown-haired man again, coming up the steep slippery path towards her. 'Have you lost your way? This path leads to the stables. Or perhaps you want to see the horses? I could take you, if you like. There's some fine breeding stock that I was just admiring…'

'No, thank you.' She turned back abruptly, but he caught her up and took her arm.

'If I was your husband, I would never abandon you,' he commented lightly, glancing at her hand.

She knew he was looking for a ring, but she had her black gloves on. 'He hasn't abandoned me. I took a notion to see the moon.'

'Really?' He looked amused. 'Well, there she is.' He pointed upwards, where the moon had slid out of a gap between the clouds, turning everything in the garden silver. 'Pretty, isn't she? Now let me show you the quickest way back to the house. Every path looks the same in all this snow, doesn't it? So white and pure.'

Gritting her teeth, she let him lead her back to the house. When they got there, he made her take a seat in the ballroom while he went off to find some more champagne.

Peter spotted her and waved and came over. 'Where did you get to? Sorry about earlier – it's just May being pregnant. She knows she was being stupid. She just feels so tired and sick, but she's been soldiering on all day. Anyway, Celine organised some chicken soup from Mrs Mulcair, and a hot water bottle, and now she's tucked up in bed asleep. So come on...' He held out his hand. 'Nick and Celine are insisting we dance the tango for the audience.'

After that scene on the terrace, when May was so upset, she was inclined to refuse. But then she saw Harvey heading their way, carrying two glasses of champagne. And so she stood and let Peter sweep her away.

The little orchestra immediately struck up the tango, with Nick on piano, and they danced and danced. Celine tossed a rose from her bouquet, which Peter caught in his teeth to ecstatic applause from the crowd. Everyone had formed a big circle around the edge of the ballroom, leaving the floor to her and Peter, and they were all beaming, actors and aristocrats alike, as Peter swept Aida around in the way she had taught him.

They passed by Harvey Bathhurst, who watched them with a cold little smile; he was busy sinking both glasses of champagne, one after the other. And then by Florence, who had managed to get beside a harassed-looking Enzo, and then the man from earlier who was pretending not to notice what Florence was up to. Aida thought he mustn't be her husband then, unless he was a very tolerant man. Peggy, the chorus girl who sometimes sung soprano with Peter, was being charmed by the aristocratic cousin with no chin and weak blue eyes – he'd been the usher at the wedding, Aida remembered.

Anyway, it looked like it was going to be a fun evening. But as soon as this tango was over, she decided, she was going to bed. For one thing, she wanted to get away from Harvey Bathhurst's cold grey eyes, which kept trying to undress her.

And she really didn't want to be dancing with Peter if May reappeared in the ballroom. The poor girl was carrying Peter's baby, and it wouldn't be right to upset her again.

# CHAPTER 22

ICK

THE BEDROOM in the east wing that the housekeeper had chosen to redecorate as the bridal suite was one he'd rarely been in before, maybe once or twice as a child when he'd been exploring. It was very private, with a stone spiral staircase leading up to it, and when he opened the heavy wooden door, it was beautiful.

The bowed glass doors opened onto a stone balcony that overlooked the snowy landscape, and apple logs burned in the large hearth. Flowers from the hothouses were arranged in Chinese vases. A Youghal lace coverlet covered the large bed, the coat of arms of his father's barony stitched beautifully into it, and the sheets and pillowcases were specially commissioned linen, all embroidered too with the family crest.

He hadn't drunk any alcohol at the wedding, terrified he'd make a fool of himself when he finally arrived here with Celine, but now he still didn't know what to do.

He'd had to put his pride in his pocket and have an excruciating conversation with Peter, asking him what exactly was required of him. He knew the mechanics as it were, or thought he did from what he'd heard in the army, but the romancing part, he had no idea.

As it happened, Peter hadn't been much help. He'd said maybe girls were much more forward than men gave them credit for, or maybe that was just his experience with May, but either way he'd never had to coax her. So Nick had tried Enzo and then Ramon, but neither of them were much interested in the romantic side. It would be cruel to ask Two-Soups, Magus was far too shy to be of any use, and Clive Stephens seemed to have no interest in women at all.

So in the end, he'd asked Millie, because somehow he felt she was the next best thing to a man among his friends. Millie didn't seem at all embarrassed to be asked. She said to be gentle and to make a few jokes, lighten the mood. She told him to start by kissing Celine, that she'd like that, and no matter how urgent he felt the need, he should take it slowly; not all girls were as passionate as men, it would seem. He was to touch her very gently for a long time before pleasuring himself, and if Celine wanted him to stop, then he should stop and not think she was just being shy.

'Of course. I would never do anything to hurt her.' He'd been horrified at the thought.

'I know, and that's what I've told her,' said Millie, and Nick felt a rush of gratitude towards her for being on his side.

Celine had slipped behind the tapestry screen, which the house-keeper had explained was put there for that purpose, and she emerged dressed in a silk negligee. She looked to him like an angel. She too seemed terrified, which was some consolation.

'I...' He felt himself blush puce. 'I'm not very... I haven't d-d-done this...'

'Me neither.' She swallowed. 'My mother died when I was little, and well, you know the girls that hung around my father's bar, so I did hear plenty from them, but I don't think what I heard about men from them...'

'Indeed,' Nick said, knowing exactly what she meant. The

behaviour of the prostitutes with the Tommies was not exactly the experience he was after.

'Should we...' He moved towards her and offered her his hand. She nodded and rested her fingers in his.

They moved to stand beside the bed, and Nick bent down to kiss her. She was barely up to his shoulder, and in her negligee, she looked so fragile, he feared he would break her.

She pulled the covers back and got into bed as he went to draw the curtains. Though nobody could see in, it felt a bit safer to do this in semi-darkness, with only the flickering light of the apple logs. He had gained back the weight he'd lost in the war, but it was muscle rather than fat these days because of all the hard work putting up and down the tent and lugging chairs and tables. He was certainly a large-framed man, and he felt so self-conscious. Nobody had seen him naked since he was a little child, and that was his nanny.

He could think of nothing to say and so just took off his shirt and trousers, leaving his underwear on, and got into bed beside her. The easy familiarity they shared on stage and off had disappeared, and he didn't know what to say or do. They lay there, side by side, in silence, for what felt like an hour, though it was probably only a minute or two.

*Come on, Nick. For goodness' sake, pull yourself together.* He remembered what Millie had said and tried to think of a joke to tell her. Nothing came to mind. He forced himself to turn on his side, to look at her profile. She was lying there with her eyes shut.

'I d-d-don't want to hurt you,' he whispered.

'No, you never would do that, Nick, I know. But we must do this, so please, just do it. I am your wife now – we must.'

She kept her eyes shut tight as he awkwardly put his arm under her head and kissed her again, this time more deeply than he'd ever done. She seemed to respond, which he took as encouragement. She was so beautiful, he could hardly believe she was his, but when he eased her negligee off and saw her body for the first time, he had to catch his breath. She was perfect.

He quickly removed his shorts under the blankets.

He kissed her then, along her collarbone and down her perfect breast, taking his time. His own body was reacting to her, but he held back. He touched her gently, over and over, and finally she sighed and moved, allowing him to enter her. From then on, he was no longer thinking but allowed his body to act instinctively, and very soon it was over.

Drenched in sweat, he rolled off her and cradled her against him.

'Oh, Celine, I... You are so b-b-beautiful. I hope I didn't hurt you?'

She rested her head on his chest as he held her. 'No... A little perhaps, but not bad, not like I feared.'

'It is frightening. It was for me t-t-too, but I... It was the most lovely thing I've ever... I know it wasn't the b-b-best, but I'll get b-b-better, I promise.'

'You were lovely, Nick. I'm sorry if I was not' – she struggled to find the words – 'how you would wish me to be.'

'You were p-p-perfect, and I love you, Celine. We're going to be so happy.'

They didn't speak again, and he just lay there, listening to the rhythm of her breathing. He thought she might be sleeping but wasn't sure. He'd had a speech prepared for this moment, about how lucky he felt and how he would do everything he could to make her happy, but he didn't want to wake her just to deliver it. It didn't matter, he supposed. She knew he loved her, and she'd said that she loved him too.

He suspected she hadn't really enjoyed the sex, but maybe over time, if he was gentle and patient, she might come to not hate it at least. He knew from Peter that May was fond of it, and from Enzo's bawdy talk that a lot of women could be very enthusiastic indeed. But the kind of women Enzo knocked about with were not the kind you marry. He wouldn't have wanted his first time to be with someone who demanded that he do things to her that he'd no idea of doing. Celine was perfect. They would learn together.

Happy in that thought, his wife in his arms, Nick fell asleep.

The following morning, when he woke, she was gone. A split-second panic – had she left him? But he forced himself to be reasonable. Of course she hadn't. She was an early riser; he knew that from when he'd met her and Millie out and about in Newry, while everyone else was still in bed. He rang, and his valet, Kenneally, arrived. His father had insisted on him using a valet when he was at home, and no matter how often he explained that he was able to dress himself, it fell on deaf ears. Gentlemen were dressed by their valets, and that was that.

Tom Kenneally was a nice chap actually, and Nick liked him. He had served in the Enniskillens during the war, and he had some bad burns to his face.

'Have you seen my wife this morning?' Nick smiled. He loved saying 'my wife'.

'Yes, sir. She was taking tea with Miss Leybourne in the orangery earlier, and I believe they joined the rest of the cabaret cast for late breakfast, which is still going on in the green dining room.'

A wave of relief. She hadn't run away in the night.

'Marvellous. I think I'll join them.' He saw the valet had chosen a dark-grey morning suit and shook his head. 'I'll just wear the navy trousers and that light shirt please, Kenneally.' He would dress casually as he always did around his friends.

The man returned the suit and selected the items Nick suggested.

As Nick entered the green dining room, a larger one than they used when they were just *en famille*, as Celine called it, he received a cheer.

'Ah, the married man. 'Ow are ya, mate?' Enzo grinned as he helped himself to scrambled eggs and kippers from the bain-marie on the sideboard. Nick noticed he had lipstick on his neck and clearly had not been to bed yet, or at least not to sleep. He was still wearing the outfit he wore to the wedding.

Everyone else looked better rested; they must have slipped away for a couple of hour's sleep.

'Marvellous, and you?' He smiled.

'Absolutely jiggered, mate.' Enzo ran a hand over his stubbled jaw and yawned. 'I need a bit of grub and a long kip, but that was one 'ell of a weddin' – fair play, your old man knows 'ow to throw a party.

And this place…' Enzo let out a long whistle. 'I ain't never seen nothin' like it.'

Nick felt proud of his home, and it struck him that it took showing it to his friends to realise how truly lovely it was. He'd only ever been lonely there.

'So where's the 'oneymoon?' Enzo nudged him playfully.

'Yes, Nick, where are you whisking your new bride off to?' May chimed in as he sat down opposite Celine. She looked a bit better than she had yesterday, less wan and drawn.

Nick gave his wife a wink, and she smiled back and melted his heart. 'I thought maybe the French Riviera? If the boss will give us the time off.' He looked at Peter, who raised his palms in submission.

'I could say no, but would I ever get out of here alive if I did?'

May slapped him playfully. 'He won't say no. He's a romantic at heart, aren't you, darling?'

'If you say so, my little rosebud,' Peter said, and everyone laughed.

Nick was relieved to see the two of them getting on so well; they'd been a bit frosty yesterday for a while. He'd overheard them arguing, but they seemed to have got over it.

'I would love to go home to France, just for a little while. It has been so long, and I miss it,' Celine said wistfully.

'Then France it is, my love. I'll have my valet arrange it this m-m-morning. We can leave on Monday, and travel with your father, and spend a day or two at the Aigle d'Or before we go on to Paris and then the Riviera.'

Enzo rubbed his hands together. 'Ooh, I envy you. All them delicious –'

'Women?' suggested Magus. The American magician was genuinely witty, even though he never smiled or laughed; his deadpan delivery made what he said even funnier.

'I was goin' to say pastries, but now that you mention it…yeah,' Enzo replied, with a salacious smile.

'Both French pastries and French women are beautiful,' said Celine, smiling at Nick fondly.

'None as beautiful as you,' he answered lovingly as the footman poured him some tea.

'Nick's right,' said Millie, from the end of the table. 'There's no need to be going to France to see beautiful women, Celine.'

Celine giggled and exchanged a look with her friend that seemed to Nick to be meaningful. 'That's true. Women are beautiful here in Ireland as well,' she said.

'And your father is so enjoying his stay here, and he's not lonely for home – he speaks French with Nick's grandmother,' Millie persisted.

'Mm, mm...' Celine wrinkled her thin forehead. 'Perhaps, Nick, Millie is right – it would be nicer to remain here in Brockleton? I still haven't properly explored this place, and the gardens are so magnificent, even in winter, and everyone has worked so hard to have it looking so beautiful for the wedding. It would be a shame to leave after only two days and not enjoy it all. And my papa can stay with us for maybe two weeks and enjoy it with us, do you think?'

He was disappointed; he longed to have her all to himself. But Monsieur Ducat did genuinely seem to be relishing Floss's company and had even been brought to admire Walter's fishing rods and guns, so perhaps it would be wrong to cut his visit short.

'Whatever you like, my d-d-darling.' He blushed at using the endearment in front of everyone, but he could feel their goodwill. 'We can all stay here for a while, and then maybe we go on a trip later in the year, just you and me.'

Celine seemed relieved, which stung a little; he would have loved her to want to be with him as much as he wanted her all to himself. But he had to remind himself, women were different. She loved him, he had that to cling to, and they would grow together; that was how it was going to be.

Nick looked around at the happy scene. His father had arrived and was grinning from ear to ear now that the future of Brockleton was safe, and Floss was happy too. His mother hadn't made an appearance, and though everyone felt sorry for him in that regard, he found he didn't care. He'd never imagined having a life so full of love. She would not have contributed anything.

He would continue with the cabaret, and now the future looked so bright as Peter and May used his money to expand and improve the show. Everyone was one big happy family, and the days of feeling alone, unloved and lost were behind him.

Celine, the great love of his life, had her head cocked to one side as Millie spoke in her ear. Celine was lucky to have such a loyal friend; they both were.

His decision to abandon his home and family had turned out to be the most fortuitous one of his life. If he hadn't done it, he would never have met Peter or Enzo, never performed with Ramon, Aida and Two-Soups and never met his wonderful wife. But despite his leaving Brockleton, vowing never to return, here he was, enjoying the best of all worlds. It was like a miracle.

# CHAPTER 23

ETER

PETER LOOKED at May across the dining table of Nick's amazing home. She looked a bit better, he was glad to note. She'd been like death warmed up yesterday. He'd written to his ma to tell her the news that she was going to be a grandmother and told her how sick poor May was, and she wrote back, delighted with the news. She also said that the sickness wore off after the first few months, so he hoped that was true.

He walked around to her side and leant down and whispered in her ear. 'Want to go for a walk?'

She looked up and smiled, rising from her chair. She'd managed some toast and marmalade and a cup of tea as well, the first time he'd seen her eat any breakfast in weeks.

He took a warm fur wrap for May from one of the staff. There always seemed to be someone on hand here to give you whatever you needed. It was luxurious certainly, but he wondered if it would drive a person mad in the end.

He refused the cape he was offered. Being reared in Henrietta Street had toughened him to the cold. He had a pullover; he'd be fine.

May tucked her hand in his arm as they walked towards the rose garden. Though no roses were in bloom, there was a bed of cyclamen in red and white profusion, poking their little brave heads up through the snow.

'It's like a fairy tale, isn't it?' May said, admiring the view. Gentle hills either side of the valley created by the river glistened white, and the trees that ringed the fields held freshly fallen snow in their branches.

'It's that all right.' Peter smiled. 'Life is strange, isn't it? How it turns out, I mean?'

'It is, but how lucky we've been, Peter. Sometimes I have to pinch myself.'

'Growing up, I knew I wouldn't live that life. I didn't have a clue how I was going to get out of it – nobody I knew ever did – but something told me I was going to do it, even as a nipper I knew. But I wouldn't have imagined this in a million years.'

'Eamonn hitting your father with an iron was the best day's work he ever did.' May giggled.

Peter smiled. He felt no remorse – Kit Cullen was no loss to the world.

'Well, it set in chain a series of events that led us to here, with our own cabaret, friends with a baron no less, and a big bunch of talented mates by our side.'

'And a baby to complete our family soon enough.'

He heard the plea in her voice, the longing for him to share her joy. He'd said he was happy, but she didn't believe him, and she was right not to, but something had changed. Seeing Eamonn and what he was doing, seeing the fragility of life on the Western Front, seeing how Nick, who was third in line but now the heir to all of this place, he realised, not for the first time, how precious life was and how quickly it could change or be snuffed out.

He would have a son or a daughter. A child of his own. It was incredible really. And now that he'd come to terms with it, the idea of having a baby, someone to have beside him in life, someone who might take over the cabaret one day, seemed like a wonderful prospect.

He turned to his wife. 'May, I'm sorry I wasn't so enthusiastic about the baby. It wasn't you, or not wanting to have a family. It's just, well, it's a big responsibility, and I want to do better than my auld fella. Not that that would be hard, but I do.'

'Eamonn said that, that you had such a hard upbringing that you'd be nervous about it. About getting it right.'

Peter nodded, grateful to his brother for trying to smooth things for him. 'That's it. I want to be a good father, someone they can look up to and admire and love, and I'm scared I can't be.'

May hugged him then, tight. 'Peter Cullen, you will be a wonderful father, and our little boy or girl will adore you as I do, so stop worrying. Everything is going to be fine.'

'If you say so, boss.' He laughed, kissing her.

'I do.' She nodded with a smile.

Everything was going to be fine.

# EPILOGUE

*H*e sat in the café overlooking the Marienplatz in Munich, seething. The girl serving him had tried to be friendly, but he just threw the coins at her and took his coffee with a scowl. He was in no humour for pleasantries.

Damn Gisella to the pit of hell, and her family too.

He should never have allowed her to talk him into coming here, to this awful place. He'd been on the winning side, for God's sake. He could have gone home to a bloody hero's welcome like the rest of them, but no. She wanted him; she'd practically begged him to go back to Germany with her after the war. He'd deserted, damned himself in the eyes of his superiors. He hoped his comrade Paul Kenny kept to his word and said he'd seen him go into action in a hail of machine-gun fire, then never saw him again. Missing presumed dead was the best way. No need for a body. He'd worked it all out. But he didn't know. He might be listed as a deserter. At the time he was so blinded by infatuation, he didn't care.

The war was on its last legs by then anyway, and he was reunited with the sweet little fräulein, the angel in a nurse's uniform who'd patched him up months before. If only he'd known what a witch she'd turn out to be, and as for her horse-faced sisters...

He forced their ugly images from his mind, their words from his memory. That he was useless, that he was not a man, that he was a pathetic piece of dog dirt on the soles of their shoes.

Gisella had to go whining to them, didn't she? Miserable little tramp.

Did she tell them how she provoked him? How she drove him mad with her stupidity and inability to get even the simplest thing right? You'd think he'd battered her half to death to hear her sisters. A few light slaps, nothing more, but all hell broke loose and he was out on the street with dire warnings from them and their lumpen-shouldered husbands to stay away or else. Warning him to leave the country. The cheek of it.

The article from *Der Bazar*, the famous German women's magazine, had been the final straw. Gisella had saved it for maximum impact to annoy him, he knew. It was just the kind of spiteful thing she would do, but then she'd acted the innocent when he was upset by it.

'She's an Irishwoman. I thought you might enjoy it, reading about someone from your home country.' She'd whined as he grabbed her by her stupid curls.

He unfolded the centre spread once more, laying it on the table. Once his temper ebbed away, he began thinking. Maybe this was useful information.

May Cullen and her husband, Peter, smiled out at him. The owners of Cullen's Celtic Cabaret, making an absolute fortune, if the article was to be believed. Travelling the length and breadth of Ireland doing some kind of show. Planning to go to England, even America.

The article was about women in business, and May Cullen made sure the world knew what a success she was. An only child of well-to-do Dubliners. He'd laughed bitterly at that bit. An only child was she? Nothing about the husband of course, except that he was the artistic director; he was written out of it. It was all about her and how wonderful she was. Typical female.

Who the hell did she think she was? Another woman, trying to destroy a man. They wouldn't be happy until every last man on earth was destroyed.

May Cullen, Gisella, her hideous sisters – they had antagonised the wrong man this time, and now they would pay. He would make sure of that.

## THE END

I SINCERELY HOPE you have enjoyed this book and are excited to continue the journey with Peter and his friends in the next book, Rivers of Wrath due for publication in November 2023.

If you did enjoy this, I would really appreciate a review on Amazon or wherever you buy your books.

If you would like to read other series of mine, stay in touch to hear about life in my stone cottage in rural Ireland, or if you'd enjoy a free full-length ebook to download, pop over to my website and join my readers club.

www.jeangrainger.com

My readers club is 100% free and always will be, and you can unsubscribe at any time.

# ABOUT THE AUTHOR

Jean Grainger is a USA Today bestselling Irish author. She writes historical and contemporary Irish fiction and her work has very flatteringly been compared to the late great Maeve Binchy.

She lives in a stone cottage in Cork with her husband Diarmuid and the youngest two of her four children. The older two come home for a break when adulting gets too exhausting. There are a variety of animals there too, all led by two cute but clueless micro-dogs called Scrappy and Scoobi.

# ALSO BY JEAN GRAINGER

**The Tour Series**

The Tour

Safe at the Edge of the World

The Story of Grenville King

The Homecoming of Bubbles O'Leary

Finding Billie Romano

Kayla's Trick

**The Carmel Sheehan Story**

Letters of Freedom

The Future's Not Ours To See

What Will Be

**The Robinswood Story**

What Once Was True

Return To Robinswood

Trials and Tribulations

**The Star and the Shamrock Series**

The Star and the Shamrock

The Emerald Horizon

The Hard Way Home

The World Starts Anew

**The Queenstown Series**

Last Port of Call

The West's Awake

The Harp and the Rose

Roaring Liberty

**Standalone Books**

So Much Owed

Shadow of a Century

Under Heaven's Shining Stars

Catriona's War

Sisters of the Southern Cross

**The Kilteegan Bridge Series**

The Trouble with Secrets

What Divides Us

More Harm Than Good

When Irish Eyes Are Lying

A Silent Understanding

**The Mags Munroe Story**

The Existential Worries of Mags Munroe

Growing Wild in the Shade

Each to their Own

**Cullens Celtic Cabaret**

For All The World

A Beautiful Ferocity

Rivers of Wrath - coming November 2023

Made in United States
North Haven, CT
10 November 2023

43860521R00150